PRAISE FOR KEVIN TUMLINSON'S
"DAN KOTLER"

★ ★ ★ ★ ★ "Move over Daniel Silva, James
Patterson, and Dan Brown."

—CHIP POLK, AMAZON REVIEW FOR
'THE ATLANTIS RIDDLE'

★★★★★ "Part Doc Savage, Part Indiana Jones."

—BRUCE BOUGHNER, AMAZON REVIEW
FOR 'THE ATLANTIS RIDDLE'

★ ★ ★ ★ ★ "Half way through I was waiting for
Harrison Ford to leap out of the pages!"

—DEANNE, AMAZON REVIEW FOR 'THE
COELHO MEDALLION'

THE DEVIL'S INTERVAL

A DAN KOTLER THRILLER

KEVIN TUMLINSON

DANVILLE PUBLIC LIBRARY
Danville, Indiana

Copyright © 2017 by Kevin Tumlinson

All rights reserved.

No part of this book may be reproduced in any form or by any electronic or mechanical means, including information storage and retrieval systems, without written permission from the author, except for the use of brief quotations in a book review.

PROLOGUE

IT WAS QUIET, AND ASHTON MINK HATED QUIET. HE'D been in the music business for nearly forty years now, and there had been very few moments of absolute quiet during his life. He had always lived for the noise. It fed him, nourished him. It was part of his DNA. Sound made him who he was.

Even now, after retiring from touring, he still hit the stage for local sets. He still recorded and produced and performed. He helped other musicians get their sound right, get in front of the right audience, and get into the business of spotlights and autographs and groupies.

It was never about the spotlight for him, anyway. The girls and the drugs and the parties were perks, but it was always, could only have been, would forever be all about the sound.

In fact, sound was at the heart of everything Ashton did in his life. His charity, for example, was built on the idea of sound changing the world.

It had started with that little girl.

Agnus Janson. Known as "Aggie" here in the states. She

was a Latvian orphan whom Ashton met while on his final tour. She'd been a big fan of his—Latvia had only just opened as a market for Ashton and other musicians, a few years ago. Decades of music that had played out in the States was now fresh and new in some parts of the world. Little Aggie had just discovered Ashton Mink when she moved to the US. As a treat, her guardian brought her to one of his concerts, and somehow managed to get her backstage to meet Ashton and the band, to get some photos and, hopefully, an autograph.

It was the kind of thing that happened all the time, and Ashton wasn't upset about it in the least. It was routine. He'd probably signed a million autographs and posed for a million photos with a million little girls over the years. And so, he had knelt beside her, put an arm around her, and said, "Smile for the camera, love."

And for the first time he noticed that her guardian, standing just to the side of the photographer, was using sign language.

The photographer snapped the photo, and Ashton turned to face little Aggie. It was the first he noticed the bulky devices behind each of her ears, hidden somewhat by her hair, but still visible if you were looking. Aggie was smiling, blissful, and she hugged him tight. He returned the hug, and patted her on the back as she ran back to her guardian, the two of them signing to each other in excitement.

Before they could leave, Ashton caught up with them.

"I'm sorry," he said to the guardian. "But, is she ... well, is she deaf?"

The guardian, whom Ashton would later learn was named Amanda, nodded and smiled. "She has cochlear implants, but she still has profound deafness. It's hard for her to make out what people are saying in situations like this," she waved a hand around the crowded room, where thousands of Ashton's fans were waiting for autographs and photos of their own.

Ashton shook his head. "Why bring her to a concert? Can she even hear the music?"

Amanda laughed. "She feels it! And yes, she can hear it. It's ... well, it's kind of loud."

Ashton smiled and laughed a little. Loud was part of the game.

Amanda and Aggie left, but not before Ashton had his manager get their contact information. He wanted to follow up with these two, later. He wanted to know more.

He had heard of cochlear implants, but they weren't really anything top of mind for him. His world was absolutely *filled* with sound—music and crowds and a million other noises and tones that washed over him every day. But he had a secret. Something he hadn't told anyone but his closest friends.

The sound was starting to fade.

He'd noticed it in the studio first. He kept having to up the gain on his headphones, to make out the nuances of the tracks he was producing. He could once pick out a sour note buried three tracks deep, and now he was struggling to hear all the subtleties of even one track.

Doctors confirmed it for him. He was losing his hearing. Years of exposure to loud environments had wrecked him. It was part of the reason he decided to retire after a forty-year career. He kept the real reasons quiet, of course. Publicly, he was "just ready to move on to other challenges."

He would still be a part of the industry, still produce new music with new artists. And he'd play from time to time, with some ear protection in place. But how could he walk away from music entirely? It was unthinkable.

But there were other things in life besides music. If he was being honest with himself, Ashton was starting to feel the pull of paths he hadn't taken. Not regret, exactly. More like a longing for things he'd left undone to the point of never doing them at all. A family. A legacy.

He wanted to leave something behind in the world that wasn't just plug-and-play. Years on the road had prevented him from having any real family, but maybe he could leave something else as his legacy. Maybe there was a way to do some good in the world, and have that be what people remembered about him.

After meeting Aggie and Amanda, and later talking with them at length about Aggie's implants, Ashton felt he had his new mission.

Cochlear implants weren't a new technology. They were invented in 1979, by Professor Graeme Clark, at the University of Melbourne in Australia. Over the next thirty years they saw a great deal of advancement and improvement, and by 2012 there were over three-hundred-thousand implants in use, worldwide. Almost forty-thousand of those who depended on cochlear implants were children.

In the years since that official number, hundreds of thousands of additional adults and kids had gotten cochlear implants. A quick tour of YouTube had shown Ashton dozens of "first sound" videos—children and even adults hearing the sound of a loved one's voice for the first time in their lives. These videos were profound, and brought tears to his eyes. He could barely imagine what it would be like, to suddenly hear for the first time.

It didn't happen all at once, but over the course of months, after retiring from the stage, Ashton started to come up with a plan. He consulted with his business manager, who put him in touch with a few people in the know. From there he met with experts and advisors. He'd seen more suits in the past two months than he'd seen in his entire life up to then, but they were telling him exactly what he had hoped to hear.

After half a century of being a rock star, he had the money and the connections to do something, and as someone suffering from progressive hearing loss himself, he had plenty of motive. But the real driving force for him was Aggie, and kids like her. He had a chance to leave a legacy that involved children after all.

Within six months of retiring from the stage, the Ashton Mink Sound Lab was established—a research and development facility set up as a hybrid charity.

That last bit had been particularly interesting to Ashton. It had come as advice from several of the big movers and shakers he knew—people who regularly did TED Talks and created startups that had a real impact on the world. Ashton had played enough charity and fundraising events for these folks that a lot of them knew him, liked him, even owed him favors. And it was through them that he came across the hybrid charity concept.

The idea was that, overall, charities weren't very effective.

Completely reliant on donations and good-will benefactors, charitable organizations rarely had the funds to attract top talent, much less to conduct the kind of highly technical and innovative research that Ashton wanted his organization to do. The real movers in the world were businesses—corporations set up for profit. The problem was, for-profit businesses tended to make decisions based on what was in the best interest of shareholders, while charities were designed to benefit people in need.

One of Ashton's high profile friends pointed him to a TED Talk by Dan Palotta, titled "The way we think about charity is dead wrong." Palotta's talk focused on the concept that a charitable organization could do more good if it could attract better CEOs, better marketing experts, better researchers, and so forth. The only way to attract that kind of talent, however, was with money. An organization that is set up for profit is in a better position to fund humanitarian efforts than a non-profit.

This presented some challenges.

The answer, according to Palotta, was a hybrid of the two models, in which a for-profit business used part of its revenue to further humanitarian causes, typically in exchange for tax relief and other benefits. The result, though, would be a corporation built around people in need as its primary share-holders.

That talk changed everything for Ashton, giving him a perspective he'd never had before. It also cinched what he planned to do.

Rather than make his organization a non-profit, he instead made it a profit-based business that shared what it produced for the benefit of those in need. The direction and goals of the company incorporated two directives, with the for-profit side directly facilitating the non-profit side.

AMSL—often pronounced *AM-SUL* by the press— conducted research and developed new sound-based tech-nologies that were sold or licensed for profit. Those profits were used to fund the growth of the charitable side of the business, which was aimed at the development of better tech-nologies to help the hearing impaired.

It worked better than Ashton had even dreamed. With his endorsement, and with the company's ability to attract top talent—from marketing to management to research—the business grew rapidly. Within the first year, AMSL had hired some of the most respected experts in a variety of disciplines, and it was starting to make waves in the world, across a variety of industries.

To date, AMSL held nearly a thousand new patents, and was licensing many of those to major corporations world-wide. The business was directly responsible for radical new advancements in fields such as surround sound, noise cancelling, improved smartphone tech, and more. Even the medical industry was benefiting from advancements in sonic-based equipment, including new non-invasive scanning and surgical tools.

But the biggest success came from the original mission—these new advancements were making cochlear implants better by reducing their size, increasing their capabilities, and dramatically reducing their costs. In the three years since founding AMSL, the cost per implant had gone from nearly fifty-thousand dollars per unit to around five-thousand. And for every implant sold, another was donated to a child in need.

It was a company and a legacy to be proud of. It was something honorable for Ashton to leave in the world. His music had touched hearts and changed lives over a long and successful career, but his technology would improve the lives of millions, and for centuries to come. He couldn't think of a better mark to leave.

And then there was the discovery.

It had started innocently enough. One of the researchers and his partner pitched the idea of technology that could directly interface a cochlear device with a human brain, without the need for surgery. A 'wearable,' as they called it—a device tuned to the individual, and something they could carry with them, without having it attached to their skull. Maybe it would be a necklace. Or a watch. Or a pair of glasses. It could even be integrated with existing technology, such as a smartphone.

If this team succeeded, it would change everything for so many people. A new way to bring hearing to the deaf, better hearing to the impaired, maybe even super hearing to people with no impairments at all.

Basically, the pitch was a cure for deafness.

That really got Ashton worked up. He was all smiles

about it, every time the updates came. He didn't have much to do with the day-to-day research of his company, since he was more of the face of the business than a director. But he'd taken a very personal interest in this one. He was highly invested.

The coolest thing, though, was that the research was based on something old and archaic.

The lead researcher—Dr. Simon Patel—happened to have a background in studying acoustic theory and technology throughout the ages. He was an expert on everything from the inventions of the phonograph and the telephone to more obscure audio technology that was nearly lost to history. He was a profoundly gifted engineer, Ashton was told, and brought a very fresh and innovative perspective to his work.

Ashton wasn't much for history, but he appreciated the idea of taking something old and making it serve a new purpose. Maybe it was his age. He was feeling a little ancient, these days, but he'd managed to find new purpose, to be put to new use. So, he could appreciate what Dr. Patel was bringing to the game.

In fact, Patel's knowledge of history eventually led to an obscure collection of research conducted in the early 1700s.

Ashton couldn't remember all the details, but he knew that it involved a priest or a monk or someone studying the tritone—what a lot of people referred to as 'the devil's interval.' Some chords were thought to cause people to think naughty thoughts, was how Ashton perceived it. The devil in the music.

Ashton new what a tritone was, of course. Most musicians did.

Basically, a tritone, or a 'tri,' was half an octave, or three whole steps between two notes. It was a perfect fifth, with a flat, or an augmented fourth, with a sharp. When you played a series of tritones it could sound like an old horror movie soundtrack—kind of creepy and edgy. But most music resolved the tritones, transitioning into music that people were familiar and cool with. Music with an emotional impact tended to stick with a listener.

The point of what Simon Patel uncovered, however, wasn't really the tritone itself. He'd come across research about how tone and frequency could influence people, creating feelings and impressions, maybe even hallucinations. And even better, he'd discovered that the right frequencies created these impressions even in people who were incapable of hearing.

Sound could influence thinking, even if someone couldn't hear it.

That was exactly what they needed. And as soon as Ashton heard it he put the full weight of his 51 shares in AMSL behind digging deeper, making sure Patel got all the funding and resources he needed.

For months, Patel led a team of squints—Ashton's name for the white-coated lab workers who mostly knew his music from TV commercials and movie soundtracks. They were a square bunch, but very good at their work. It took less than a year for them to make the breakthrough everyone had been hoping for, with Patel feeding them insights and ideas to drive things along. Patel was a marvel, coming up with new theories and practically inventing new technologies overnight. And this tech, which they had jokingly code-named "Devil's Interval," was purely next-level. Patel would go into the history books over this work.

They had technology that could transmit sound directly into the brain, without the need for surgery.

Trials started as soon as they had a prototype, and that was when Ashton wanted to yank his hair out. There was a protocol to these things, he was told repeatedly. Everything had to be done in order, and on a timeline, before they could get approval for human trials. But eventually those hoops were jumped through, expedited a bit by donations to the right lobbyists at the right time.

Ashton felt no particular shame about influencing the system a little. This work was going to do so much for the world. A little rule bending wasn't going to kill anyone.

The research continued, and things went very, very well. The first people to take place in the trials could hear the test tones easily, though many of them had no way to actually interpret this new sensation. It was like watching those "first sound" videos all over again, Ashton had thought with pride.

It took fine-tuning, but every test subject eventually reacted to the test tones, even if they'd never heard a sound in their entire lives.

It was the breakthrough they'd been hoping for, and it was a cause for huge celebration. Ashton had arranged a big party, right here in his own penthouse, to laud Patel and his team.

Too soon, as it turned out.

Within weeks of the first successful trials, the team started to report side effects among the test subjects. Ashton didn't understand quite everything they brought to the next review meeting, but he understood the implications of it all. Their technology, which was such an amazing hope for the world, was dangerous. Scary dangerous.

Ashton sat in with the team and AMSL's CEO and COO when the results were given. It was a pretty dark day. A scary day. And Ashton found himself wondering how he, of all people, had come to be in this place, making the choices he was forced to make. He was a musician, an artist. His work had been rock-and-roll, up until just a few short years ago. In a lot of ways, music was still the only thing he really knew. What was he doing, sitting at the head of a table full of people who were discussing something so dangerous, it could be compared to the atomic bomb?

It was a hard decision, but everyone agreed that this research had to be scrapped. Every public record of it would be erased, and related research kept aside would be classified to the point of being nearly non-existent.

Ashton had agreed to all of this. He owned this company, and controlled a majority of the shares, and so he'd been included in the decision. But he could tell that his CEO and COO would have preferred to keep him out of it. Maybe to protect him. Or maybe to keep him from interfering, if he hadn't agreed with them. But he had agreed. Of course, he had agreed.

The data was wiped from AMSL's systems. The prototypes were all destroyed. And Patel and his team were all forced to sign non-disclosure agreements, with penalties that would have caused Bill Gates to file for government assistance.

It was done. Buried. No one would explore that avenue again—not in that direction, at least, and certainly not at AMSL.

Except …

Ashton was no scientist. He'd done rather poorly in grade school, and had dropped out of high school to start his first band. But over the years he'd come to appreciate learning and knowledge, and there was a part of him that couldn't stand the idea of letting something brilliant be lost forever. It would be like losing a tune that came to you in a dream—losing perfect lyrics that could move someone to tears. He couldn't stand the thought that they'd come so close to this, and now it had to be torn down by their own hands, lost to history forever.

His legacy. Lost.

He couldn't just let it go.

So, he'd made a copy.

It was just the data from the company's network. The prototypes were all destroyed. But Ashton had used his own personal clearance to snag the bits and pieces that AMSL had agreed to keep. And he'd gotten lucky. Six months earlier, Patel's research partner, Dr. Bristol, had died in an accident, and her records had all been secured and stored. That was the rule, put in place by AMSL's security chief, Nick Peters. And it was a lucky break.

Her files contained sensitive information, about ongoing projects. Including this one. If he was being honest, Ashton had to admit that he had no idea how complete this data was. But Bristol had been active in the start of the trials, so there was a good chance she had records of nearly everything.

Ashton wasn't sure how he'd stumbled across her files. He'd been in the system, rooting around for anything related to the project. It had a very memorable codename—Devil's Interval. Ashton wasn't much for computers, but he could use a search engine, and he grabbed anything tagged with that codename. His clearance must have given him access to the secured and archived files as well as active ones. That's all he could figure.

He had used microSD card to smuggle out everything that had been on the system—a maneuver that rather made him feel like a spy. He had, in fact, hummed the 'Mission Impossible' theme as he made his exit.

Getting that SD card out of the building was as easy as pie. No one ever searched the owner of the company. In fact, unlike everyone else, who had to trot in and out of security on the main floor, Aston had the option of leaving by heli-copter from the roof, unmolested and unscanned. Which was exactly what he'd done.

That had been two weeks ago. The research was all gone

now. The prototypes all destroyed. Every bit of progress they'd made had been set back.

Ashton was now considering his options. At first, he thought he might approach some of the other researchers from the company—those who had not signed the NDA. But that might tip someone off, and cause headaches he wasn't prepared to deal with. So instead he reached out to his network again, asking around to see who might be able to take on this level of research and development. Maybe he could hire someone privately. Someone who wasn't already working for him.

His business manager had some promising leads, and he was already scheduling meetings with a few people. One of those meetings was to take place in the morning, right here in Ashton's penthouse. It was the safest place, with no chance of paparazzi or eavesdropping.

That appointment put Ashton here in his home for the first time in weeks. Travel had always been a part of his work, mostly on tour buses, but also First Class flights and the, eventually, private jets. His travel had always been about the music before, but these days, as often as not, it was about AMSL business. He was constantly making appearances, doing interviews, meeting with investors and shareholders and potential partners. He let his business manager handle all the finer details, but it was important for Ashton himself to be there, as the face of the company.

It was boring, and exhausting, but as long as he had a guitar with him he weathered it well enough. He could handle just about anything, with a guitar in his hand.

Now, though, he was hope for once. And he was having mixed feelings about it.

His apartment was dark and quiet, which was always a little unnerving to him. It reminded him too much of the hearing loss he was suffering. These days he could use tech from his own company to compensate for his hearing loss, but he was holding out. Devil's Interval would have been an invisible way to restore his hearing. He wasn't ready for the world to see him with even one of AMSL's sleek and stream-lined hearing aids.

He looked out over the Manhattan skyline, a perforated pattern of lights interrupted by streams of neon. Spotlights ranged and roved in the distance, sweeping signals across the sky, telling people where to find the party. The sounds of the street were muted from this height, and from the thick glass of his windows. Ashton shook himself, and took his phone out of his pocket. After a few taps there was music, playing just loud enough from speakers around the room that it could wash over him and make him feel more at home and less isolated.

Much better.

He also brought up lights from under the cabinets and racks around the space, providing some ambient atmosphere. Nothing too jarring. This had been a long day, and he just wanted to relax a bit before turning in. He'd pour himself a whiskey—probably Wild Turkey. He might have money and might have a skyline view of Manhattan, but he was still a Texas son. It was hard to beat the small town out of some-body, even after several decades.

He sat at his piano—a refurbished Steinway Grand from the 1800s that had cost him ninety-thousand back in the 80s. It was perfectly tuned, and playing it had always taken him back to his early days, learning piano from his grandfa-ther, playing Baptist Hymns on the rickety box that Gramps kept in a shed behind the house. It had been too big to be in the house proper. And unfortunately, after years of sitting in the heat and humidity of that backwater Texas town, it had suffered a great deal of rot and decay.

By the time Ashton had become successful enough to

afford restoring it, there wasn't enough left to restore. He'd had to settle for having the old piano bench fixed and polished—though he kept the nicks and dings, the character of the thing. He paired it with this very expensive older cousin to his grandfather's rickety instrument, and the incongruity of it made him smile every time. He could just imagine Gramps scoffing at the finery of the Steinway, telling Ashton, "You might get the sound out of that thing, but you won't get the soul."

Ashton smiled. He patted the bench, and then looked up at the old, ragged hymnal that he kept on the Steinbeck's music rack. He'd opened that hymnal only a handful of times over the past few decades. More so recently.

Ashton's career had been hard rock-and-roll, but he still appreciated the classics. The soulful sounds of R&B. The sexual undertones of smooth jazz. And, maybe out of a sense of familial nostalgia, the strident and hopeful marches of those old country hymns.

He played one now—*Amazing Grace*—and smiled as he thought of Gramps belting out the lyrics in his gravely baritone, as if singing it loud enough might save someone's life.

Ashton stopped playing when he heard another sound, though, from somewhere in the apartment.

"Hello?" he called.

Maybe Richard, his business manager, had stopped by. They had partnered to produce a few new artists, and sometimes that work went late. Richard had a key, and an open invitation to use the spare bedroom, even if Ashton was out of town.

"Richard, that you?" Ashton called, still tinkering with the keys of the Steinway.

But there was no answer.

Ashton stood from the bench and looked around. The darkness of the apartment was broken by the downlights below the cabinets and above the racks of albums and CDs and awards. There were still deep pockets of shadow everywhere, though. And for the first time, those shadows were giving Ashton a bad feeling.

"Anybody here?" he asked.

There was a slight thump, and it sounded like it was coming from one of the guest bedrooms. Maybe it was Richard, after all? But something wasn't right.

Ashton moved toward the sound, picking up one of his guitars in the process. They didn't call these things 'axes' for nothing. It wouldn't be the first time Ashton had used one to beat the crap out of an overzealous fan.

He reached into his pocket and took out his phone, hitting speed dial for the front desk. "I think I may need security," he said to the girl who answered.

"We'll have someone up there in just a moment, Mr. Mink. Do you need me to dial 911?"

"No, I don't think so. I'm not sure, actually."

"I'm calling to be safe. Please find a safe place, Mr. Mink. Security should be there any second."

He hung up. "Any second," he said to whoever was hiding in the space. "You hear that? Now look, I don't like having lay a beat down on somebody. And I'd rather we didn't have any problems. If you're a fan, I get it. I'm happy to sign something. I can even give you a little gift. If you're here to rob me, then just take what you want and leave now. I won't even try to stop you."

Again, there was no answer, and Ashton was starting to wonder if he was imagining things.

He was about to give up, to go out into the hall and wait for security. He'd let them do a sweep, just to make sure things were ok. But he was sure at this point that he was imagining the whole thing.

Suddenly, someone pressed something hard and frightening into his back.

"Tell me where you have hidden the data," a man's voice said.

"I …" Ashton started, but was cut off as the gun was pressed harder into his back.

"Before you lie to me, I know that you have it. I know it was taken from your company's network, two weeks ago, and I know that you saved it to a microSD. Where is it?"

Ashton shook his head. "It ain't here, brother. I don't have it."

"You have one more chance," the voice said. "If you don't tell me now, I'll kill every guard that comes through that door, and then I'll kill you. Do I sound like someone who would bluff about that?"

Ashton swallowed, and felt sweat moving down his side, under his shirt. "No," he said. "Please …"

"Where?" the voice asked.

Ashton pointed a shaking hand at his piano. "There," he said. "The … it's in the hymnal."

The man jerked Ashton backward, then pushed him forward toward the piano. "Grab it," he said.

Ashton reached out and grabbed the old book, knocking a ream of blank composing paper and a couple of pens to the floor as he picked it up.

The hymnal was one of the few things he had left from his grandfather. It had been part of Ashton's origin story—part of the beginning of his career. It had started all of this. It was the foundation of everything, including AMSL. Ashton hesitated as a part of him rebelled, wanting to protect the book from this man.

"Give me the chip," the man said.

His hands shaking, Ashton opened the hymnal to the back cover. He worked a fingernail into the seam where the cover met the pages, and peeled the paper backing away just enough to reveal the microSD, stuck with a bit of adhesive to the cardboard stock. He lifted the tiny memory card out between his index finger and his thumb.

There was a hard knock on his front door then.

"Mr. Mink, this is building security. We are using our master key to enter."

"Give me the card," the man said, holding out a gloved palm.

Ashton shakily placed the card in the man's hand. "Please, just leave, ok? I'll distract the guards, have them look in my bedroom. You can just hide near the door and rush out. They'll never see you."

The man said nothing, and the front door opened, casting a cone of light across the floor.

The guards were ex-police officers, hired at salaries that far exceeded what they made on the Force. They were trained, and they knew how to deal with hostage situations. They were skilled in negotiation, and in taking down bad guys.

They were dead before they'd even drawn their weapons.

Two silenced shots from the man's gun, striking the chests of the two former police officers.

Ashton let out a yell, and as hysterics overtook him it turned into a scream. Years of belting high-pitched lyrics on stage made that scream powerful and even, and there was a hope that maybe someone would hear it. Maybe they'd come to his rescue.

The man shoved Ashton hard, sending him to the floor. As Ashton rolled over, the man aimed at him. "I loved your music," he said. "Big fan."

He pulled the trigger.

PART 1

CHAPTER 1

THE MANHATTAN OFFICES OF THE FBI'S NEW HISTORIC Crimes Division were just a couple of cramped rooms crammed into a far corner of the FBI's regular, newly-remodeled offices. One space served as a conference room, for those very rare times that there were more than two people working a case. The other served as Agent Roland Denzel's office.

Dan Kotler had wandered into the latter with two cups of coffee in his hands. He placed one on Denzel's desk, and was in no way surprised when his agent friend didn't so much as look up from his laptop. Denzel reached for the coffee, brought it to his lips, and *then* looked at Kotler, surprised.

"This is good," he said.

"It's from that new place a block over."

"The Greek place?"

Kotler nodded, smiling and sipping at his own dense and dark brew.

Denzel nodded appreciatively and turned back to his screen. "Welcome back. How are things in Atlantis? You were there nearly three weeks this time."

Kotler laughed. "Good, but slow. I was helping to organize dive teams to explore the sunken parts of the city. There's a lot down there, but the currents and some tectonic issues make things dicey. We sent a robotic probe in and got some amazing images, though. I expect it will be a few more months before the research team decides to make an official public announcement. Also, we're not sure it's Atlantis."

This made Denzel finally look up. "What?"

"Well, it has all the earmarks," Kotler said. "The evidence for is pretty strong, but the evidence against is getting stronger."

"But we were shot at," Denzel said.

Kotler laughed again. "That isn't really considered proof, Roland."

"What about all that nonsense with Gail McCarthy and Eric van Burren?"

Kotler shrugged. "That only proves that they *thought* it was Atlantis. We're still verifying everything." Seeing the look of near devastation on Denzel's face, Kotler retreated a bit. "Don't worry, it's still a significant archeological discovery. At this point, there's just as much a chance that it really is Atlantis. But you wouldn't arrest someone without proof, right? You'd make a case, based on facts. It's the same thing. Think of archeology as the FBI of history."

Denzel scoffed and sipped his coffee, shaking his head in quiet disbelief.

Kotler knew what he was feeling. It was so tempting to just give over, to decide that things were settled and all the facts were known. It would be so much easier, and so much more fun, to just accept everything at face value and call the mystery solved. Especially in cases like this one, where both speculation and emotions ran high, and where so many lives were affected. Being able to publicly announce the discovery of the true, real, not-a-myth-or-legend Atlantis would change the world. It was disappointing to even think that they might not have it after all.

Especially after everything they'd gone through with that case (such as getting shot at), and all the lives that had been impacted.

Eric Van Burren was currently in witness protection, which was a touch better than either Kotler or Denzel had wished on him. That was frustrating, but also necessary. He had a lot of information about his grandfather's smuggling network, and the FBI was keenly interested in dismantling that. So, appalling or not, giving Eric a comfortable bed in a nice house, nestled into a suburb somewhere in the Midwest —that was the annoying and necessary reality of things.

Far worse was the fact that Gail McCarthy had escaped. Using that same smuggling network, Gail had managed to make a run for it and stay hidden all these months. There hadn't been a peep out of her. No clue as to where she was or what she was up to. That was frustrating to both Kotler and Denzel, for a variety of reasons. But mostly to Kotler

Gail had played him worst of all, masquerading as a neighbor, as a victim, even as a lover. She had been far more devious than Kotler could have anticipated, and had nearly had both Kotler and Denzel killed on multiple occasions. Worse, though, was that Kotler had been fooled so completely. He was highly trained to read body language, to see the signs of lies and deception, to intuitively and overtly understand the drives and motives behind a person's actions. He hadn't seen Gail coming until it was too late.

But that was yesterday's story. At least for now. Today was a new day, with new promise. The Atlantis project was continuing, and was now at a point where Kotler could step away, and concentrate on other things. Which brought him to here and now, in the Manhattan offices of the FBI.

Kotler needed a new thing to concentrate on.

He sipped his coffee and said, "What's on the docket these days? Anything interesting?"

Denzel leaned back, stretching a bit before folding his hands over his stomach. "I'm glad you asked," he said. "We still have the map thing."

Kotler shook his head. "The map thing isn't historic. It's not real."

"It's being played off like it is," Denzel replied. "That's the problem."

"It's a forgery. A good one, but still a forgery. That isn't really our thing, is it? Isn't that a White Collar case?"

"They're booked up," Denzel said. "And there's the whole 'lost civilization' thing."

Kotler nodded, and sighed. When this new division was commissioned, Denzel was two-for-two with solving crimes the FBI only barely had bandwidth for. He'd become something of a hero in the Bureau, after bringing down Director Crispen and solving two high-profile, history-related crimes in a row. There was buzz that echoed all the way to the Hill, where it was determined that there was a growing need for this sort of thing.

As a reward for his work in Pueblo, and at the Atlantis site, Denzel had been given the helm of a new division, and carte blanche to pick personnel to man his team. As his first pick, Denzel had engaged Kotler as a resource on retainer, though Kotler had set things up so his fee went to charity. He had no need for a salary, and didn't feel right taking one. It was better for the money to go to a good cause, such as funding science and history programs in underprivileged schools.

For a few months after the Atlantis case, Denzel and Kotler had been rock stars at the Bureau. Every case that had even a hint of 'misplaced history' was sent their way. Most turned out to be mundane, lacking any real connection to actual historic or archeological facts or events, and often turning out to be scams or forgeries.

Case in point, 'the map thing,' which Kotler had determined to be a forgery of a sixteenth century nautical map, that supposedly pointed to a lost civilization in the Antarctic.

It had taken Kotler only thirty minutes to prove the map was a fake, but the case persisted because the forger had not yet been apprehended, and the suspect who had tried to sell the map was insisting that it was a replica of a real document, and that it was accurate.

The case wasn't quite in the purview of the new Historic Crimes Division, but it was deemed 'close enough.' Kotler was happy to help, in all the ways he could, but at this point there really wasn't much left for him to do. Unless they could locate the forger, and somehow verify that the fake was based on a real map, Kotler's usefulness amounted mostly to helping Denzel brainstorm leads.

He was about to comment on this, again, but at that moment Denzel's desk phone rang. "Agent Denzel."

Kotler settled into his chair, sipping his coffee and looking at the decor of Denzel's office, which trended toward memorabilia. There were framed photos of Denzel with various political figures and a couple of celebrities. A signed Nolan Ryan baseball card was in a small frame resting on a shelf next to an autographed baseball from the same pitcher. There was a photo of Denzel with President Obama, and another with President George W. Bush. There were also photos with various high-ranking officers of the Bureau, though notably no photo with Director Crispen.

And, to Kotler's delight, there were news clippings about the Coelho Medallion, as well as a photograph of the ruins at the Atlantis site. These told Kotler a story about Denzel— that he was proud of his work, but also inspired by it. And as a part of that work, Kotler was gratified to know of its impact. Maybe he would take this 'map thing' a bit more seriously.

"Detective Holden?" Denzel asked. "What can I do for you?"

Holden. Kotler recognized that name, but it took a moment to place it. Detective Peter Holden, with the NYPD. He'd been the lead detective working the murder of Morgan Keller, the former Head of Acquisitions at Baker Tait. She had been murdered by Gail McCarthy, or by someone she'd hired—though they'd been unable to prove it so far. Was this something to do with that investigation?

"Detective, I'm afraid I don't really handle murder investigations, so …"

Kotler watched as his friend's face went through a rainbow of micro expressions. There was skepticism, or something akin to it, and a bit of stubbornness as Denzel internally decided to ignore Holden's request for assistance. Then something changed. There was a spark. Denzel's eyes darted to the newspaper clipping and the photo on his wall, and Kotler could see that his interest had been piqued.

"That does sound interesting," Denzel said. "Hold on." He held the phone aside and looked at Kotler. "What do you know about something called 'the Devil's Interval?'"

THEY ARRIVED at the high-rise home of Ashton Mink less than an hour later. It was quite close to Kotler's apartment. In fact, Kotler had bumped into Ashton a few times at local events—the type where Ashton was asked to be a guest rather than a performer, and where he and Kotler were valued more for their checkbooks than for whatever their contributions to society might be.

For all that, Kotler hadn't really known Ashton very well,

and wasn't sure Ashton knew who he was at all. But the man had seemed interesting and kind, if a bit eccentric. And his company was doing amazing things in the field of acoustic research. Some of the technology used in Kotler's own field was built around AMSL's patents.

Kotler and Denzel were greeted by two uniformed police officers standing in the doorway to Ashton's apartment. Denzel showed his badge and Kotler showed his FBI consultant ID. It was the coolest thing about his contract with the Bureau, and Denzel had made him swear on his life that he would never abuse it for fun. Kotler had mostly lived up to his word on that promise.

Inside the apartment, a forensic team was at work combing through everything. Kotler saw with relief that the victims had already been removed. There were little numbered cards placed on each blood-soaked spot on the carpet, but no taped outlines or other evidence that a body had lain there.

Kotler had no problem with dead bodies—he'd seen more of the dead than most living people ever had. He had no driving desire to see more, however. He could live with a corpse-free day, just fine.

Detective Holden was consulting with a lab tech, whose white polypropylene coveralls stood in stark contrast to Holden's rumpled brown suit and coffee-stained shirt. His necktie was loosened just enough to reveal a missing top button on his shirt collar, its severed threads coiling and bending away from the fabric like thin, white weeds. Holden looked exhausted, which was exactly how Kotler remembered him from the last time.

"Agent Denzel, thank you for coming," Holden said. He then turned to Kotler. "And you're the squint."

Kotler nodded. "We've met before."

"I remember," Holden said. "You're the archeologist guy.

The one who found all those Vikings in Colorado. I read about you."

Kotler only nodded. Holden's body language was sending all sorts of signals, particularly his disdain for Kotler. But he was also showing signs of deep respect for Denzel, which seemed unusual. The FBI and the NYPD had a notoriously bad relationship at times. At least, if the whole of modern fiction was to be believed.

"Ok, let's get to this," Holden said. He turned and caught the eye of one of the forensic personnel—a young woman in white coveralls—and waved her over. She wound her way between markers on the floor, and when she arrived she presented a large plastic bag, zip closed at the top, and marked with details about the case. Holden took the bag, held it up and looked through it, then handed it to Kotler.

"You know anything about this?" he asked.

Kotler examined the contents of the bag, turning it to get more light from the large windows of Ashton Mink's apartment.

Through the clear plastic, he could see a torn piece of paper, bloodstained around the edges. It seemed weathered by age, but otherwise clean enough to make out the shaky handwriting: *Devil's Interval.*

Kotler turned the bag over and saw that on the reverse side were musical notations. In the top margin of the page were the words "Take the Name of Jesus With You," and in the bottom margin was the page number.

"This is a page from an old Baptist hymnal," Kotler said aloud, looking closer. "Maybe from the 1940s or '50s."

"We know that part," Holden said. "The handwriting on the back. The Devil thing."

Kotler nodded, turning the bag over and once again examining the writing. "Shaky," he said. "Written under extreme duress. I'm guessing by the fact that there's blood on it that Ashton wrote this as he was dying?"

"That's our guess," Holden nodded. "What does it mean?"

"Well, the Devil's Interval is a tritone," Kotler said. "It's a pretty common interval in music, actually. But back in the early eighteenth century there was a concern that it was evil, and that using it could create a sense of dread in the listener, that was basically the devil encroaching on their soul."

"That's what Elizabeth said," Holden nodded, indicating the woman who had presented the bag. "Dr. Elizabeth Ludlum," Holden said. "She's our Lead Forensic Specialist."

Kotler turned to Dr. Ludlum, who had taken off a rubber glove and extended her hand to him, smiling. "Dr. Kotler, it's a privilege to meet you! I started my career in Forensic Anthropology, and I've read practically everything you've published."

Kotler smiled. Since the events in Pueblo, he'd gained quite a bit of notoriety, even from people on the streets, but it had cost him a lot of the respect he'd once held within the scientific community. It had become rare indeed to hear praise for his academic work, especially work published prior to the events surrounding the discovery of the Coelho Medallion.

This made Kotler take an instant liking to Dr. Elizabeth Ludlum. He was aware of the implications—that his ego was driving.

However, ego or not, he had always enjoyed meeting intelligent women. It didn't hurt that Dr. Ludlum was very attractive, of course. Though the observation did make Kotler question his own perspective. He knew his faults, and his weakness.

Dr. Ludlum was a young woman of African descent, with a deep, flawless complexion of mocha and *créme*, accentuating startlingly bright hazel eyes and a glistening smile that was entirely captivating. She wore her hair long, but had it in a ponytail to facilitate her work in the field. The baggy over-alls hid her figure, but she seemed somewhat diminutive. Except that she was tall—as tall as Kotler himself.

Kotler blinked. He realized he'd paused just a bit too long in reply, but sped ahead anyway. "Good to meet you," he said, taking her hand and smiling.

Denzel cleared his throat. "So, Kotler, can you tell us anything else about this? Anything that might give us a clue as to why Mr. Mink wrote it?"

Kotler again refocused his attention on the bag, turning it over once more to examine the musical notes. "Do we know where this page came from?" he asked.

Dr. Ludlum answered, "He tore it out of an old hymnal. We've bagged that, too, since there's blood on it."

"Can I examine it?" Kotler asked.

Ludlum ushered them to a bar top that was being used by the forensic team as a convenient place to make notes and take photographs of small objects. Resting on the bar was another large, plastic bag, and within was the hymnal.

"Can we open it?" Kotler asked.

Ludlum nodded and pulled on a new set of rubber gloves. She took a pair of forceps from what looked like an antique doctor's bag, tore open the sterile paper sleeve for them, and laid them on top of the paper on the bar's surface. She then used a small scalpel to cut the bag open. "I'll need to rebag it when we're done, and note what we do here, to preserve the chain of custody."

Kotler nodded.

She laid the hymnal on a piece of sterile, lint-free cloth, and opened it to the very back, where the last page had been torn. She turned to Kotler and handed him the forceps.

He took these, and very carefully began turning the pages

of the hymnal, examining each one. There were no more torn pages, and it seemed the blood droplets were confined to the exterior surface of the book. By all evidence, Ashton had opened the back cover and gone straight to tearing out the final page. Kotler flipped the pages to the front again, so he could examine those remaining, as well as the back cover.

Stooping and looking at both the page and back cover at angles, with the light cascading in from the window, Kotler could see that there were subtle impressions from pen strokes, and they matched what had been written on the torn page. "He wrote it while it was still in the hymnal," he said, noting details out of habit. They may or may not be important to the investigation, but you never knew.

He picked up the hymnal now, and turned it in the light, looking at the interior of the back cover. There was a large, bloody blotch there, possibly form Ashton's thumb, but also something else.

"There's an impression in the paper covering the cardboard stock," he said.

"There is?" Ludlum asked, leaning in, close. She smelled of a very distracting perfume, and Kotler blinked a few times before using the forceps to point out his findings.

"There," he said, lightly tracing the indentation. "It's bulging outward, slightly. Whatever made it was beneath the paper, between it and the card stock." He ran the tip of the forceps along the edge of the paper, and gently took an edge, pulling it away. There was a bit of adhesive there, just enough to hold things together but not enough to glue the cover in place permanently. "Temporary adhesive," he said. "Like what they use to make sticky notes. This was a hiding place."

He stood upright, looking around, and spotted a photographer's loupe a foot or so to his left. "May I?" he asked Ludlum, who nodded.

He held the loupe to his eye and examined the corner of

the cover, looking first at the slight bulge outside, then peeling the paper back to look inside.

The adhesive had formed a slight ridge around what had been stuck there, and it was preserved by the air gap of the bulge. Kotler could see the shape of it. And as he looked closer, he saw a small scrap of white paper, contrasting sharply against the aged paper of the hymnal.

He tugged at this with the forceps, removing it. The word "microSD" was mostly visible, only partly obscured from the tear.

"There was a memory card hidden here," he said. "A microSD card. The kind you might use for additional memory in a smartphone. Ashton must have hidden it here."

"Something to do with his company?" Holden asked. He consulted a small notebook. "AMSL?"

"I'd make that guess," Kotler said. "But I couldn't say for certain."

Holden noted this. "I'm stopping by there this afternoon. I'll ask them about this. You still don't know what he meant by 'Devil's Interval?'"

Kotler thought about this, but shook his head. "I'm sorry, Detective. I can tell you about the history of the phrase at length, but I can't determine why he wrote it."

"I'd like to get a full statement from you about it, then," Holden said. "Everything you know."

"That could be quite an essay," Kotler smiled. "As in volumes. It would help to be able to narrow things down a bit. To have some context."

"Mind if we tag along on your interview at AMSL?" Denzel asked, suddenly.

Holden looked up at him, as if he were about to tear into him, but stopped. He frowned, shook his head, and said, "Sure. Just remember, this is my investigation. You two are here to assist, not take over."

"Wouldn't dream of it," Denzel replied, smiling.

Holden turned back to Kotler. "If you think of anything relevant, I'd appreciate the heads up."

Kotler nodded, and the three of them moved away, back out into the hall.

As they exited, Kotler spared one last glance at Dr. Elizabeth Ludlum, who quickly looked away and tried to pretend she hadn't watched them go.

CHAPTER 2

AMSL FACILITY

DENZEL AND KOTLER ARRIVED SHORTLY AFTER
Detective Holden, walking into the lobby of Ashton Mink
Sound Lab just as Holden was clearing their entry with secu-
rity. He waved the two of them over.

Denzel produced his FBI credentials before Kotler had
even had a chance to think about it, and for a few seconds
Kotler was less than his usual pulled-together self, fumbling
through his coat pocket for the consultant ID, and flipping it
open for the guard to inspect.

"Smooth," Denzel said.

Kotler grimaced a bit, shaking his head. "I'm new at
this part."

"It shows," Denzel replied, a small smirk on his lips. Any
chance to show up Kotler—multi-doctorate, multi-disci-
plined, world-renowned archeologist—would be taken
without mercy. Kotler was aware of the sibling-like rivalry he
and Denzel shared, and it made him smile. Even if his ego
might take a bruise from time to time.

They were shown to a secured elevator, and escorted to

the executive floors by a trim guard with a military haircut. "Fresh out?" Denzel asked the guard.

"Got home two months ago," the guard replied. "Spent six years in Iraq. My brother got me this job before I'd even left the desert."

"Must be a nice change," Denzel said.

"Not a grain of sand for miles," the guard smiled.

The doors opened and the guard—Jared Partano, as he introduced himself—led them to a secretary seated behind a large desk. He introduced them, and then returned to the elevator.

"This way, gentlemen," the secretary said, as he led the three of them down a corridor and into a large conference room. "Mr. Miller and Mr. Chandler will be here in a moment. There is water and coffee at the bar."

The secretary left, and the three of them milled about, waiting. Kotler poured himself a cup of coffee, and when he looked up Holden was giving him a look. "We're not here for book club," the Detective grumbled.

Kotler nodded, smiled, and sipped the coffee, which was excellent. As he knew it would be. Even better, somehow, with the detective's disapproval.

Kotler looked around the conference room, gathering details to see what story this place could tell. An occupational hazard, but also a habit that served Kotler well. You never knew when a tiny detail could have a very large impact on your day.

It was obvious how much influence Ashton Mink's personality had on the business. There were framed and signed concert posters and photographs on the walls. A signed Gibson Les Paul was mounted in a glass case, positioned on top of a credenza and lit from behind to further accentuate its glory. Just about everywhere Kotler looked, in fact, there were signs of Ashton's career, displayed proudly, and meant to make an impression.

It was very personal, Kotler determined. It showed how invested Ashton had been in this place. It made clear that this wasn't the result of advice from a money manager, intending to diversify and boost Ashton's portfolio. The company was, in every way, a part of the man himself. A legacy.

Seeing Ashton's reflection in every corner of this room gave Kotler a profound respect for the man, and a troubled heart over his murder.

The door opened and two men entered. Each was young, tan and trim, dressed in slacks, but each wearing only button-down shirts, and no ties. Not what one would expect from executives of one of the most profitable technology firms in Manhattan, but still a bit formal for the company of a rock star.

Middle ground, Kotler thought, as he shook their hands.

"I'm Ross Miller, CEO," the taller one said. His hair was jet black and cut short in a messy, spiked coiffure. "This is Garret Chandler, our COO."

Chandler may have been the younger of the two, with a boyish face and brown hair that lay a bit longer than his CEO. He had a slightly softer look, compared to Miller, particularly around the eyes. And unlike Miller, Chandler's bearing was poised, almost like a dancer. It was a curious bit of body language, from Kotler's perspective. Chandler seemed almost feminine, as if he were a woman forced to dress in the trappings of a male-dominated corporate culture.

Both men seemed somber, even a bit haunted, indicating that they'd already heard the news. Kotler watched their faces, looking for signs of—well, anything, really. There were details about all of this that weren't quite jelling yet, and anything could be a clue.

Holden held up his badge. "I'm Detective Holden, NYPD. This is Agent Denzel with the FBI, and Dr. Kotler, who is consulting on this case."

"FBI?" Chandler asked.

"I'm also consulting," Denzel said. "There's no Federal jurisdiction, at the moment."

"I've brought them along because they're experts on certain aspects of the case," Holden said. "But the NYPD is running this investigation." With this last, Holden gave Denzel a sidelong glance.

Denzel gave a brief nod.

"I see," Miller said, quietly. "Well, we were devastated to hear about Ashton's murder. We haven't announced it to the rest of the company yet. The board members and the share-holders were informed by email just after we got your call."

Holden nodded. "There won't be much chance of keeping this quiet. Mr. Mink was a big name."

Miller nodded, then motioned for everyone to take a seat around the large conference table. The secretary entered then, and prepared a pitcher of water and several glasses. He even refreshed Kotler's coffee, which earned Kotler another disapproving look from Holden.

Kotler sipped.

"Mr. Miller, in our investigation we've uncovered a few strange details. What can you tell me about the phrase 'the devil's interval?'"

Miller and Chandler exchanged glances. Chandler's eyebrows were raised, and both men seemed to Kotler to be near panic.

"Detective …" Chandler began, but he was cut off as Miller raised his hand.

"Detective Holden," he said, "how private is the information we share here? There are … well, there are details that are classified, and they could be dangerous if they got out."

"Everything you say to me, here and now, is part of an ongoing investigation. We don't share details with the public."

"But we can never share these details with *anyone*," Miller said, his face becoming hard. "They would represent a …" he paused, looked at Chandler, who nodded. "A public danger."

Denzel glanced at Kotler, who nodded. This was all true —no games. Whatever it was these men had to share, it was dangerous. But they were above board, and hiding nothing.

Holden had turned to Denzel, and had seen the exchange between him and Kotler. His own expression was more curious than anything. He wouldn't be aware of Kotler's skill at reading body language, of course, and would wonder why the FBI agent seemed to defer to the consultant.

Denzel spoke next. "Go ahead, Mr. Miller. I can assure you that anything you say will be kept in strict confidence. If there really is a public threat, we should know about it."

Miller nodded, though he didn't look altogether assured.

"The Devil's Interval is a codename for research conducted by one of our team, Dr. Simon Patel. It's part of the development of a next-generation cochlear implant."

"Hearing aids?" Holden asked.

Miller shook his head. "Not really. Not what you're used to. These are devices implanted in hearing impaired patients, often giving them the ability to hear for the very first time. Research into improving this technology is at the heart of AMSL. It's why Ashton founded the company in the first place. The rest," he waved off toward the walls of the conference room, a gesture meant to encompass everything that AMSL did as a business. "Everything else we do is really a support system for making that technology better. Ashton wanted it that way."

"But you're not a charity," Holden asked. "You do this for profit?"

"Yes," Chandler said. "We're a hybrid charity. We patent what we create, and license our technology to other industries. We use profits from those licenses to fund more research and development. It allows us to hire top talent, and to better serve the community. From those profits, we can provide high-need services, such as donating equipment and medical procedures to people who need it. Particularly kids. We've helped a lot more people with this model than we could have otherwise."

Holden noted this in the small pad he carried.

Kotler leaned forward then. "You mentioned Dr. Simon Patel. I've heard that name."

Holden shot Kotler a sidelong look, which Kotler ignored.

"He's an outstanding scientist," Miller said. "He has a background in the history of acoustic research. He's studied every great discovery in the field throughout recorded history. We actually fund sabbaticals for him twice a year, so he can travel and find new resources to bring to his work."

"What's his connection to the 'devil's interval?'" Holden asked.

"Dr. Patel was following a line of research from the 1700s," Miller said. "At the time, the tritone was considered evil, because of the way it made listeners feel. It is kind of creepy, when you hear a series of them. Like listening to the soundtrack of an old horror film. Dr. Patel was intrigued by what he was learning from the historic records, and saw a connection with some of our current research."

"What is the current research?" Holden asked.

Again, Miller and Chandler exchanged wary glances, and Miller said, "We were trying to determine a way to transmit sound directly to the brain, without the need for surgical implants."

Kotler sat back. "Incredible," he said. "That would certainly revolutionize the technology."

"In what way?" Holden asked, now looking at Kotler.

"Cochlear implants, and pretty much all assisted hearing technology, would become obsolete," Kotler said, glancing back at Miller and Chandler.

Miller nodded in agreement. "Dr. Patel uncovered research from Newton, who was constructing his principles of physical acoustics."

"Newton?" Denzel asked. "Isaac Newton? The guy who had an apple fall on his head?"

Miller smiled a bit wistfully. "That's exactly what Ashton said when he heard it. But yes, the same. That apple story is about his work on the theory of gravity, but he explored many more facets of physics, in his lifetime."

Denzel nodded.

Holden was jotting down more notes. "What did Dr. Patel find?"

"The answer," Chandler said. "The exact answer we needed. Newton had measured the impact of certain frequencies on the brain, though he didn't have the technology to make his measurements directly. His study was observational and anecdotal, but it provided enough data to give Patel a starting point. There were reams of records, studies of deaf people who had volunteered as subjects. Newton had experimented with a variety of tones and frequencies, generated from equipment he built himself. He had done quite a bit of research into the field, before moving on to other things. When Simon uncovered his research, it was like a treasure trove. The research was incomplete, and had a lot of gaps. But Simon is brilliant, and it didn't take long for him to make several intuitive leaps, and create a series of new patents. We made rapid progress after that."

"So, you've developed the technology?" Denzel asked.

Chandler shook his head. "We've buried it."

"Buried?" Kotler asked. "Why?"

Miller spoke up, "We never expected the results we'd get. The … well, it was horrible."

"Tell me about it," Holden said, his voice becoming grave.

"The trials went well. The technology worked exactly as we hoped. But there were side effects. The subjects gained the ability to hear, some of them for the first time in their lives. It took a bit of practice for them to understand *what* they were hearing, and to connect language and other symbolic acoustics with the visual cues they were used to. But they could hear. It was a victory. And then the first subjects started to experience dementia."

"They went crazy?" Holden asked.

Miller shook his head. "No. Not exactly. Memory loss. Confusion. Disorientation. Some of them started telling us about things they were seeing or hearing or experiencing, none of which ever really happened. One subject held a half-hour conversation with her mother while in one of our labs. Her mother died nearly twenty years ago."

"So, the technology was causing hallucinations," Kotler said.

Miller nodded. "And things got worse from there. We went back to the basics with it, trying to find where things might have gone wrong. That was when one of our technicians discovered they could …"

He stopped, looking at Chandler, who was looking at the table, staring at manicured hands.

"What could they do?" Denzel asked, and Kotler heard a note of dread in his voice.

"They could implant suggestions. Memories. Emotions." He paused, and said, "Commands."

"Wait," Holden said, looking up from his note pad. "Are you telling me you people invented a mind control device?"

Chandler was shaking his head, but Miller simply said, "Yes. And more than that. Devil's Interval could implant new memories. In effect, the technology could rewrite the personality of a subject, even overcoming their basic instincts."

"Basic instincts," Kotler said, "like self-preservation?"

Miller said nothing but stared at Kotler, as if trying to determine whether acknowledgement might mean incrimination.

Holden sank back in his chair, then looked to Denzel and Kotler.

Kotler arched his eyebrows, and put a hand on the back of his neck. "My God," he said.

Denzel leaned forward. "You did this, and then buried it? Did you report your findings?"

Miller shook his head. "No. We destroyed everything but the most basic research. All the findings, all the prototypes. Everything is gone. We wiped all the data regarding the project and had everyone sign NDAs. But we're a private company, Agent Denzel. We have no government contracts. Everything we do is funded by our own patents and licensing. We did nothing illegal or even unethical. We did the morally and ethically responsible thing, and buried this so deep it couldn't come back."

"Except you didn't," Kotler said, leaning forward.

Miller looked at him, stunned. "What? What do you mean?"

Kotler looked at Holden, who had a grim expression. "The data card," he said.

"What data card?" Chandler asked.

"Gentlemen," Holden responded, "I'm going to need to see all of your security records from the time you buried this thing until now."

CHAPTER 3

THE SECURITY OFFICES OF AMSL WERE POTENTIALLY more impressive than any Kotler had seen before. They resembled nothing less than mission control for some clandestine spy organization, with a curved bank of screens dominating an entire wall of the wide room, wrapping around a central set of tables that were themselves festooned with monitors and other devices.

Dozens of guards sat before consoles, monitoring the ins and outs of laboratories, streams of data running between terminals and mainframes, and even feeds from exterior cameras covering the building's entrances, the roof, and the operational facilities.

"I don't think the NSA has this much tech running at once," Denzel whispered to Kotler, leaning in so only he could hear.

"I feel like we're about to see a drone strike," Kotler replied, grinning.

"Detective Holden," Miller said, reaching out to put a hand on the shoulder of an older man, dressed in shirt and tie, his sleeves rolled up to his elbows. "This is Nick Peters. He's our Head of Security. Former CIA."

"Former CIA?" Denzel asked. "You left the Company to run operations for a private firm?"

"I did 45 years in service and retired with a decent pension and a nasty divorce," Peters said, his voice all gravel as he smiled and shook Denzel's hand. "I needed something to keep me sharp. And I haven't been shot at once since coming on here, which has been nice." He turned and shook hands with Detective Holden. "We're happy to help, any way we can, Detective."

"I appreciate that, Mr. Peters."

Peters turned to Kotler. "Dr. Kotler," he said, taking Kotler's hand. "It's a pleasure to meet you. I saw that special on Discovery Science, about the Vikings."

Kotler nodded. "I hope it met with approval."

Peters shrugged. "It was interesting. Some of my buddies at the Agency filled me in on a bit of what happened behind the scenes. You and Agent Denzel are national heroes."

Kotler glanced at Denzel, who seemed suddenly to want to move the conversation along. "There were a lot of heroes at that site," Kotler smiled. "My role was mostly to avoid getting shot and to consult on the unique details of the case."

This earned him a chuckle from Peters, who nodded, then motioned for them to follow to one of four small rooms at the far end of the security suite. Each room had glass walls and doors, floor to ceiling, and no blinds or shades. There were table tops built into the walls, and on these were laptops and monitors, all facing the outer glass. "Screening rooms," Peters offered. "Nothing is private here. There are microphones recording all conversation in these rooms as well, just so you know."

"Very thorough," Holden said.

Peters shrugged. "Some habits die hard. When I was

approached about heading security here, I took the job seriously."

"And we wouldn't have it any other way," Miller said, smiling. "Nick has helped us keep corporate espionage to a minimum. We've had only six occasions where someone tried to steal research or data, and Nick's team took them out of commission before any damage was done."

"We monitor everything in and out of this place," Peters said. "Digital and physical."

"Sounds pretty tight," Denzel said.

"Like a drum," Peters nodded, with no hint of a smile. This was his baby, Kotler realized. This suite, the measures he'd put in place, were an extension of himself, in the same way that the company itself had been an extension of Ashton Mink. Unlike Ashton, however, Peters was a buttoned-down guy, and this was a buttoned-down operation.

Holden turned to Miller. "You said you locked down everything regarding the Devil's Interval. Does that include Mr. Peters and the rest of these security guys?"

Miller nodded. "Nick has full access. Maybe even more security clearance than I have," he smiled. "He knows about the project, and about what we found. He personally helped us lock it all down."

Holden turned back to Peters. "That right?"

"It was me and two of my juniors. Scott Nolan and Christopher Partano."

"Partano?" Kotler asked. "Would that be Jared Partano's brother?"

Peters nodded. "That's him. Chris brought Jared to me after he left the Marines. Good kid."

Kotler smiled. "I only chatted with him for a moment, but I liked him. Good that you brought him on alongside his brother."

Peters shrugged. "Kid had one of the cleanest backgrounds I've ever run. Exemplary service in Iraq. Not so much as a speeding ticket before going in. And his brother is one of my best. I mine all the gold when I find a vein."

"Can we look at everything you have on Ashley Mink's last visit here? We have some evidence that there was a data card stolen from his apartment, on the night of his murder. The words 'Devil's Interval' were found on the scene."

Peters guided them into a screening room, and had one of his people bring a couple of extra chairs.

"Devil's Interval," Peters said, almost under his breath. He was shaking his head. "That's a nasty bit of business."

"I take it you're aware of the scarier parts of the research?" Kotler asked.

Peters looked him in the eye. "The implications of this thing are more than scary. I can tell you that there are agencies in this world that would use this to completely disrupt civilization as we know it, and enslave the entire human race under one rule. And before you get any ideas, not all those agencies wear suits or use spy satellites. There's a fundamentalist group in Pennsylvania that is actively trying to find ways to mind control people and turn them into soldiers of God, willing to die on command. And don't even ask me about the Middle East. They'd just as soon issue a worldwide suicide command and have done with the lot of us."

Kotler could see that Peters was a controlled man, right down to his body language. But that control slipped when discussing Devil's Interval. To Kotler, knowing the ex-CIA agent's fear of this technology brought home the danger of it far better than anything else he'd heard so far.

They settled into seats in the screening room, and were brought cups of coffee, notepads, pens, and anything else they needed. Peters was chatting with one of his team, giving instructions, authorizing access to files and logs, and sending him off to retrieve what they needed.

"I'll leave you to it," Miller said, as he stood in the doorway. "I have to get back to the rest of the business. Please, Detective Holden ... if I can help at all, please contact me. Ashley wasn't just our founder, he was a friend. He'll be missed around here."

Holden shook Miller's hand. "I'll be in touch. Thank you for your cooperation."

Miller nodded and left as Peters closed the door. "I'll run through things with you for now, and then I'll have one of my team come in."

"We'll need to speak with the two guys," Holden said, flipping open his note pad. "Scott Nolan and Christopher Partano."

"I can arrange that," Peters said. "Want to review the data logs first?"

They spent the next hour sifting through logs of data transfers, as well as scanning video footage of the data wipes in progress. Holden and Denzel were rapt by the entire play, but Kotler found he was starting to grow bored. He was used to sifting through mountains of data, searching for kernels of the story in a deluge of details and side trails. But in this case, he was superfluous. Between Denzel and Holden, and with Peters assisting, Kotler wasn't really needed here. He felt there was something better he could spend his time on.

"Nick, do you think it would be possible for me to speak with Dr. Simon Patel?" he asked.

Peters looked up from the terminal, "I can arrange that. I need to move on from here anyway." He turned back to Denzel and Holden. "One moment, gentlemen."

He stood, opened the glass door, and caught the attention of a young, sandy-blonde man across the security suite. The man came on call, and as he entered the screening room Peters said, "This is Scott Nolan. Scott, I want you to assist Detective Holden and Agent Denzel in reviewing security logs for the Devil's Interval project. They have my authority to review any and all records."

"Yes sir," Nolan said. "Happy to help."

"We'd also like to ask you a few questions, Mr. Nolan," Holden said.

Nolan nodded. "Of course."

Peters motioned for Kotler to follow him out of the room.

"I'll see what I can learn from Patel," Kotler said.

"Can you handle that?" Holden asked, gruffly.

"He can handle it," Denzel said.

Kotler grinned. "A ringing endorsement from the FBI, Detective. I'll try not to let you down."

He left, following Peters out of the security suite and into an office just off the larger room's entrance.

This was clearly Peters' personal domain. Every wall of the space was lined with shelves, from floor to ceiling, and each of these was crammed with all manner of items. There were books, manuals, and binders covering a large portion of the walls, but scattered among them were crates of security and surveillance gear. There was the odd decorative item here and there, of course, but this seemed limited to the bare minimum. Plaques honoring Peters for his work in the CIA, a photo of him and President Obama, next to another of him and President Bush—Kotler smiled, remembering similar photos in Denzel's office. And in one Plexiglas case there was a gold-plated handgun, what looked like a Beretta 92.

"Got that when I retired," Peters said. "It was my service piece. I turned it over when I gave my notice and they put me on a desk for my last three months. They had it retired, too."

"A nice gesture," Kotler said.

"I would have preferred to have her back intact," Peters said. "This is kind of like having a pet stuffed and mounted."

He turned and went to his desk, which was clean and well-ordered. He opened his laptop and used a fingerprint scan to unlock it, then started clicking and typing, pulling up records. After a moment, he grunted. "Huh. Patel didn't show today."

"He's out?" Kotler asked. "Did he call in sick?"

"He hasn't checked in at all. I have an automated email alerting me that his security card hasn't been used anywhere in the facility today. It's outside his pattern."

"His pattern?"

"Activity pattern," Peters said. "I have one for every employee here. The system keeps track of everyone's movements in and out, and I have software that translates that into their activity pattern. It helps identify unusual behavior."

Kotler nodded. "Impressive. And kind of scary."

"It better be scary," Peters said. "That's the point." He used the touchpad on the laptop to open another window, and tapped a few keys. "He checked out yesterday at 9PM. An hour earlier than usual. Hasn't been back since."

"Can we contact him?" Kotler asked.

Peters picked up the phone from his desk and dialed Patel's number. After a moment, he hung up. "Voicemail. Went straight to it." He turned back to his computer. "I'll send you his contact information. And I'll bring up his last activities on the logs, so you and your boys can review it. Something isn't right about this."

Kotler agreed.

Ashton Mink's time of death was estimated to be around 10 PM. If Simon Patel left the building at 9 PM, he had plenty of time to get to Mink's apartment. Kotler was sure that would make him a suspect, at least for now.

And there could be a motive. Patel's research was being quashed by the company, expunged from the servers.

Everyone involved, including Patel himself, was required to sign an NDA, with heavy financial and even legal penalties. That meant there would be no patent on the final technology. And since AMSL's policy was for research leads to be included on the patents, allowing them to receive a percentage of profits, Patel stood to miss out on a great deal of money. The technology he pioneered would make cochlear implants obsolete, and make it possible to provide or restore hearing to anyone, without invasive surgery. The permutations of that technology from there weren't even calculable.

It was entirely possible that Patel had decided to take his research and technological developments elsewhere, to receive his due. And if he saw Ashton as standing in the way of that plan, he might be motivated to murder.

Kotler returned to the screening room and delivered what he'd found. The records search then turned to scanning both Patel's and Ashton's last moments in the building.

Dr. Patel, an Indian man wearing the standard blue lab coat, was onscreen, putting away a few items in a secure cabinet. He took off his lab coat, hung it on a hook, and then left the building. He had no bags or attaché case. He passed through the security scanners without incident. He seemed calm and relaxed. Nothing about him indicated that he was doing anything untoward or suspicious.

"Can we see outside the building?" Holden asked.

Nolan brought up the outside cameras from two angles, splitting the screen. They could see Patel as he left, both from in front and from behind. He was casual. Walking with his hands in his pockets, against a slightly chill evening. After a moment, he passed under the camera he was facing, and a few minutes after that he rounded the corner and disappeared from the view of the camera at his back.

"I'll have someone check in on him," Detective Holden

said, picking up his phone. "Get his whereabouts and an alibi for last night."

Kotler leaned in. "What about Ashton? Can we look at what he was doing just before he left?"

Nolan nodded and started to bring up Ashton's video.

"That's weird," he said. "It stops at noon."

"What do you mean?" Denzel asked.

"We have tagged footage of him right up until noon, but then there's nothing." He typed commands and selected options onscreen. "I show that his security card was used for the helipad exit, on the roof. That was at 3 PM. But there's no footage after noon."

"Someone erased it?" Denzel asked.

"Looks that way, but … well, it's not possible."

"Why?" Kotler asked.

"Only security personnel can erase footage. Everything is backed up instantly, here and at an offsite facility. We can pull up both from any terminal here, streaming it from offsite. But you can't delete the offsite footage without going there physically."

"Where is this offsite facility?" Denzel asked, taking out his notepad.

Nolan had to look it up, and gave Denzel the address. "You'll have to have someone go with you. Probably Nick. It takes high clearance to get in."

"Who has that clearance?" Denzel asked.

"Nick and Mr. Miller. Other than that, I'm not sure. There are people who work in the facility. It's a server farm, highly secure. They provide data security for big corporations and for government offices."

Kotler was thinking about all of this, and could see that something had gone on a tangent somewhere. It was even more disturbing when considering the epic levels of security that Nick Peters had enacted here.

Not only had the company's primary shareholder been murdered, he had apparently made off with highly secure data that was meant to be destroyed. His final three hours in the building had been somehow deleted from both local and off-site storage. And one of the company's top researches, and the lead on the very project in question, was currently nowhere to be found.

Kotler wasn't a detective. He wasn't even an FBI agent. But he could see that whoever was behind this had covered it brilliantly. Was it Patel? Did he have the kind of security clearance it would take?

He was a brilliant technologist—maybe he had worked out how to bypass the system. But was he a murderer?

"Thanks," Holden said into his phone, before hanging up. "I just got word back from my people. Patel booked a flight to London. He boarded at 12 AM." He stood and pulled on his coat, stepping away from the screening desk and reaching for the door. "He's in the wind."

CHAPTER 4

HOME OF DR. SIMON PATEL

SIMON PATEL'S APARTMENT WAS A MODEST WALK-UP, with a view of the street two floors below. The neighborhood was equally modest. This part of the city had a large Indian population, and its demeanor was pleasant and relaxed. Children played in the streets as adults walked among them, clucking at kids who were too rambunctious or too loud. The feeling Kotler got was that this was the "it takes a village" concept of child rearing, played out over a few city blocks. It was touching.

Just down the block was a restaurant that poured aromas of curry and other spices into the streets. Kotler's stomach grumbled, but there was little chance he'd be able to grab lunch. Things had taken a strange turn in the investigation. If this were a dig site, he'd grab a sandwich or something even while reviewing findings, but the NYPD and FBI both frowned on snacking during an investigation, it seemed.

Patel's apartment was neat and orderly—one bedroom, with a larger, open-plan living space that included a desk wedged into the corner of what would normally have been a breakfast nook or small dining area. This was where most of their attention had been since arriving, sifting through papers and rifling through the single desk drawer. There wasn't much to be found.

Two uniformed officers met them at the apartment, helping to comb the rest of the place, looking for any hint that Patel might be connected to the murder of Ashton Mink. Their warrant—hastened through approval due to the suspect fleeing the country—had given them access to every corner of Patel's life. So far, they were coming up empty.

"No computer," Holden said, grunting.

"He likely took it with him," Kotler said. He was browsing through titles on Patel's book shelves, and liked what he was seeing. There were books on acoustics, physics, and engineering, as would be expected. There were also a great many more books on music theory, art, the histories of various cultures, and biographies of the leading figures in acoustic research. Quite a few were names that Kotler had never heard of.

It was a comfortable library, and spoke volumes—no pun intended—about Patel himself.

What it didn't do was give any clue as to why Patel had suddenly flown to London with no notice.

"I have Scotland Yard putting Patel on their radar," Denzel said, slipping his phone back into a jacket pocket. "He landed around 1 PM London time, 8 AM our time. They're pulling footage to see if they can track where he went from there."

"Those guys have the whole country wired," Holden said. "They should be able to drive right to him and pick him up like a bill of groceries." He dropped a file folder back on the desk, having found nothing useful in it, and stood scanning the apartment in a slow circle. "I don't get it," he said. "I could figure this guy for corporate espionage, but he doesn't feel right for murder. No priors. No gun on record. And he

lacks the training. Whoever killed those guards was a marksman. Two kill shots, from across the room. Patel has nothing
in his background to suggest he has those skills."

"He wasn't in much of a hurry to get out of the office,
either," Denzel said. "Other than leaving earlier than usual,
he was pretty casual about his exit. No signs of stress."

"But he skips work and boards a plane to London,"
Holden said. "It just doesn't figure."

Kotler was still scanning titles on the shelf when he came
across something. Or rather, the lack of something. There
was a gap—a space where a book had been removed. Judging
from the pattern of dust on the shelf, it had been taken down
recently.

He turned and scanned the apartment. Nothing on
Patel's desk. But on a small table next to the sofa, there was a
book laying at an odd angle. Kotler picked it up.

"*Never a Reft?*" Denzel asked, spotting the title.

"Rest," Kotler said, smiling. "The font is a little old fash-
ioned. This is Professor Richard Westfall's biography of Isaac
Newton. It's been in print since '81."

"You've read it?" Denzel asked. "What am I saying. Of
course, you've read it."

"I have," Kotler nodded. "Along with several other
biographies about Newton." He fanned the pages of the
book, looking for anything that might be helpful. Practically
every page had hand-written notes in the margins, and highlighted passages. Midway through, however, Kotler found a
scrap of loose paper. He opened the book to these pages, and
lay it on the kitchen counter. Holden and Denzel stepped in
beside him to have a look.

Kotler picked up the paper and unfolded it.

"What is that?" Holden asked, confused by the scrawl
covering the paper.

"Equations," Kotler said, frowning. "There's a formula I

don't recognize, but a lot of this looks to be a frequency graph." Kotler pointed to a roughly drawn sine wave pattern, intersecting a vertical and horizontal graph. "And those notations are low and high cutoff frequencies."

"And how do you know what any of this is?" Holden asked.

"Didn't you know?" Denzel said. "Kotler here has multiple PhDs"

"I thought he was a history geek," Holden said.

"Oh, I'm a quantum physics geek, too," Kotler smiled. "And acoustics aren't entirely in my bailiwick, but there's quite a bit of crossover with wave theory, and I've studied enough to recognize it. I'm not at all sure what these notes and equations mean, but I think Patel was referencing them before he left."

"That paper is torn along the top," Denzel noted. "Maybe he took something with him?"

Kotler looked at the torn edge, then turned his attention back to the biography itself. He read the pages where the paper had been found, looking for context. The only passages that seemed relevant were references to the velocity of sound. Most of the section was related to the wave properties of light. Nothing about it stood out for Kotler, though he was worried his lack of expertise in this field might blind him to potential clues.

But maybe it wasn't the specific passage that provided the context Kotler needed. Maybe it was the book itself.

"Newton," Kotler said.

"What about him?" Holden asked.

"He died in London. In the 18th century. He's buried there. He had a lab there."

"You think Patel is going to Newton's lab?" Denzel asked.

"I'm not sure. It may be long gone. But Patel based some

of his work on historic research. Newton did do some research into the Devil's Interval."

Denzel turned to Holden. "What do you think?"

"I think fair old London is a little out of my jurisdiction," Holden scowled. "I'll have to rely on Scotland Yard."

"Not necessarily," Kotler said.

They turned to him.

"Well, the FBI does have a historic crimes task force. Most of it is standing in this room."

"You want us to fly to London?" Denzel asked. "On what grounds?"

Kotler held up the torn paper. "I think Patel is after something that's tied to this case. But more than that, we're not just investigating a murder at this point, are we? That technology could be a used as a weapon. A monstrous one. If Patel murdered Ashton, and stole that memory card, maybe he's on his way back to the source of his research. He may be attempting to reconstruct what he built."

Denzel nodded. "We have discretion in cases like this," he said to Holden. "I can escalate this case."

"Take it over, you mean," Holden said, sourly.

"You're still in charge," Denzel said. "Of the murder case, at least. I'll give you any information we uncover. But Pete, this case … you know it's bigger now."

Holden considered this, and nodded. "So far, you've shot straight with me. I trust you to share anything you find. Help me close this case, that's all I ask."

Denzel nodded, and turned back to Kotler. "Why do I get the impression that you've been angling for this all along?"

"I found out about London at the exact time you did," Kotler shrugged.

"But you knew we'd end up on the move at some point. You're bored with …" he paused, glancing at Holden, leaving the word 'Atlantis' unspoken. "Your other project. You're ready for something new."

Kotler grinned. "I just want to help bring down the bad guys, Roland. You know me."

"Yeah," Denzel said, shaking his head and scowling. "I know you."

CHAPTER 5

LONDON

IT WAS ALWAYS A BIT DISORIENTING TO BOARD A FLIGHT on a New York evening and arrive in a European afternoon, but Kotler had done it enough times, he could acclimate quickly. He'd slept fitfully on the plane, however, and was feeling groggy by the time they hit the ground.

Denzel had slept like a log, albeit one being cut into lengths by a rusty chainsaw in need of an oil change. His snoring was part of Kotler's fitful rest.

The other part, however, was Patel. Or rather, speculation about what Patel was up to, and why he would do any of this.

Before leaving New York, Denzel had pulled together an extensive background on Patel, which Kotler had consumed during the flight.

The son of two immigrant parents, both of whom held PhDs of their own, Patel had attended first New York State University and then MIT. He had double majored at State, earning undergraduate degrees in both History and Applied Technologies and Engineering. He was a strong math student, according to his records, but he was clearly much more passionate about History, particularly the history of science.

The background dossier included some of Patel's publicly available papers, many of which were as brilliant as anything Kotler had read in his career. It seemed that Ashton Mink's idea to attract high-end talent with his hybrid charity was a success. Patel was one of the best in the world.

Patel had a sharp sense of where the veins of gold were hidden in historic records, and he knew how to mine them to contribute to modern advancements. In one paper, published in the *Annual Review of Biomedical Engineering,* Patel outlined seven technical innovations that he had made based on historic works that were all but lost to the Western world.

"There are numerous avenues of research that remain open loops, buried in documents that are historic, but are not yet cata-loged by history. So much can be learned by seeking out these lost remnants of early science, and picking up the threads they leave, to weave them into a tapestry of new work, advancing science and technology for the benefit of humanity."

Kotler had smiled at that passage. He understood the sentiment, and even admired it. But he also knew that modern science was a forward-facing animal, rarely looking back. The mainstream norm of science dictated that new discoveries were made in laboratories, not in libraries. He imagined that Patel had faced numerous challenges over his approach, and may even have been ostracized by the very academic and scientific community he served.

Kotler could relate.

There was no doubt, however, that Patel's passion had led him to some remarkable discoveries. Or rediscoveries, as it were. Perhaps more remarkable, however, were the leaps Patel made from antiquated research to actionable patents. His facility with extrapolating modern technological advances from discarded historic research was uncanny.

After landing in London, Kotler and Denzel left the airport in a cab, and a short time later arrived at New Scotland Yard, in Westminster, with their carry-ons still in tow. Denzel hadn't wanted to waste any time with checking in at the hotel. Kotler could have used a shower and even a nap, but duty called. He would tough it out.

The day at Scotland Yard was spent largely going over more security camera footage than Kotler could have imagined existing in all the world. Detective Holden had been right—the UK had surveillance well in hand.

Kotler was well-traveled, and thought of himself as being a citizen of the world more than any given nationality. But even he had to admit that his American sensibilities, regarding privacy and civil liberty, were flat-out assaulted by the volume of information the UK could have on him. At any given moment, they could track even his slightest moves, what he had for breakfast, when he went to the restroom, and more. It was unnerving, and Kotler decided it was best to pretend he didn't mind.

"He's here," one of the Scotland Yard Detectives offered Denzel a folder containing surveillance images pulled from video, and an address for Patel's last known whereabouts. "He arrived at this location shortly after his flight, and there's been no sign of him leaving."

"Where is this?" Denzel asked. "Any significance to this place?"

The Detective shrugged. "To my knowledge, it's a series of flats, converted from an older building within the last twenty years. Nothing notable about the location."

"Any connection to Isaac Newton?" Denzel asked.

"*Sir* Isaac Newton did own properties in the area," the Detective said.

Denzel nodded, and turned to Kotler. "What do you think?"

"I think there's a chance that Patel has discovered something in that area, and that he's managed to slip surveillance."

The Detective gave a derisive laugh. "Not likely," he said. "We have him stitched in quite well, I believe. And we can assist in his capture."

"I appreciate that," Denzel said. "But I'd like to approach him, first. He hasn't committed any crimes, that we know of. He's just a suspect, at this point. I want to see what we find by talking to him."

The Detective nodded, and left the two of them. Denzel arranged for a rental car, and he and Kotler left Scotland Yard less than half an hour later.

"Do you think he killed Ashton Mink?" Kotler asked as they entered London traffic.

Denzel was shaking his head. "I'm not sure. He had the time. He had motive. And he did run."

Kotler nodded. "I've been studying the dossier on him, and looking over some of his work. Honestly, Roland, I don't get the vibe that Patel is a murderer."

"Maybe you're just seeing him as a kindred spirit," Denzel said.

Kotler arched his eyebrows. "Is that what you think?"

Denzel chuckled and shrugged. "It was something I picked up on, when looking over his background. History and science. One feeding the other. That's your thing."

Kotler couldn't dispute that. He had chosen a path in life that had his feet planted firmly in both history and science, and he often fell back on his training in both fields, to assist in his work. So, it was possible he was over-empathizing with Patel, seeing himself in the man. He couldn't help wondering what circumstances might make him act as Patel had—leaving suddenly, flying out of the country over night. There were plenty of times when Kotler would have done just that, for reasons that wouldn't be evident to just any observer. Maybe this was one of those times for Patel, as well.

Still, Kotler couldn't see Patel as being so cold that he could murder someone and then casually board a plane to London.

"He's smarter than this," Kotler said, thinking aloud.

"Than what?" Denzel asked.

"Than to murder someone as high profile as Ashton Mink, then hop a flight out of the country an hour later. He's smart enough to have covered his tracks. This would be a really bad move."

Denzel nodded. "That thought occurred to me, too."

"When you were considering whether I would board a plane after murdering someone?" Kotler grinned.

"Something like that."

It took close to half an hour to arrive at the building where Patel had last been seen. Denzel found a parking space down the block, and the two of them walked casually toward the building, trying not to rouse any attention.

The address was a building on Whitcomb St., and Kotler recognized the area immediately. "Our Detective friend at Scotland Yard has a gift for understatement," he said.

"Why's that?"

"We're about a block from Westminster Reference Library. Newton used to own a house on that site, in the 1700s."

"So, this really is about Newton," Denzel said.

Kotler shrugged. "There's still room for coincidence. Should we go inside?"

Denzel nodded, and the two of them entered the building, snagging a still open door as a tenant exited to the street.

Inside, the space felt a bit cramped. At some point, this building had been renovated to create a series of apartments.

This corridor hadn't existed, in the building's early history, and had been built at a width that was the bare minimum for allowing a human being to move through it. Moving furniture into any given apartment in this space would require hoisting it up from the street and wedging it through a window, Kotler surmised.

"I thought New York apartments were tight," Denzel said.

"So we're in, but we have no way of knowing exactly where Patel went from here," Kotler said. "I still think he slipped out somehow."

"If he did, he didn't do it through the standard exits. Scotland Yard has footage all around the perimeter of this place."

"So, he had to go either up or down," Kotler said. "I don't think he can fly. And I'm reasonably sure he doesn't have spider-like leaping abilities."

"So down," Denzel said. "This place must have a basement."

They made their way through the narrow corridors until they came to a passage covered with a hinged metal grating rather than a door. A set of stairs dipped down into the darkness below. There was no lock on the grating, and Denzel opened it with a creak, looking back at Kotler.

"How are we on trespassing?" Kotler asked.

"So far, we've just walked through open doors. We don't exactly have carte blanche to do whatever we want, but Scotland Yard does know we're here, and investigating. I think we have some leeway."

"So, down into the dank darkness," Kotler smiled.

"Why do I get the feeling you were hoping for this?" Denzel asked.

"You have somehow gotten the impression that I'm just

waiting for the opportunity to drag you into adventure," Kotler smiled.

"Drag me into dark holes in the ground is more like it," Denzel said, a note of regret in his voice.

Kotler knew his friend suffered from claustrophobia, and that this whole scenario had to be triggering some anxiety. He also knew that Denzel was one of the bravest men he'd ever met, and had pushed through worse than narrow hallways and dark basement stairwells in a London apartment building. He'd get through this, though he'd sweat it a bit.

Kotler took out his phone and turned on the flashlight. Denzel did the same, and the two of them pushed through the doorway, letting the metal grating creak back into place, assisted by a spring-loaded hinge.

They made their way into the darkness below, their steps echoing on the metal stairs. The light from their phones helped a great deal, showing their path clearly. After just a moment they set foot on solid stone, and looked around to find themselves in a small boiler room. An ancient iron furnace dominated one end of the space, and two sets of washing machines and dryers lined the wall opposite the stairs.

Kotler was panning the flashlight around the darkened room, and spotted a switch at the base of the stairs. He glanced up, and noted there was another switch at the top, which they had missed on their walk down.

The switch was a dial—a timer that would turn the lights off after a preset interval.

No wonder there's one at the top and one at the bottom, Kotler thought. He had a chill, imagining being down here when that timer ran out, being thrown into pitch black in a place that made the set of *Saw* look like a Disney theme ride.

Kotler turned the dial all the way to the top, and a set of fluorescent lights buzzed on, casting the space in a sickly green hue. The ticking from the timer filled the space and echoed oddly, making everything feel all the creepier.

"Remind me to kiss the woman who does my laundry, when we get home," Denzel said.

"This place does make an excellent case for outsourcing," Kotler replied.

They turned off the lights on their phones, conserving battery, and looked around in the dim space.

"So, any sign that he came through here?" Denzel asked.

Kotler was examining the walls now, running a hand over the stones and brick, trying to find any hint of a secret passage. He also looked closely at the floor, particularly the drain set in its middle, to see if there was a way to get to a tunnel below. Nothing.

"What about that?" Denzel asked, nodding to the furnace.

They went to it, and Kotler started searching around its edges. It was massive—a hunk of iron that was at minimum two hundred years old. Over the years, it had been caked and coated in grime and soot, picking up moisture and oils from the air. And within the past twenty years or so, dryer lint could be added to that list. A sheen of fuzz clung to the outside of the furnace, making it look like a stuff animal whose fur had worn through.

"Still functioning," Kotler said, approvingly, noting that the furnace had a pilot light burning. "That's craftsmanship."

"Admire it later," Denzel grumbled. "Could Patel have used it to get out?"

Kotler shook his head. "No. The pipes going out of it are too narrow." Kotler gripped one corner of it and gave it a hard yank. "And there's no way he could have budged it."

Denzel let out a sigh. "So, this is a dead end," he said. "Good. Let's get out of here. I'm starting to sweat through my suit."

Kotler looked at his friend and saw that he wasn't exaggerating. It was cool here, in the basement, and the humidity was low. Denzel was clearly feeling the pressure of the walls closing in on him, though. His claustrophobia was giving him hell.

Kotler brushed his hands on his jeans, and nodded. "Let's go," he said.

It was just then that the timer clicked to its last, and the basement was thrown into deep and eerily quiet darkness.

Denzel let out a curse, and Kotler fumbled in his pocket for his phone, then stopped short.

From the angle where they stood, he could see a tiny sliver of light, right at the base of the wall behind where the washers and dryers rested.

"Wait," Kotler said. "Do you see that?"

"I don't see anything. It's darker than a well diggers ass crack in here."

"Over toward the machines. See that light?"

It was coming from a gap that would have been completely hidden from anyone standing and doing laundry, even if the lights happened to time out. It would only be visible from this spot, near the furnace. Kotler moved toward it, and heard Denzel do the same.

"Is that it?" Denzel asked.

Kotler turned on the light from his phone and stooped to look at the floor behind the dryer, at the base of the wall. There, barely visible, was a tiny gap. Looking closer, Kotler could see that there was an ancient rubber gasket wedged into a seam at floor level. A small bit of it had torn away at some point, allowing light to pass through from the other side.

There was a clicking sound and the fluorescents flickered back on. Kotler looked up to see Denzel, his coat off and draped over his arm, and his tie and collar loosened. He looked pale. "You ok?" Kotler asked.

"Tell me you found Patel's passage and I'll tell you I'm ok."

Kotler turned back to the seam, which was much better hidden with the lights on. He felt around at the base of the wall, and after a moment his fingers encountered a metal switch, hidden in a recess near the floor. He pressed this, and there was a loud click, then the bricks of the wall swung inward.

A door, camouflaged to look like the wall. The entrance that opened was around four-foot-high, and just over two-foot-wide, and was only partially blocked by one of the dryers.

Denzel bent down next to Kotler, and the two of them considered the narrow passage. There was a string of modern work lights hung from hooks, running the length of the passage until they disappeared as the floor and ceiling curved upward and out of sight.

"Looks like a long crawl," Denzel said.

"It opens up enough for us to stand and walk, on the other side," Kotler replied. He looked at his friend, who had looked better. This wouldn't be the first narrow passage they'd found themselves in together, but at least this one had lighting.

"So," Kotler said, "ready to see where this goes?"

CHAPTER 6

KOTLER HAD BEEN RIGHT—THE TUNNEL DID OPEN enough for them to stand at full height, and walk without stooping. Though he could have done with a bit more headroom. There was less than three inches between the top of his head and the ceiling, and for Denzel the gap narrowed even more.

Denzel was breathing in a steady, meditative rhythm, to keep calm. Something Kotler had seen him do before, to control his claustrophobia. Kotler decided they could both use a distraction.

"This tunnel pre-dates the building," Kotler said. "It must have been here for centuries, and whoever built that structure decided to preserve it. Build around it."

"What's it for?" Denzel asked.

Kotler shrugged. "There could be any number of reasons for it. Smuggling, maybe. An escape tunnel, to foil someone's enemies. Or it might have been a tunnel leading to the home of a mistress."

"Seems like a long haul just to cheat on your wife," Denzel grunted.

Kotler chuckled. "Debauchery can be a powerful motivator."

"Imagine trudging through this with no light, though," Denzel said, and there was a slight, incredibly subtle pitch to his voice that warned Kotler.

"Good thing we have plenty," Kotler replied calmly. "I didn't see any power cables or leads at the entrance. Patel must have these work lights plugged in at the destination." He looked around, noting details from the stone of the tunnel. "There are signs of soot on the ceiling, probably from an oil lantern, or possibly tallow candles. Whoever used this tunnel brought along their own light."

Denzel said nothing to this, and instead plodded forward, his eyes glued on the upward-curving horizon.

They started an incline, which was steep enough that they quickly became winded. There were no steps, and so they steadied themselves by bracing a hand on one of the walls of the tunnel. Kotler stole glances at Denzel from time to time, just making sure his friend was ok. The strain of walking up the steep rise of the tunnel was distraction enough, it seemed.

They eventually came to a wall of ancient looking bricks, blocking the path from floor to ceiling.

"Dead end," Denzel said, a note of concern touching his voice.

Kotler stepped forward, running his hands along the bricks, and the line of mortar between each. There were no obvious seams.

He turned his attention to the work lights, tracing the power cable along the ceiling and down the wall, to where the cable disappeared into a slight gap in the brick.

Kotler looked closer at this gap and saw that it had been carved out recently, to make way for the cable. He saw the tiniest ridge—a seam that indicated this was likely the hinge-side of a door. Now he knew what to look for, and on the opposite side of the wall he found a brick encircled with tiny, hairline cracks in the mortar—invisible unless you knew to look for them. He pushed the brick, and it sank into the wall with a click. The wall then swung open, into the tunnel.

They stepped back enough to pull it completely open, and then Denzel put a hand up, signaling Kotler to hold back.

Denzel drew his weapon, and quietly disengaged the safety. He led with his sidearm raised then, taking a quick peek around the edge of the doorframe, then leveling and bracing his weapon and moving in a quick step, out into the space beyond, sweeping left to right in one smooth and quick motion.

"Clear," he whispered.

Kotler stepped out of the passage and into the greater chamber.

The space opened into a cavernous room, divided with antique screens and workbenches. Strewn on nearly every horizontal surface were numerous devices in various states of construction. Some looked to be from the Victorian era, while others might have been even older. There, too, Kotler spotted a few modern instruments, such as oscilloscopes and smart tablets. In fact, as he looked closer, there were artifacts and objects from just a few decades past—equipment from as early as the 20s to as late as the 70s, with a sudden jump to modern digital technology after that.

"This chamber is just one anachronism piled on another," Kotler whispered. "There's tech in here from just about every decade."

There was light, dotting the room as hanging fixtures, illuminating various workstations. They could move freely in this space, avoiding obstacles easily, and they stepped quietly around work benches and standing equipment as Denzel scanned and panned with his weapon, alert for signs of danger.

Across the large space, from the other side of a set of backlit screens, a shadow moved against the far wall. They made their way toward it.

"Did ... did you hear something?" a man's voice said, frightened.

"Shut up," a gruffer voice replied. "If you keep stalling, I may decide it's not worth the trouble of keeping you around. Do you have it yet?"

"This work took years to complete the first time," the frightened voice protested.

"You know what you're looking for now, Patel," the other man said. "With the data I gave you, there shouldn't be a problem."

Kotler turned to Denzel and mouthed the word *Patel*.

Denzel nodded, and motioned for Kotler to stay put as Denzel himself slowly moved forward.

"That data wasn't complete," Patel said, sounding stern for the first time. "I need ..."

"You need to remember what's happening here, and why you're doing this."

Patel was silent, and Kotler heard the clacking of keys from a laptop. He watched as Denzel eased slowly up to one of the screens that hid Patel and the other man.

Kotler wasn't much for staying put. He knew this was a character flaw. But seeing his friend facing down an unknown threat tended to make him uneasy. Kotler searched the tables nearby, and spotted something that looked like a small wheel axel—a metal rod about three feet long, and half an inch thick. He carefully picked this up and hefted it, testing its weight. It would do in a pinch.

Kotler started moving, though he was taking a more indirect route. He wanted to get to an angle where he might be able to see around that screen. He tried to stay close enough that he could be backup for Denzel, if something happened, but far enough to be out of the way.

Denzel, for his part, was edging closer, peeking around the screen to assess what was happening.

"What's that?" Patel said loudly, nervously.

Things moved quickly from there.

Denzel rounded the edge of the screen, weapon leveled and trained on someone out of Kotler's line of sight. "FBI, drop your weapon! Down! Get down!"

There was a shot fired then, and Kotler watched Denzel leap sideways and take cover, then return fire.

Kotler raced forward now, stooped low and angling toward the far wall, with the screen and Denzel to his right. From his new vantage point, he could now see into the work-space. Simon Patel was cringing on the other side of a large, wooden table, covering his head with both hands.

Another man—no one Kotler recognized—had fallen back, pulling a large, rolling toolbox in front of him for cover. He was brazen about standing and firing at Denzel, who had only a thin wooden screen for protection. Denzel sprinted now, diving over a table and scattering its contents to the floor in a huge racket.

From his vantage point, Kotler could see that Denzel still had line of site on the man, but it wasn't a very strong position.

There was little Kotler could do to help. He could see no way to skirt the edge of the room and get behind the shooter without being noticed. If he'd had a gun, he could easily have taken the guy out from this vantage point, at this distance. But despite being trained, licensed, and qualified on a variety of firearms, the FBI hadn't yet granted him permission to carry, deeming it unnecessary for a consultant. Maybe this scenario would convince them.

If they survived.

Denzel was returning fire, but he was at a great disadvantage. He had flipped the table to provide more cover, and the wood was proving tough enough to block incoming fire from the shooter's handgun. But it wouldn't be long before a shot got through, and Denzel was a sitting duck.

The man fired two more rounds, apparently as cover, and leapt forward. He grabbed a weathered and beaten book from the workbench where Patel had stood, a few loose pages or sheets of paper feathered out from its edges. And then he yanked the cable of a card reader hard enough to rip it from the laptop it was attached to, before standing back and putting a round through the laptop's casing.

Holding everything he'd gathered in one hand, he fired another couple of rounds to put Denzel's head back down, and sprinted off in the opposite direction.

Kotler moved then, watching where the man went. He spotted a gap, previously hidden by the screen—a tunnel entrance. It was the only place the man could have gone.

"He's made a break for it!" Kotler shouted at Denzel, who was immediately on his feet and running for the screen and the tunnel beyond.

"You see to Patel," Denzel said, before ducking and disappearing through the bricked alcove.

Kotler sprinted toward the screened area, wheel axel still in hand. "Dr. Patel?" he asked.

Patel was shaking, but looked up, cautiously.

"I'm with the FBI," Kotler said, showing his consultant ID but not bothering to clarify that he wasn't an agent. "You're safe, but I need you to stay right here. Understand? You're only safe if you stay *right here*."

Patel nodded, and Kotler took off after Denzel.

The corridor on the other side of the room was similar to what he and Denzel had used to come in from the apartments, with the exception of having its own lighting, and a higher ceiling. Someone had modernized it at some point, Kotler observed.

The tunnel branched at a T at the end of a short hall. Kotler saw Denzel ahead, scanning both directions as Kotler caught up.

"I told you to stay with Patel!" Denzel said between gnashed teeth.

"You need backup," Kotler said.

"You're not armed."

Kotler held up the axel. "I beg to differ, sir."

"You're not armed," Roland repeated. "*Stay here*. I mean it, Kotler."

Roland then sprinted down the left branch.

"You're sure he went that way?" Kotler called after him.

"No!" Roland shouted back.

Good enough, Kotler thought, and turned to race down the right-hand branch.

These passages were still underground, despite Kotler and Denzel having come into the chamber on an incline. There must have been a hill or some other rise on the surface. Since entering these tunnels, Kotler had lost all sense of what might be above them.

He raced along, even as the corridor began to slant upward.

Suddenly he came to a wall. This time, armed with his previous experience, he knew just where to look for its mechanism. He felt around, pushing and testing, until he came to the release. With a click, the door opened inward, and Kotler cautiously peered through to the other side.

This time, the space beyond was well organized—filled with book cases and shelves full of artifacts and other objects. All of it looked familiar, even comforting. The annals of research and academia. Kotler would recognize them anywhere. This was either a library or a museum, and suddenly Kotler suspected he knew exactly where this tunnel had led.

He moved cautiously among the stacks, keeping low and hidden. The gunman could still be here, and Kotler was mostly unarmed, despite his bravado. It was starting to hit him that this was a really dumb idea. Certainly not his first, but he'd have to labor hard to make sure it wasn't his last.

After a moment, Kotler came to a metal stair case, to the right of which was a boxy elevator in an open shaft of metal scaffolding—the sort of lift that was added well after the building's completion. From the looks of this one, and its collapsible metal-grating doors, Kotler figured it had been added some time in the 40s or 50s, along with these stairs.

He stepped gingerly onto the first step, glancing back to make sure no one was hiding in the stacks behind him. Then he quickly made his way up to the flight above, and through a door that was closed, but not locked.

He found himself emerging into a larger space filled with shelves, every inch of it clean and categorized, ready for public use. The shelves stretched in all directions, lining the floors in a neat grid, and each was filled with books. Here and there were tables where patrons sat, reading or taking notes or tapping away on laptops and smart tablets.

Welcome to the Westminster Research Library, Kotler thought, his initial suspicions confirmed. He'd been here before, and recognized it immediately.

He reached back into the stairwell and leaned the axel rod against the wall, so he would look less conspicuous as he moved among the library patrons. Though that did, of course, leave him without a weapon, which might put him at a serious disadvantage if he encountered the gunman. He'd cross that bridge when he came to it.

He left the door closed behind him, making his way

through the stacks and shelves, watching warily for any sign of the gunman. He'd seen the man's face, though from across a dimly lit room. He felt sure he could recognize him.

The library was quiet except for the occasional cough or mumbled conversation, and of course, the sounds of Kotler's footsteps. Kotler straightened his collar and brushed back his hair with a hand, hoping he wasn't covered in dirt or grease. He needed to blend in.

From where he now stood he could see a fair bit of the place, including exits to other wings and to the exterior of the building. Where would a gunman rush off to? What path would he use for escape, without causing a commotion or drawing too much attention?

The likely choice, Kotler concluded, would be an exit to the outside. And the closest exit to Kotler's current position was about twenty feet to his right.

Kotler moved to this door, and cautiously opened it, peering through a crack to make sure no one waited with a gun on the other side. When things seemed clear, he pushed out into the London day.

This part of the library grounds was an alley of sorts, running between two wings toward Orange Street. The space was a bit tight for Kotler's comfort, with nowhere to take cover if something went sideways, but it seemed clear enough. He made his way to the street, and was startled to nearly bump into the gunman the moment he turned a corner.

There was a pause. "Pardon me," the gunman said in his distinctly American accent, his hands shoved into his coat pockets, where he surely had the gun concealed. Kotler saw the book, with its loose pages, tucked under the man's arm. The card reader must be in a coat pocket as well.

The man didn't recognize Kotler. In fact, he might not

have even known that Kotler had been there, in the underground workshop.

"No, it's entirely my fault," Kotler said, forcing a smile. "You're American? It's good to hear a familiar accent."

The man nodded, and tried to walk away, but Kotler pushed it a bit, following along just to the man's side.

"I'm sorry to bother you, but I've just arrived here, and I was so anxious to see the library, I somehow left my bags at the airport. Such an idiot," Kotler smiled, rolling his eyes. "And unfortunately, my wallet is in one of the bags. Would you be willing to share a cab with me? I could pay you for the fare, once I …"

"No, sorry," the man said. "I have to go." He turned and walked away, and Kotler hung back for a moment before crossing Orange Street and following the man from the other side. Kotler stayed out of sight, and had to hurriedly cross back when the man took a left turn on Charing Cross Road, cutting through a small, wooded park. Kotler used the trees to keep hidden.

His phone buzzed, and Kotler cautiously answered, hanging back to stay out of sight, but keeping the man in visual range.

"Where the hell are you?" Denzel asked, his voice tense and angry.

"I have eyes on our guy," Kotler said.

There was a pause. "What's you're location?"

Kotler gave him the cross streets and his general location, plus the direction the man was moving. "I'm staying back, watching. He's definitely headed somewhere."

"Stay completely out of sight, but don't lose him," Denzel said. "And for God's sake, do not engage him. I'm here with Patel, and I'm taking him up and through the exit I found. There was another one of those secret doors, and it opened into maintenance tunnels. There's an access at street level. I have some Scotland Yard folks meeting me there in a few minutes. I can get back to the car and come to you soon. Keep your phone on silent, but check it."

"Done," Kotler said, hanging up and pressing on.

He had managed to keep up with the man until now, but after a few blocks things started to get crowded. Kotler risked closing the gap a bit, sticking to the other side of the street and coming nearly parallel with the gunman.

The man was walking with his head down. He'd pulled on a pair of dark sunglasses, and had the collar of his coat popped, and the book apparently shoved into the coat's inner pocket. He looked conspicuous, but it might have been a necessary risk. Kotler glanced up and saw clusters of cameras mounted on street lamps at regular intervals, like high-tech coconuts—London surveillance at its finest. The man was trying to keep his face from being recorded.

Kotler, on the other hand, really had no such restrictions. In fact, he stopped in view of one set of cameras, waved his arms in front of them, then texted Denzel his current location, along with a note to have Scotland Yard start tracking him. "I've made it easier to spot me," Kotler wrote, and hit send.

While he'd had his eyes on his phone, however, he'd lost track of the gunman.

Cursing, Kotler moved forward quickly, keeping his eyes open, alert for any sign of the man. He was scanning the other side of the street, pausing to look down any side streets or alleys. The truth was, the man could have entered any building along the way. Kotler had been a fool to text instead of calling. What had he been thinking?

Suddenly there was a firm hand on his left shoulder, and the feeling of metal being pressed into the small of his back.

"You're with that other guy," the man said.

Kotler again cursed himself, silently, but raised his hands and said, "What other guy?"

The man shoved the gun harder into Kotler's kidneys. "Hands at your side! Walk," he said. "Do anything to get attention and I'll kill you in the street and duck out while everyone is gawking."

"Look," Kotler said, genially, "I don't want any trouble. I'm just lost, ok? You seemed like you knew where you were going. I was hoping that if I followed you, I could somehow get a ride."

"I said walk," the man said, emphasizing his words with the gun.

"Ok," Kotler said, nodding and walking. "Where are we going?"

The man said nothing.

"Look, I'm sorry, ok? I didn't know you were … I don't want to be involved in whatever you're into. I'm just here to see the sights and do a little research for a book I'm writing. Maybe you've heard of me? Dan Kotler? I found proof of Vikings in America?"

"Never heard of you," the man said gruffly.

Kotler blinked. "Seriously? You're probably the first person I've met lately who doesn't know who I am. Which kind of figures, I guess."

"Shut up," the man said. "I told you, try anything and I won't hesitate to kill you."

They came to an alley, and Kotler reluctantly allowed himself to be steered down it, toward whatever lay at its end. He had a feeling it wouldn't be good.

They came to a space with several doors, all leading into the backs of various shops and cafes. There were a couple of compactors in the alley—one stenciled with the word "Rubbish" and the other marked "Recycle."

"Get in," the man said, waiving his gun toward the Rubbish compactor.

"Whoa," Kotler said, raising his hands and turning to face the man. "Look, if you're going to kill me and crush me, could you at least recycle? It's the only planet we've got."

"Cute," the man said, then he leveled his gun at Kotler's head. "Get in."

Kotler stepped toward the compactor, pulling the bolt that kept the heavy steel door closed, then swinging the door open with a loud, protesting squeal of metal on metal. As the door reached the pivot point, Kotler used its momentum, leveraging it to swing his legs up and out in a fast arc, kicking the man's gun hand.

The weapon fired, and the man was about to recover quickly, but Kotler leapt on top of him, pushing his gun hand down and away, slamming it on the ground until the man let go.

The gunman struggled, and it quickly became clear that he was very strong and had some hand-to-hand training. He managed to get just a small measure of leverage, twisting and pushing Kotler with his free arm. Kotler had to grip him tight to keep from being thrown aside. As it was, the man rolled onto his stomach and clutched for his gun.

Kotler put a knee in the man's back, between his shoulder blades, and then pushed off hard, trying to reach the gun first.

Now both were sprawled on the grimy stone of the alley floor, wrestling and pulling at each other, scrambling for the gun and clawing at each other to gain purchase.

The man flipped then, and his sudden change in direction threw Kotler off balance. The man pounced, punching Kotler repeatedly, smacking his head against the ground.

Kotler, dazed and injured, saw dark edges intrude on his vision, and knew he was about to lose consciousness. He lay still, groaning, as the man stood, then stooped to pick up his gun. The gunman dusted himself off a bit, and was breathing heavy, wiping at a streak of blood from his lip with the back of his free hand.

"I was going to keep this quiet, but someone probably heard that shot. Which means it won't matter if they hear another one." The main lifted his weapon, aiming for Kotler's head.

"Gun down!" a familiar and very welcome voice shouted.

The man looked up, startled, and Kotler took advantage of the distraction to roll quickly into a crouch and use a back kick, striking like a mule at the man's knees.

With a yelp the man stumbled, and Denzel rushed forward, gun raised.

"Down! Get down now!" he shouted.

The man turned, fired a couple of rounds at Denzel, and used those for cover as he sprinted to one of the backroom doors, slowed only slightly by a limp. He pulled the door open and disappeared through it.

Denzel had briefly taken cover behind the recycling compactor, and now raced out into the open. "Kotler, you good?" he asked, concern plain on his face.

"I'm good," Kotler mumbled.

"Locals are nearby," Denzel said. "*Stay put.*"

This time, Kotler had every intention of doing as he was told.

Denzel disappeared through the same door the gunman had used, and Kotler dragged himself forward to prop himself up against the side of the rubbish compactor, taking stock of his bruises and other injuries. He gingerly touched the back of his head, wincing as he pulled away fingers damp with blood.

From the distance, he heard the warbling of London sirens, and he slumped back, waiting for them to arrive.

CHAPTER 7

ST. MARY'S HOSPITAL

A DOCTOR HAD CLEANED AND BANDAGED KOTLER'S wounds, paying particular attention to the head wound. It was a minor abrasion but could have been very serious, she'd told him somewhat sternly, as if he ought to be more careful when wrestling gunmen to the ground.

There would be some tenderness and headaches. The cure would be rest and ibuprofen, and they started him with a small supply.

He had thanked her, downed two pills with a glass of water, and then stood, despite her protests. He steadied himself a bit, and told her he was fine. She mumbled something about 'Americans' and an 'obsession with *Die Hard*,' and left him to his misery.

He understood where she was coming from. His head ached. His body ached. He probably needed at least a day's bed rest. But he needed to get to Scotland Yard. There was bound to be more information about the gunman by now, and Kotler also wanted to be a part of questioning Simon Patel.

There was a light knock on the door, and Denzel popped

his head in. "They told me you'll live," he said, his tone indicating that might not be the outcome Denzel had hoped for.

"If it makes you feel any better," Kotler said, quietly, "I'll live, but I'll suffer. I have a massive headache."

Denzel considered this, and nodded. "That does make me feel a little better. Maybe next time you'll listen when I tell you to stay where you are."

Kotler smiled, and winced, but said, "Maybe."

"You've been discharged, on your request," Denzel said. "Though the doctor didn't seem all that thrilled about it. You good to go?"

"Good to go," Kotler nodded. "Where's Patel?"

"He's in an interrogation room. I have him cooling until we get there, though the locals have been asking for a go at him."

"He hasn't broken any laws," Kotler said. "He was clearly under duress."

"They want to know a lot of what we want to know," Denzel said. "And I'm not ready to rule out Patel as a suspect, just yet."

Kotler considered this. His own instincts told him that Patel was just another victim in this story, but he admitted that he might be a little biased. Patel seemed like a kindred spirit. And since Kotler would never murder someone for money, he was having a hard time imaging a fellow historian and scientist doing it.

But then, Kotler *had* money. That was the key difference. Kotler could afford fine things, and could live in the kind of place Ashton Mink lived in. Maybe Kotler's view on this subject was a little skewed. Not every man of science was noble—Kotler knew that much, at least.

Still, as they drove to New Scotland Yard, Kotler mentally went through everything he knew about Patel and his work, looking for any hint that greed might have motivated him to murder one of his greatest benefactors. Patel could have stolen the information at any time, or never handed it over at all, and sold it to the highest bidder. Why would he wait until it was deleted from the AMSL servers, and then kill Ashton to retrieve it?

Ashton's death was sure to be high profile, anyone would have seen that. It would call immediate attention to all of this, and cause a full clampdown on everything running at AMSL.

Was that the point? And if so, what would Patel gain from any of that?

It seemed far more likely that the gunman they had chased from the Westminster Research Library was the killer, and that he had coerced Patel into helping him. The conversation they'd overheard in that underground lab seemed to confirm this, but Kotler knew it wasn't enough. Denzel would want to the full story, and the only way to get that was to treat Patel like a suspect.

Kotler thought about all of this as they exited the hospital and drove Denzel's rental car through the crowded London streets. He was still a bit groggy from the head wound, but his mind was constantly turning over all the facts they had, looking for anything odd, making connections.

"What about that chamber?" Kotler asked, as they pulled into a parking garage. "Where we found Patel?"

"There are officers watching both entrances, and a team of forensic guys are going through the place."

"I'd like to go over any of their findings," Kotler said. "I'd also like a chance to get back down there and explore the place myself."

"I think I can arrange both of those things," Denzel said. "The locals are being very cooperative. The last time I dealt with Scotland Yard, I had to jump through a lot of hoops just to bring my weapon into the country."

"What changed?" Kotler asked.

Denzel shrugged. "I'm not sure. Maybe my new position."

Inside, they were shown to a viewing room, where they could see Patel sitting at a metal table, looking about as miserable as anyone could look. There was a paper cup near Patel's left hand, filed with water, and he shakily raised this to take a sip.

"He's not cuffed?" Kotler asked.

Denzel shrugged. "You said yourself, he hasn't committed any crimes. None we can prove yet, anyway."

This was a concession, Kotler knew. It was Denzel's way of giving Patel the benefit of the doubt. He'd been in that same chamber, after all, right alongside Kotler. He'd heard the exchange between Patel and the other man.

"Let's talk to him," Denzel said.

They entered and took seats across from Patel, who was watching them warily. His face showed his fear, but it also showed a resigned weariness. He'd come to some conclusion about his life and his career, Kotler decided.

"Dr. Simon Patel," Denzel said, opening a folder that contained Patel's background and history, including photos of Patel taken from his employment records and social media profiles. "What brings you to London?"

"You're American?" Patel asked, surprised.

Denzel reached into his coat pocket and produced his badge. "Agent Roland Denzel, FBI. This is Dr. Dan Kotler. He's consulting with the Bureau."

Patel looked from one to the other, nodding to Kotler. "He did mention you were with the FBI. I remember that now. What are you doing in London?"

"We're investigating the murder of Ashton Mink," Denzel said, staring at Patel.

Kotler watched Patel's face, and saw the micro expressions. He took a quick, gasping breath, and his gaze drifted down and to the right. He was surprised—shocked. When he looked back up, Kotler saw markers of grief.

"Ashton is dead?" he asked, shaking his head. "I ... didn't know."

"You left work early two nights ago," Denzel said. "Earlier than usual, at least. What made you decide to leave when you did?"

Patel shook his head again. He was staring down at the folder that Denzel had open between them. There was a photo pulled from the AMSL security video, showing Patel on the sidewalk just outside of the building, and this seemed to have Patel's attention.

"Dr. Patel?" Denzel asked.

Patel looked up. "I'm sorry. I ... What did you ask me?"

"Why did you leave work earlier than usual two nights ago?"

Patel considered, taking a breath and letting it out slowly. "We had wrapped up everything I was working on," he said. "There was a project ... I really can't go into details about it. But it was shut down, and with it went much of what I was working on. I left because there was no point in staying."

Denzel made a note of this.

Kotler was still watching Patel, reading him. "Dr. Patel, we know about Devil's Interval."

Patel shot Kotler a glance, confirming some of Kotler's suspicions.

"We were sworn to secrecy on that," Patel said. "I signed an NDA, and we buried or destroyed all the data."

"Not quite all of it, though," Denzel said. "Your friend from the chamber brought you some of that lost data?"

Patel's expression was sour. "He is no friend of mine."

"Who is he?" Kotler asked.

Patel shook his head. "I don't know. He was in my apartment when I got home. He had a gun." Patel shook from the memory. "He forced me to grab my things, and to book a flight to London. Somehow, he ..." Patel stopped, his head down, chin nearly resting on his chest. He was breathing in heavy sighs.

"What?" Denzel asked. "Somehow he what?"

Patel looked back up at them. "He knew about Newton's chamber. I don't know how. The only other person who knew about it was my research partner, Lawny Bristol."

"Dr. Lawny Bristol?" Denzel asked, referencing the file. "She died about six months ago, correct?"

Patel nodded. "Yes. An accident. She fell into an open service grating. It was raining, and the barrier must have been knocked down or obscured. It was terrible." Patel shook his head and looked down, chin on his chest, breathing in deep, steady breathes, as if calming himself.

Kotler could see that Patel felt real emotion over Bristol's death. More than he likely should have. "Were you and Dr. Bristol in a relationship?" he asked.

Patel looked up, sharply. "How ... no one knew that. I've never told anyone."

"So, your research partner was the only other person who knew about the Newton chamber," Denzel said. "Did either of you keep any records of it? Notebooks? Logs?"

"I am ashamed to say, I hid all record of it," Patel said, hanging his head again. "There were so many things to explore. I should have alerted someone about it the moment I found it, but I knew that this was a rare opportunity."

"You could study research that no one else even knew existed," Kotler said. "And introduce new 'discoveries' based on what you found."

Patel looked up, shame plain on his features, and nodded.

"And how did Dr. Bristol become involved?" Denzel asked.

"I ... we were in love," Patel said. "And we were partners. I brought her here, to London, and showed her the chamber. I had already cataloged everything by then. I'd spent months in there. I wanted her to see it. I wanted ..."

He stopped in mid-sentence, as if he wasn't sure how to go on.

"You wanted to legitimize it," Kotler said. "You wanted to know that at least one other person knew it was there, so that it wouldn't feel like you were hiding it."

Patel wiped at his eyes. "Yes," he said, never meeting Kotler's gaze.

Kotler felt a stab of disappointment at Patel. Finding the chamber, uncovering such a unique and rare part of history, and then burying it out of a sense of personal ambition—the idea was abhorrent. Any kinship Kotler felt with Patel dissolved in that moment.

But Kotler took a deep breath, centering himself, making sure that the pendulum didn't swing too far in the opposite direction. What Patel had done was unethical, but it wasn't proof that the man was a murderer.

"So, you had no record of the chamber at all. How did this man find out about it?"

Patel was shaking his head, but said, "Lawny must have kept some record of it, I suppose. She may have noted it in her logs at AMSL. Part of our research notes, perhaps. Or background. We log background information—context for our discoveries, to provide proof of prior research during the patent process. She may have kept a note about the chamber, hiding it from me."

"Why would she do that?" Denzel asked.

Patel looked up at him, and there was a trace of a smile on his lips. "She would have done it to protect me," Patel said. "She was always doing things like that. Looking out for my best interests, when my decisions weren't entirely right."

Denzel made some notes, and then glanced at Kotler.

Kotler was watching Patel, and asked, "What happens to employee logs, if an employee leaves? Or dies, in the case of Dr. Bristol?"

Patel thought for a moment. "All files in their personal folders are locked and archived. If anything is part of ongoing research, it's flagged for immediate team review. I was the first to see Lawny's logs, regarding Devil's Interval. I never saw any mention of the chamber."

"Could she have noted it somewhere else?" Kotler asked. "Maybe a separate set of logs? Something only she would know about?"

Patel took a deep breath and let it out. "Yes, she might have done that. As a measure of protection."

"Who has access to those logs, if they aren't part of ongoing research?" Kotler asked.

Patel considered. "Only high clearance personnel. Our CEO, Ross Miller. Our COO, Garret Chandler. Nick Peters, the head of security. And anyone the three of them may have authorized."

Kotler glanced at Denzel, who was jotting notes and reminders.

Kotler looked back to Patel. "What about the book? The gunman grabbed some sort of leather-bound book from the table as he left. It had loose pages in it."

Patel nodded. "It was a journal, though I don't know who it originally belonged to. It was clearly quite old. It contained continuing notes on Newton's research, and on the research of several others. It was …" he looked at them both, then sighed. "It was where I first encountered the data I used to build Devil's Interval. Much of it was a study into the effects of sound, particularly music, on the human brain. Including notes on experiments conducted on hearing impaired and deaf patients."

"So basically, the premise of your whole project," Kotler said, disgusted.

Patel said nothing.

"Could this guy reconstruct what you built with that book?"

"I do not believe he could personally," Patel said. "Even with the data he stole, the complete research isn't there. It's fragmented."

"But it could be a start," Kotler said.

Patel agreed. "Yes. I fear it could."

"The loose pages?" Kotler asked.

"Mostly printouts of some of my notes," Patel said. "And a few things I didn't recognize. Possibly notes from Lawny."

"Are you able to recall everything you saw?" Denzel asked. "Could you fill us in on what this guy may have? And what it means?"

"I'll give you everything I can," Patel said. "I didn't see everything, but I can tell you what I saw."

"I'll have them provide with a means of giving a full statement," Denzel said. Patel nodded, silent and sullen.

Kotler leaned forward and gave Patel a hard look. "What you did—hiding that chamber and everything in it, claiming that research as your own—you realize what that means?"

Patel slumped, falling back in his chair. "I do," he said. "I've lost all credibility now. My career is over."

"More than that," Denzel said. "Because of what you did, at least one person was murdered, and his killer is still out there. And as if that weren't enough, this technology of yours could be the most dangerous thing on the planet, and it's clear someone knows all about it. So, you need to tell us everything you know, Dr. Patel. No more secrets. Because as of now, you're looking pretty good as an accomplice in all of this."

Patel looked as if he were going to implode with grief and fear.

He nodded, and for the next two hours he answered every question Denzel and Kotler could think to ask.

It was a grueling interview, and at the end of it Denzel had Patel moved to a cell, to await transport back to the US.

They were leaving the building, walking back through the parking garage to where the rental was parked.

"We don't have enough to convict him of anything," Denzel said. "Not yet, anyway. And I think I'm with you now. He doesn't feel right for the murder. But I'm still not sure about his role in stealing that data. Someone had to know that Ashton Mink had that memory card."

"You think Dr. Patel knew? That he leaked it?"

Denzel shook his head. "Too soon to tell."

Kotler nodded. "One thing's for sure," he said, feeling disappointed and disgusted. "He's definitely a part of covering up that chamber."

"And Scotland Yard may pursue something about that," Denzel replied. "If it comes to it. They have their own version of historic crimes, so I'm sure they'll have a strong interest."

Kotler nodded. He was feeling out of sorts now, but there was one thing that might cheer him up. "So, when do we get to explore that chamber?"

"Funny you should ask that. The locals are sifting through surveillance footage, tracking where the gunman disappeared to. While they do that, I've gotten us clearance to get back down into that chamber and have a look around."

"Why Agent Denzel! For lil' ol' me?" Kotler said, smiling.

Denzel rolled his eyes. "No. Patel and the gunman were trying to reconstruct the missing data for Devil's Interval. There may be some clue down there that will tell us how to track this guy. They've had a forensic sweep of the place and turned up nothing useful, but I've convinced them to give you a go at it. You bring special skills to the table."

"I'm flattered," Kotler said, smiling.

"Don't get a big head about it, Kotler," Denzel said, as the two of them climbed back into the rental car.

CHAPTER 8

THE NEWTON CHAMBER, AS KOTLER AND DENZEL HAD started to refer to it, was lit by modern work lights, strung along the walls and powered by lines tapped into a main circuit of the Westminster Research Library. Denzel mused that Patel must have figured no one would notice a small bump in power usage, since people could be found in the library day and night. And, from what Kotler was finding, the power needs of this space were slight. A few lights, a few small pieces of equipment, a laptop or smart tablet here and there.

The forensics team had tagged everything in the space by now, and left most of it exactly where it had been found. Kotler was impressed by how thorough they'd been. And how respectful—even the most minor-seeming object was labeled with special care, ensuring no damage.

Kotler had a strong urge to peruse the entire space, to examine everything he could find, but he limited himself to the area where Patel and the gunman had been working, for now. Here, presumably, was everything Patel and Lawny Bristol had studied as part of Devil's Interval. Kotler could look over the manifest later, to see if anything that had been cataloged in this space might be pertinent to the case.

"Anything?" Denzel asked, not for the first time.

"Roland, if you're going to keep pestering me, the least you could do is go find some place to buy me a decent cup of coffee."

"I'm not your personal assistant, Kotler," Denzel groused.

"I'm not sure what the gunman made off with," Kotler replied, bending to look closer at a small, wooden box with a brass horn mounted to it. "I know he took the card, and the reader. He also grabbed the journal from this table."

"We should have Patel's statement about the contents of that soon," Denzel said. "The tech guys at Scotland Yard are also going over Patel's laptop to see if they can pull up anything, though it's apparently tough going with a bullet hole through the hard drive. They have tech that can pull some of the data, and Patel is cooperating, so they should be able to reconstruct at least a portion of it."

Kotler nodded, straightening. He looked up from the workbench he'd been scrutinizing for the past couple of hours, and nodded to the expanse of the chamber. "This is just stunning, isn't it? You know, Newton wasn't really known for his work in acoustics. It was essentially a side pursuit. We have him to thank for a lot of early research into the wave and particle properties of light, though. Foundations of quantum physics. Ironic, considering Newtonian physics has ruled for so long."

"Yeah," Denzel said. "Stunning."

Kotler grinned. "I know. Geek talk. But *look* at this place, Roland! Buried here for a couple of centuries, and it looks like it was just in use yesterday!"

"That's because it was just in use *today*," Denzel said. "Are you finding anything useful?"

Kotler shook his head. "Not really. It would take weeks to

comb through everything here, to see how all the pieces fit. Patel's data may be the only real clue we have."

Denzel rubbed his eyes. "Ok," he said. "Let's go over what we do know. Patel and his partner …"

"Dr. Bristol," Kotler supplied.

"Right. Bristol. Patel finds this chamber, and brings in Bristol to help him go through this place. The two of them decide to keep it quiet. Why is that?"

"Patel wanted to introduce new discoveries one at a time," Kotler said. "He was going to sit on this until he'd mined it for everything he could." Kotler looked around, feeling the disgust return. Mining history for profit wasn't something he could just ignore. Too much history had been lost to the world forever, thanks to that sort of greed.

"So how is that any different than what he was telling people? Miller and Chandler were praising him for being able to repurpose forgotten research."

Kotler nodded. "True. But they were working from the same assumption I was. Patel was writing papers and filing patents based on having discovered lost principles, and then exploring them on his own, connecting them to modern day science and technology. He admitted to finding some research intact, and simply carrying it to it's natural conclusion. What he wasn't telling anyone was that a lot of his patents and papers were based on *complete* research. He wasn't just finishing work someone else started, he was lifting their work in its entirety, and claiming it as his own. This," Kotler said, waving a hand to indicate the Newton Chamber, "was the source of a lot of his revolutionary patents. Whoever maintained this chamber was clearly a genius, but must have died sometime in the late 70s. Patel found this place, and exploited it. He was claiming work that wasn't his own."

Kotler found that he was getting agitated, and he took a

deep breath to calm himself, sighing into the cavernous chamber, as if he might breathe life back into it.

"I get it," Denzel said.

Kotler looked at him, and felt a bit embarrassed. "I'm sorry. This kind of thing gets to me."

"What I *don't* get," Denzel said, "Is why Patel would even have to do it. He's clearly smart. He'd already set up the idea that he was uncovering historic research, and putting it to new use. Why claim someone else's work? He could have revealed it, and still used it, right? He could have innovated from it."

Kotler shook his head. "It was his mindset. Basically, there are two types of mindsets—a fixed mindset and a growth mindset. If you have a growth mindset, you tend to think in possibilities and options. You believe everything has a solution, and all you have to do is find it. A fixed mindset believes that limitations are built in. You're only as smart as you were born to be. And if being smart is your identity, then any time you aren't smart, you're lost. I think Patel has a fixed mindset. I think he believes that he's only as good as his latest patent, and so, to protect his own self identity, he stole someone's research and released it as his own. He cheated, even though he never needed to."

"You're telling me this was self-preservation?" Denzel asked.

Kotler nodded. "For Patel, it was."

Denzel thought about this for a moment, then shook his head. "Ok," he said. "So Patel kept no record of this place. But Bristol may have. And when she died, her records were secured and archived, except for anything linked to ongoing research."

"And she may have kept a separate log, not linked directly to the Devil's Interval project," Kotler said.

"So, whoever has access to her data could have found a

log entry about this chamber. If they had that kind of access, they might have known about the Devil's Interval project from the start. They could have been waiting for Patel to finish what he was doing, so they could steal the data."

"Then why would they need the data from Ashton Mink?" Kotler asked.

Denzel shook his head. "Maybe they couldn't get to the data before it was deleted," he said. "Or they hadn't expected the reaction from the executive team."

"Or maybe ..." Kotler said, drifting, thinking.

"What?"

Kotler looked up at him. "Maybe they had counted on Ashton getting to that data. Or, at the very least, they had set it up so that only Ashton could get to it."

"I don't follow," Denzel said.

"Nick Peters is former CIA. He has security measures in place that would make some small nations salivate with envy. Nothing gets in or out of that place without him knowing. Except ..."

"Except Ashton not only made copies of that data, he put it on a memory card and carried it out of there without so much as a burp from security."

"And he would be the only one in the company capable of doing that," Kotler said. "He owned fifty-one percent of that place. There was no public offering. His shareholders are venture capitalists. So out of everyone in the company, Ashton was the one guy who could move around with complete autonomy. There was no need to monitor him. He had access to literally everything."

"And no one would have considered him a security threat," Denzel said, "because ... well, mostly because he was Ashton Mink. Most people wouldn't think he'd have either the interest or the ability to steal data from his own company." Denzel looked at Kotler. "Someone set him up."

Kotler nodded. "Makes sense. Now, we just need to know who."

"My money's on someone in security."

"Peters?" Kotler asked.

Denzel hesitated, and Kotler knew exactly what he was struggling with. Just as Kotler had felt a kinship with Dr. Patel, Denzel related to the ex-CIA security head. They had both served their country in similar ways. They had both taken oaths. If Peters was dirty somehow, Denzel would take it personally. "I'm not ready to rule anyone out yet," he said.

"Ok," Kotler said. "So, we need to talk to everyone who had access to Dr. Bristol's files. We should also look into her death."

"You think it wasn't an accident?"

"Do you?"

Denzel shook his head. "I think the timing is suspicious. But this case has more loose pieces than this chamber has, at the moment."

Kotler looked around. "I need to do a more thorough sweep. But it'll take time. Do you have the manifest?"

"I had it sent to our phones," Denzel said.

"Phones? Not paper? You?" Kotler grinned.

"I'm not a luddite, Kotler. What am I going to do, carry a file cabinet everywhere?"

Kotler chuckled as he searched and found the file in his email. He opened it, and downloaded a secured PDF, requiring his 'badge' number to open. He used the number for his FBI consultant ID, and he was in.

To his delight and relief, the document was searchable by keyword. He could quickly sift through the thousands of entries by searching for anything sound related. The forensics team had been savvy and meticulous, and they had done an excellent job of sussing out the general purpose of nearly everything. That took some creative thought, in many cases.

Even Kotler didn't recognize most of the bits and pieces down here.

One entry stood out for him, as he searched.

"Theremin," Kotler said.

"What now?" Denzel asked.

Kotler looked up. "This is interesting," he said.

"What's a thermonim?"

"*Theremin*," Kotler corrected. "Originally known as an *aetherphone*. It's a musical instrument. Kind of a weird one. You play it by moving your hands in and out of proximity to two antennae. The movements control pitch and volume, and the sound it produces can be kind of eerie."

"That's fascinating," Denzel said. "What's it got to do with anything? Sounds like you've seen one before."

"I have. It's been used for years in film and television, mostly in the 60s. They used it in 'The Day the Earth Stood Still.'"

"The Keanu Reeves movie?"

Kotler rolled his eyes. "I would have thought you, of all people, would have an appreciation for classic film."

"Noir, maybe," Denzel said. "So, get to the point."

"The Theremin was invented by Léon Theremin, a Russian inventor. It was patented in the late 1920s. Theremin himself wasn't born until well after Newton had died." Kotler walked way then, looking from the manifest to the numbered stations left by the forensics team.

Denzel followed. "So, there's no way that Newton could have had access to this thing."

"None," Kotler said.

"Did he maybe invent it before this Theremin guy?"

"No chance," Kotler said. "The technology this is dependent on would have seemed advanced to the point of being magic to Newton."

"So, what does this mean, Kotler? What are you thinking?"

"We already know that Patel wasn't the first person to discover this place," Kotler said. "There's technology in here spanning decades as recent as the 70s. Someone else knew about this chamber. That journal the gunman took may have belonged to whoever was keeping this place going."

"This Theremin guy?"

"Not likely," Kotler said. "But someone who knew Theremin's work." He finally came to the station where the Theremin had been cataloged, and looked at the object on the table.

It was a box, standing around three feet high, with a sloped front. There was an antenna made from wire, sticking up from the right-hand side of the box, protruding from the top. On its left side was a wire loop. There were a couple of ancient looking knobs mounted to a front panel.

Kotler looked at it, and then back to Denzel, grinning. "This is an original. No manufacturer markings. It's in pristine condition, too."

"Does it have anything to do with the case?"

Kotler smiled and took out his phone. He took a moment to register just a bit of surprise that he had signal down here, and opened the YouTube app. He typed in simply 'Theremin,' and played the first result.

The sound of the device echoed in the chamber, and after just a few seconds Denzel waved his arms, "Enough! Shit! That is the eeriest damn sound I have ever heard! They think that's music?"

Kotler laughed. "That eerie effect you're feeling is exactly why this is relevant to the case. Newton was studying the Devil's Interval. Patel found that research and expanded on it. But someone else used this place first, and was likely exploring the same phenomenon."

"How recently do you think that happened?" Denzel asked, wary.

Kotler shrugged. "This thing is old. Probably built in the 30s. Maybe a bit later. There's other equipment here from various decades, right up to the 70s, at which point I suspect this chamber was sealed and left abandoned. No way to know when any of this was brought down here."

"Kotler," Denzel said, exasperated. "Seriously, what does this have to do with the case?"

"If someone else knew about this place, the journal may have belonged to them. Maybe Bristol found it when Patel brought her down here, and she kept it secret."

"Ok," Denzel said. "So, the gunman got his hands on it when Bristol died. How did he even know it existed?"

Kotler shrugged. "No way to know that just yet. But I'm starting to suspect that journal is at the heart of all this. Maybe Dr. Bristol took it somewhere to be authenticated, and someone got word of it."

"That makes sense," Denzel said. "At least something makes sense, finally. But now the bad guys have the journal."

"I think they've had it for at least six months," Kotler said. "And it's incomplete. Which is why they needed Patel's research."

"And how would they know about Patel's research?" Denzel asked.

"I think they've been trying to reconstruct it," Kotler said. "The gunman knew that Patel had access to this place, here in London. He had him fly here. I think that man is working for someone else. Someone who knows all about Devil's Interval, and wants to rebuild it. Probably to sell it to the highest bidder."

Denzel was examining the Theremin. "It's a good story, Kotler, but I don't see how it helps us."

"It gives us a bit more to look for, at least," Kotler said, shrugging. "If Bristol kept a log or something about this site, there might be evidence for it among her things. It's something else we can look for. Another piece."

"So far, this entire case is nothing but pieces," Denzel said.

Kotler laughed. "Welcome to archeology."

CHAPTER 9

THEY HAD A FLIGHT BACK TO NEW YORK BOOKED FOR the next day, but the best takeoff time they could manage was nearly noon, London time. That put them getting back in the evening in New York. A long and seemingly wasted day.

Denzel arranged for Patel to be flown back after answering some pointed questions from London authorities for the next couple of days. They were very keen to learn more about what other discoveries Patel may have made, and what he'd done with them.

Kotler was certain that Patel had nothing to do with Ashton's murder, and Denzel agreed. But he still had a lot to answer for, concerning the discovery of Newton's underground lab, and the fact that Patel not only kept it a secret, but mined it for profit. Kotler didn't envy the man for everything he'd go through, both in London and back in New York. His credibility was a smoldering heap now.

As it was, Kotler and Denzel found themselves with a free night in London. It took some convincing, but Kotler finally managed to persuade Denzel that his time would be best spent in the most lively local pub they could find.

"You need a pint and some fish and chips," Kotler grinned.

"Sounds kind of touristy," Denzel replied, his body language throwing off hints that he was both reluctant and intrigued.

"Well, we get to be tourists for the night," Kotler said, and nudged his partner out into the London evening.

They found a place just a few blocks from their hotel. It was exactly the spot Kotler had in mind—dart boards and boisterous conversation occupied everyone who wasn't holding a froth-headed mug or digging into a meal that, to Kotler, seemed far heartier than any bar food he'd previously encountered.

Kotler and Denzel got a table, ordered their drinks and their food, and settled into the atmosphere.

"I always end up in places like this," Kotler said, smiling.

"No surprise. You go looking for them," Denzel said.

Kotler laughed. "I guess I do. It's just that these places, to me, represent all the nuances and truth of a culture. If you could track every major moment in history back to its origin, you'd find most of them started in a place like this. Or in the old coffee houses, or at bath houses. The theme of the place never mattered as much as the atmosphere. Gathering places. What Howard Schultz called 'the third place.'"

"Who?" Denzel asked. He was sipping a stout beer from a frosted mug, the liquid grading from frothy at the top to rich and dark at the bottom. It left a bit of foam on Denzel's lip, which Kotler, smiling, chose not to mention.

"Howard Schultz was basically the founder of the modern-day version of Starbucks. He took the concept of a small, highly knowledgeable coffee seller, and married it to the idea of the traditional espresso bars in Italy. He worked from a philosophy that people need a third place—something outside of work and home. Something that lets them be part of a community. That idea isn't new. Humanity has always sought out a third place, and they're often the birthplace of new philosophies and ideas, even revolutions. I'd be willing to bet that the idea of the Boston Tea Party started at an actual tea party."

Denzel nodded, and finally wiped his lip with a napkin, to Kotler's slight disappointment. "Fascinating," he said.

Kotler chuckled. "History. I guess I can't get away from it."

"That's why you're here," Denzel said. He looked around, and shook his head. "Sometimes I wonder why I'm here, though."

Kotler arched his eyebrows, surprised. "What do you mean? Here in London? Or …" he let the sentence drift, because he didn't actually know what he meant to say. He was fishing. Denzel had been a bit more prickly than usual lately, and Kotler wondered what it meant.

Denzel wasn't meeting Kotler's eye, but instead swept the pub, catching on details here and there. He sighed. "Ok," he said. "I'll tell you. I'm concerned that I'm a little out of my element here."

"Here being …"

"The job, Kotler. The Historic Crimes division. I'm worried that I'm in on something I can't handle, and that I'll drop the ball. Screw up."

"What has you thinking this?" Kotler asked, sipping from his own beer.

Denzel shook his head.

"History. Archeology. Science. That's all your gig," Denzel said. "I'm just a guy with a gun and a badge. The kind of stuff I've done in my career—it's more like what Detective Holden does. I go to a crime scene, I gather evidence, I work the case. Sometimes those cases turn out to be related to national security. Terrorism. Sometimes they're just garden variety murders, but the person has ties to something of interest to the FBI. That's the kind of thing I worked on before. Oh, and babysitting troublemaking archeologists."

"Flattered I made the list," Kotler smiled.

"But the rest? Vikings and ancient cities and hidden labs? Unless those labs are being used to make meth or dirty bombs, I was never really involved. The rest of it was just stuff I might have read about in the news, if I needed to kill time in the john."

He took another sip from his beer, leaving another dollop of foam on his lip.

Kotler nodded. "You have …" he indicated his lip, and Denzel wiped the foam with a napkin, thanking him.

"Look," Kotler said. "I know this wasn't really your thing before, but the Bureau saw a need for this division, right? They promoted you. Put you in charge. That has to say something about your … well, I guess your worthiness, though I think you're worthy regardless of what anyone else thinks."

Denzel nodded. "Yeah, they put me in charge. Gave me resources, too. And there are plenty of cases. Seems like a new case comes in every day. It's almost like the Bureau has been waiting for someone to come along, so they could hand these over and have any hope that they'd be solved."

"That's good news, then, right?" Kotler asked. "You're the guy for the job."

Denzel laughed. "No, Kotler, *you're* the guy for the job. I'm just the guy with the badge. I'm the guy who happened to be with you when we took down Director Crispen. The higher ups in the Bureau wanted to mitigate any fallout from Crispen, so that may be half of why I got this assignment."

Kotler was finally starting to see it. "Roland, look, this whole thing … it's just new, right? It's true there was a bit of luck, when it came to you being part of it. But that doesn't mean you aren't qualified. You've handled some pretty intense stuff, without breaking much of a sweat. That means something. Are you thinking you don't have a role in this? Because you do. You know you do."

"Kotler, most of the time I feel about as useful as pickle in a candy store, when we're working one of these cases." He waved off Kotler's move to protest. "No, look, it's all good. You're right. I have a role. I can do something useful with this. I think I'm just trying to figure out what my part actually is, aside from pointing and shooting."

"Your connections and resources are the only thing that makes this work," Kotler said. "You're the actual operation here."

"I don't follow," Denzel replied.

"The FBI didn't approach *me* about heading this division," Kotler said. "They might have wanted me in on it, but they knew it wouldn't be enough to just give me some sort of charter and let me go digging into case files. I'm just a consultant. I'm only part of this because you made me part of it. I'm replaceable."

Denzel scoffed. "Hardly. I couldn't do any of this without you. I don't know the first thing about even half of what you talk about, most of the time."

"Exactly my point," Kotler said, smiling. "We both have our roles to play. I provide the history and science. That's my gig, like you said. But you bring your field experience, your connections, your resources. You bring your investigative abilities—I can't hold a candle to those. You also happen to bring the power of the Bureau into the equation, which is nothing to take lightly. Even if I had the backing of the FBI, on my own I wouldn't even know how to use it. But together we can do this. That's the point."

Denzel studied him, then nodded, picking up a few French fries drenched in malt vinegar. "Ok," he said.

"Ok," Kotler replied, raising his mug in toast before taking another sip.

"So," Denzel said, "What do we think about this log that Dr. Bristol may or may not have kept?"

Kotler shook his head. "Until we ask the people back at AMSL about it, I have no idea. My working theory is that she found that journal in Newton's chamber, kept it hidden from Patel, and kept records about it in her personal logs at AMSL. Someone discovered she had it, and killed her to get it."

"You're sounding more like an FBI agent every day," Denzel said, grinning. "But why kill her? Why not just force her to hand over whatever she found?"

"Maybe they did," Kotler said, thinking. "Maybe that's what someone has right now. Some piece of the puzzle. But what they're missing is Patel's part. If Bristol was keeping a log, she might have shadowed all of Patel's research. She may have made her own copies."

"So why not just kill Patel?"

Kotler considered. "I'm not sure. But he's more secretive than we might have thought at first. Maybe he didn't keep complete records. In fact, I'm willing to bet on that. He kept information out of his research logs, precisely because he didn't want anyone to find out he's been pilfering a historic site. But Bristol …"

"Bristol may have had more of an ethical conscience about the legitimacy of their work," Denzel said, sipping his beer and thinking. "And unfortunately, that may be what got her killed."

Kotler thought about that for a moment. He'd already been burned after making assumptions about Patel—relating a little too closely to the man as a scientist and historian. He would be more careful about making assumptions from here out. But based on what they'd learned about Lawny Bristol so far, Kotler couldn't help but think she was an innocent caught up in something bigger than she could handle. She had to have been complicit in covering up the lab, but there were signs that it hadn't rested as well with her as it had with Patel. She may have been making a play to bring all of this to light. And in that, she may have trusted the wrong person.

"But then there's the SD card that Ashton Mink took," Denzel said, breaking Kotler's preoccupied reflection. "The thing he was murdered for."

Kotler nodded. "Seems like we have a Tel Dan inscription," he said.

Denzel stared at him over a handful of fries, his mouth slightly open. He rolled his eyes. "Ok, tell me what a Tel Dan inscription is," he grumbled.

Kotler smiled. "It has to do with King David."

"From the Bible?" Denzel asked.

Kotler nodded. "And *only* from the Bible, for centuries. For a couple of millennia, in fact. For thousands of years, the only written historic record we had for the actual existence of King David was the Torah, the basis of the Old Testament. Both of which are based on oral tradition, making them somewhat unreliable from an academic standpoint."

"Wait, we don't have proof that King David was a real person?"

"We didn't," Kotler said. "Until 1993. That's when an archeologist named Avraham Biron unearthed evidence of David's existence from the Tel Dan site in northern Israel. In the excavation they uncovered a stone, which they could date to ninth-century BC. That stone made a reference to the 'House of David.' The first in recorded history, outside of biblical texts. It was an account from an Arabian king, boasting about his victory over the 'king of Israel' and 'the king of the House of David.' It was a fragmented account, missing a lot of details. But most scholars believe it's from Hazel of Damascus, detailing his defeat of Johoram of Israel and Ahaziah of Judah."

"Ok," Denzel said.

Kotler knew he was losing his friend in the details, and needed to bring this around, before Denzel lost interest. "Basically, we had accounts of David from the Bible, from his childhood to his slaying of Goliath, all the way up to the seduction of Bathsheba and the passing of his kingdom to Solomon. But it was all hearsay. There was no proof, outside of biblical accounts, that David even existed. Not until that fragment was recovered. I think that the same thing may be true for the Devil's Interval. There were stories of this research, and some historic documentation. But the idea of someone pursuing it to fruition was just hearsay. That is, until Patel came along and built technology based on that lost research. That would have piqued interest, from someone at least. And if this third party somehow figured out that Dr. Bristol had an actual document or log from the Newton chamber, that would have been just the Tel Dan inscription they'd be looking for. Getting their hands on that may not give them all the information they need to build whatever Patel designed, but it would be enough to prove it was real. Worth the effort and resources needed to obtain it."

"The proof made it a target," Denzel said.

Kotler nodded. "What I'm thinking is that they found their proof too late. I think they got their hands on whatever Bristol found, six months ago, but they killed her for something else."

"Her logs," Denzel said. "They needed to have her logs archived and locked, so that only they could get to them." He cursed. "Which means it had to be an inside job."

"Or at the very least, someone inside is in on it," Kotler

said. "Someone knew that once Bristol died, those logs would be archived and locked, so only key people at AMSL could access them."

"Key people like Ashton Mink," Denzel said.

"We need to know exactly what was and was not deleted from the servers, and what Ashton would have backed up on that SD card."

"I've already set up appointments to drop back by AMSL, after we land. So, we'd better get out of here and get some sleep. It's going to be a very long day."

Kotler took another sip of his beer.

"Kotler," Denzel said, waving towards Kotler's face. "You have foam on your lip. Use a napkin, will ya?"

PART 2

CHAPTER 10

KOTLER WAS FEELING THE SORT OF GROGGY THAT CAN'T be easily combatted, even by the best of coffee. He was on his second cup as he and Denzel walked into the lobby of AMSL. The building was dim, running in night mode with lights lowered. Security was still alert, however. Kotler got the impression that one does not shirk one's security detail, when one reports to Nick Peters.

They were shown through the scanner—something very like the airport security scanners they'd moved through between London and New York—and into one of the elevators. On the ride up, the security guard yawned more than once.

"Long shift?" Kotler asked.

"Early, actually," the man said. "I just got here about fifteen minutes ago. I'm here through 6AM. I'm still adjusting to sleeping during the day."

"You just started, then?" Kotler asked.

The guard smiled and nodded. "Came on about a week ago, as soon as there was an opening."

They exited the elevator and the guard led them to the

same conference room they'd used a few days earlier. Everything was much quieter now, of course, and darker. But the room lit up as they entered. Kotler slumped into one of the comfortable chairs, and sipped his coffee, in an attempt to perk up a bit.

"What was that, with the guard?" Denzel asked.

"Just being friendly," Kotler shrugged.

"Except you learned he's new, and that someone else left," Denzel said.

"Sounds like you learned it, too, Agent Denzel."

Denzel nodded, took out his notepad, and made a note.

Several minutes later, Ross Miller entered the conference room. "I'm sorry to keep you waiting again," he said. "Even this late in the evening, I still end up with a lot to do." He gave a weary smile. "You've found something in your investigation?"

"We found Patel," Denzel said. "London authorities have him in custody now, and he'll be back in New York in a couple of days."

Miller nodded. "Did he … is he …?"

"No, he didn't murder Ashton Mink," Denzel said. "But he's committed a few other crimes, which I'm not able to discuss. I thought it might be fair to warn you, some of his work here may be called into question."

"Any danger to our patents?" Miller asked.

"I couldn't say," Denzel replied.

"You might want to have your attorneys on standby," Kotler said.

Miller looked from Denzel to Kotler, and nodded. "Well, this has become an even bigger mess somehow."

"Are you seeing a lot of fallout over Ashton's death?" Kotler asked.

Miller shook his head. "No, nothing we weren't expecting. In fact, if anything, it's brought our work more prominently into the public eye. There are vigils all over the country right now, and all the news is focusing mostly on Ashton's music career. Some of the majors have picked up the story of what Ashton was hoping to do with this company, and that's been highlighted as a major humanitarian effort. We've had thousands of people call to make charitable donations. We're funneling all of that into paying for cochlear implants for several thousand recipients, at cost."

"Very big of you," Kotler said, nodding.

"It's the job, actually," Miller replied, smiling lightly. "Part of our charter, as a hybrid charity, is that a hundred percent of outside donations go into providing services and resources to the community we serve. The profit-building side of our business comes from licensing, primarily."

Kotler nodded again, and sipped his coffee. As if that were a cue, Miller went to the Keurig adorning the small bar on one wall, and made his own cup. He held up another, offering to make one for Denzel, who shook his head.

"Mr. Miller," Denzel said, taking out his notebook. "We have a few questions, if you don't mind."

"Of course," Miller said, turning with his cup, and leaning against the bar.

"When we questioned Dr. Patel, he mentioned his former research partner, Dr. Lawny Bristol."

Miller nodded, a sad expression on his face. "Lawny was a wonderful person, and a brilliant researcher. She died in an accident, several months ago."

"When she died," Denzel continued, "who gained access to her files and records?"

Miller thought about this. "Well, I did. Garret. Nick. And whoever Nick assigned to vet her files."

"Can we get the name of that person?" Denzel asked.

"Of course," Miller said. "Was she … involved in this somehow? She's been gone for quite a while."

"I can't really comment," Denzel said. "But we do believe there was a connection." He turned back to his notebook. "We've learned that you had someone from security leave recently. Do you know who that was?"

Miller sipped his coffee and shook his head. "No, sorry. Nick can give you that information. I do know that someone left."

"Were they fired?" Kotler asked.

Miller pondered for a moment, then said, "No, I believe he resigned. Nick reports to me on this kind of thing, but honestly it wasn't something that caught my attention at the time, so I don't have any details."

"We'll circle up with Mr. Peters," Denzel said. "Is he still on the premises?"

"No, I don't believe so. He likes to leave at a decent hour. Perks of no longer being in the CIA, he says. Honestly, I let him do anything he wants. He's earned it."

"How so?" Kotler asked.

"Well, serving his country helps," Miller smiled. "But he's also kept our overhead down quite a bit by preventing a lot of IP theft. It's amazing how often it happens. He has measures in place that tell him exactly when and how data leaves this building."

"Sounds like he's pretty indispensable," Kotler said, smiling.

"I'm more easily replaced than he is," Miller chuckled.

"Speaking of data, have you had any luck determining what files Ashton Mink took? And how he was able to do that?"

"We think he took some of the lab records and research. We don't really know how he did it, though. He wasn't exactly tech savvy. And most of the research had been deleted or locked tight by the time he got to a computer. For the most part, we think he could get it out of here because ... well, frankly because he owns the place. We're not under any sort of government contracts, so ultimately he had carte blanche to do whatever he wanted with data or anything else here. He would have been the only one capable of taking that data out of here without it being noticed."

Kotler said nothing, but he knew that Denzel would find that last bit of information just as interesting as Kotler found it. There were several dominoes stacked in a row for this, and that fact made it look even more orchestrated.

They continued to ask questions of the CEO, over the next hour, and finally let him get back to finishing up his day. Arrangements were made to talk to Nick Peters and any other security staff who had access to the Dr. Bristol's files, as well as to Patel's research.

"I'm meeting with Detective Holden in the morning," Denzel said. "He'll want the name and any other information you have for the security guard who left."

"Of course," Miller said. "I'll have my secretary pull that information for you. He can email it to Detective Holden directly."

They parted then, and within half an hour Denzel dropped Kotler at the doorway of his apartment building. "Bright and early tomorrow," Denzel said.

Kotler yawned and nodded, then walked into the lobby.

Ernest was off duty for the evening, and there was no one manning the doorman's podium. Kotler had to let himself in with the security key fob. He fumbled for this in his travel bag, found it, and pressed it against the sensor next to the door. There was a click as the lock disengaged.

Kotler opened the door and was about to step inside, but was suddenly pushed from behind. He tripped, his bag flying forward into the lobby, and barely caught himself before hitting the ground. The door swung into his head, and he was dragged backwards by the feet, letting the door close and lock.

Kotler rolled on his back and saw the man from London, weapon raised and aimed for his chest. There was no way for Kotler to escape. "Still need a ride?" the man asked, waving the gun toward the street. "You're in luck."

CHAPTER 11

DENZEL HAD SLEPT ON THE PLANE, AND EVEN THOUGH he was bone tired, he was having trouble getting to sleep in his own bed. Details of the case were still flitting around in his head.

But it wasn't just that. His conversation with Kotler, from in the pub the night before, still had him thinking.

This new role with the FBI was an honor, and it was big. He was running his own division—not a common thread for an agent's career. But he couldn't seem to help the 'imposter syndrome' he was feeling. He couldn't shake the idea that he was somehow superfluous to his own department. Kotler was the genius with multiple PhDs, and a head crammed full of history and science that Denzel had never even heard of.

What was he really bringing to the table?

That's it, he thought, swinging his legs out of bed. *Night's over.*

It was four in the morning, and the best he'd managed was to doze for a few minutes. He might as well get an earlier jump on the day.

He pulled on workout clothes—a pair of shorts and a T-shirt—and laced up his running shoes. He hadn't been on a solid run for a month now, and he was starting to feel it. A jog would do him some good. Maybe he'd sprint down to the park, make a circuit of it.

He downed some water from the tap, and filled his water bottle. He'd carry it like a baton. Very important to stay hydrated, especially when you're tired. He'd seen more than one cadet fall face down from heat exhaustion and dehydration, during boot camp and, later, during his FBI training. He had learned that it was worth the inconvenience of carrying a water bottle as he ran.

Outside, he stretched on the steps, then started moving. His pace was slow at first, but as he got his wind he started to get into the run. He pushed himself a little, got up to speed, and soon was several blocks away from his apartment. The park was coming up in the next block. At this pace, he'd finish a full loop right around sunrise, and he could snag breakfast at a little diner he liked, on his way back.

The run burned off a lot of the stress and weariness he'd been feeling. He called this "leaving it in the miles behind." As if every step forward was a step away from the tension.

It was good to have something he could control, something he understood. He used to do runs like this with a full pack, rifle raised over his head, canteen bouncing at his belt. He and his unit joked about how much they missed running snakes up and down the bleachers, for football practice, in comparison to lugging a hundred pounds of gear and body armor up and down every hill their drill instructor could find, and usually twice. But the unspoken part of those conversations with his platoon mates was the wonderment of what they could do—more than they ever would have thought possible, back in whatever hayseed, Podunk towns they'd come from. They could endure physical discomfort and weariness and pain beyond anything they'd ever imagined. Even if it did suck.

Embrace the suck, Denzel thought. A mantra from Special Forces. And one that reminded him, suddenly, that sometimes you're just there to do the job, even if you don't like it much. Sometimes, the mission requires you to be the pawn, the sacrifice made so that the mission can be completed. You do your best to keep your bodily fluids on the inside, but you do the job. That's what you swore to do.

That was the nagging perspective that Denzel had been struggling with, ever since he'd been offered Historic Crimes. This new role chafed him a bit, because he couldn't seem to find his fit. He felt like a bureaucrat, when he'd always been a soldier. He was built to take action, to complete the mission, not push paperwork and track down stolen antiquities.

But that was the job. The paperwork was there no matter what. That was always a given, at the Bureau. And tracking down stolen antiquities—well, that could require as much of his military training as anything else, as evidenced by being shot at in an underground chamber in London. This was the job. The boring bits and the bullets.

He realized then, if he wanted fulfillment out of his job, and wanted to feel worthy of his new role, he was going to have to embrace the suck. He was going to have to do the parts he wasn't comfortable with, and grow into his new role —and keep growing until all of this was just part of who he was.

He was going to have to change his attitude about it, and accept that he had a part to play, even if it was just pointing, shooting, and filling out the paperwork.

It wasn't a perfect philosophy, but he felt comforted by it. He could define his own purpose. That was the point. If he couldn't contribute at Kotler's level, he would contribute at his own, and to his own ability. And he'd learn some things, as he went, to make him better at it.

He immediately felt better about things as he wound up his run, rounding things off at that diner, as planned. He ordered three eggs with wheat toast, and as much fruit as his waitress would bring him. That and the coffee set him right. He could feel life returning to his body. His energy was up, despite the fitful sleep.

He had cooled off by now, the sweat dried on his shirt and his body. He was only a block or so away from home, so he did a light jog back, up the stairs and right to his door. He fished the apartment key out of his shoe, but stopped just as he was about to unlock the door.

He was crouched, with the knob at eye height. The door was closed, just as he'd left it. But as he looked at the dead-bolt, he saw a series of tiny scuff marks.

Admittedly, it had been awhile since he'd been on one of these runs. But he'd always come home the same way. He always crouched here, dug out the key from just inside his shoe, and opened the deadbolt before standing. He knew that deadbolt, in other words. Every little scratch on it had been accounted for. Except these.

These were new.

For a moment, Denzel stayed frozen in that position, wondering what he should do. His firearm was inside, locked in a gun safe beside his bed. He was wearing nothing but running shorts and a T-shirt, plus his Nikes. He didn't even have his mobile phone.

He stood slowly, looking around, trying to find anything that might give him an advantage over whoever was inside. Across the hall, beside the stairwell, was a metal box with a fire extinguisher. It would have to do.

Denzel moved quietly, stepped to the box, opened the

glass door and removed the fire extinguisher. He pulled the lock pin, and held the metal canister at the ready.

When he stepped back to his door, he inserted the key as slowly and quietly as he could, standing to the side of the door frame. He took a deep breath, then turned the key. The lock made a loud *thunk* as it disengaged, and he slammed the door open, standing to the side as he pointed the fire extinguisher into the apartment and let loose with a billowing cloud.

A shot was fired, hitting the wall opposite Denzel's door and plowing through it like it was paper. There was nothing on the other side of that wall but the stairwell, and beyond that, the exterior of the building. For that Denzel was relieved. He would never forgive himself if someone were hurt or killed because of him.

He stooped low, holding the now-empty extinguisher like a stubby baseball bat. He raced inward, keeping close to the wall, and as soon as he saw a shadowy shape he leapt, raised the extinguisher above his head and brought it down hard on the skull of the other man.

The man grunted, and fell, sprawling to the floor. He was unconscious.

The fog of the extinguisher was swirling, and Denzel opened a window to help clear it out. He'd be cleaning this mess up for weeks, he knew. But more important things had to be dealt with now.

He looked at the man on the ground, and recognized him.

Christopher Partano. One of Nick Peters' security team, from AMSL.

Pixels and pieces from the case were starting to resolve for Denzel, but he had to put it all aside while he secured Partano's weapon, searched him, and then tied his hands with the man's own shoelaces. He used Partano's belt to bind his feet as well, for good measure.

There was a bleeding wound on Partano's head, and it looked bad. Denzel may have been a bit overzealous with his attack. Which didn't particularly bother him, at the moment.

He picked up his mobile phone from the charger beside his bed. His first instinct was to call his home office, to have some of his people come and deal with Partano. But he stifled that. This was part of something else, after all. More than just an attack on a Federal Agent. This was part of an ongoing murder investigation, and he had made a promise.

He called Detective Holden.

"Agent Denzel?" the man answered. "Shit, we just got a call about shots fired at your address."

"You know my address?" Denzel asked.

"I looked into you," Holden said. "But I was also about to reach out to you. There's been a development. Your boy, Kotler, was nabbed last night."

Denzel huffed, as if he'd been punched in the stomach. Kotler had been taken? It must have happened just after he'd been dropped off at his apartment. Denzel cursed. "Fill me in when you get here."

"I don't usually respond to this kind of thing," Holden said.

"You're going to want to respond to this one. I have one of the AMSL security guys here, and he tried to kill me."

"I'll be there in ten minutes," Holden said.

"Bring an ambulance. He's not in good shape."

"You shot him?" Holden asked.

"Beaned him with a fire extinguisher. He's the one who shot at me."

Holden chuckled. "You brought a fire extinguisher to a gun fight and won? I had you pegged as a badass from day one."

They hung up, and Denzel checked Partano's bonds. He then got on the phone with his home office after all, and had them ping Kotler's mobile phone. He also put in a request to pull local camera footage, which would take a bit.

He was breathing in long, steady breaths, trying to stay calm. Kotler had been in situations like this before. Multiple times.

In fact, as he thought of it, Denzel realized Kotler was a kidnapping magnet. This was the third or fourth time that Kotler had been grabbed since the two of them had met. It was becoming a problem. They'd have to do something about it.

Kotler's last known location was his apartment building, and his phone went offline shortly after Denzel had dropped him off. It had connected with a couple of cellular towers that put it only a few blocks from Kotler's place. His kidnapper probably smashed and tossed it. Maybe they could recover the phone, run prints, get lucky.

Denzel looked down at his 'guest,' and regretted that the man was still out. He might have leads on Kotler, as well as on this case. As it was, that appointment Denzel had with Nick Peters was definitely going to be kept, and it was going to be a much tenser conversation than originally planned.

CHAPTER 12

"I don't know anything," Jared Partano said. "Is my brother ok?"

"No," Denzel said. "And neither are you, if you don't start telling me something, right now."

"I want a lawyer," Partano said.

Denzel leaned in, and nodded to Detective Holden, who was standing near the doorway. Also in the room was Nick Peters, who had requested sitting in on this. Denzel had allowed it, primarily to shortcut time. He wanted Peters to answer some questions himself, and he didn't want to waste time bringing him up to speed.

"The Detective will make sure you get a lawyer," Denzel said. "I'll make sure it takes a very long time for him to get here." With that he stood, and motioned for Holden and Peters to follow him.

They were at Detective Holden's precinct, using one of the interrogation rooms. Denzel knew he was skating, when it came to Partano's attorney. Legally, he couldn't continue to question him until the attorney was present. It was frustrating. But it was also costing time.

"We'll keep leaning on him," Holden said.

"Let me talk to him," Peters said. "I know him. He trusts me. I can get him to talk about what happened. And I don't have to wait for a lawyer."

"Peters, I'm not entirely sure how much we can trust you at this point," Denzel said, bluntly.

Peters blinked, his mouth opened to respond, but closed again. He took a deep breath, let it out slowly, and finally said, "Ok. I can see why. You want to question me now?"

"I want you to tell me why one of your men tried to kill me this morning."

Holden piped in. "And what his connection is with Ashton Mink's murder."

Peters shook his head. "I don't know. But I'm going to find out. I already have my team pulling everything in our database on both Partano brothers."

"And what about the guy who left?" Holden asked. "What was his name?"

"Jack Harris," Peters said. "He left about a week ago. He was good at his job, but kind of hard to work with. He was too intense. I have a folder full of complaints about him. Truth is, if he hadn't resigned, I was planning to fire him."

"Why did you hire him in the first place?" Holden asked.

Peters shook his head. "I inherited him, actually. He was onboard as Head of Security when I got there. When I replaced him, I thought there might be trouble. But he took it well. Said he was tired of the responsibility of running the whole thing. He stepped down voluntarily."

"Just stepped down? Like that?" Holden asked. "No fuss? What was his new role?"

"Senior Security Technician," Peters said. "He had a background in IT."

Denzel made a disgusted noise and turned on Peters,

glaring. "For ex-CIA, you're kind of dense, aren't you, Peters?"

"Denzel …" Holden said, cautioning, trying to calm him.

"You have a guy who knows tech," Roland said, clenching his teeth. "Who isn't well liked and has an attitude problem, but for some reason steps down from director role with no problem. And who leaves just before Ashton Mink's murder. When did you figure it would be a good time to mention any of this?"

Peters' expression was hard now. He stepped forward, not close enough to be in Denzel's face, but certainly not backing down. "My entire database is open to you, Agent. My people will talk to you. I have the clearance to give you any information you want, and I'm going to do exactly that. Harris was a problem child in my classroom, and when he left I didn't think about him again until just this minute. I've been dealing with a shit storm of problems since Mink was killed, and I had no reason to suspect Harris of anything. It was an oversight, not an omission. I'm not holding a single fact back. And I will do everything I possibly can to help you get your man back."

Peters was stern, and his voice had an edge, but to his credit he didn't respond out of emotion. And at the mention of Kotler, Denzel knew he was aiming his frustration and worry in the wrong direction.

For certain, there were still questions that Peters would need to answer. He would need to be cleared. Holden and Denzel could do that first, to ensure that whatever they got from the man was the truth, and was relevant to the case. But Denzel trusted his own gut in these things, and his gut was telling him that Peters was clean.

He decided that, for now, he would roll with that gut feeling.

"Someone in your company is behind this," Denzel said, his tone more relaxed than before. "Or they're deep into it. I need to know everything there is to know about Jack Harris. And I need access to everything that was locked down when Dr. Bristol died. Plus, a list of who had access to that data."

"It's already being pulled," Peters said.

Denzel nodded, then turned to Holden. "I've set up coordination between you and my office at the Bureau."

"I've already gotten a report and some security cam footage," Holden said. "I have it queued up at my desk."

"What about him?" Denzel asked, nodding to Jared Partano, on the other side of a glass wall.

"He'll get his attorney," Holden said. "I have 48 hours to track the guy down."

THEY SAT at Holden's desk and reviewed footage from several local security cameras, including the one in Kotler's lobby. The man who took him had attacked just as Kotler had used his key fob on the door. He was quick, and Kotler was clearly taken by surprise. But there was no real violence, and Denzel was grateful for that.

Holden stopped the footage on a frame that showed the man's face. "Anybody we recognize?" he asked.

Peters swore. "That's him," he said. "That's Jack Harris."

"So not the smartest guy," Holden said. "He's not making any attempt to hide who he is."

"He might not care if we know," Denzel said. "He knows I saw his face, in London. He knows Kotler saw him, too. And forensics from Scotland Yard have verified that the rounds fired from his weapon match those that killed Ashton Mink. He's our guy. He may have been counting on me being killed by Partano, which would have distracted everyone from Kotler's disappearance. Kotler travels all the time—it would have been weeks, maybe months before anyone other than me wondered about where he'd gotten to."

"That seems kind of dangerous to me," Holden said.

Denzel realized, for the first time, that Holden was right. And it was a shock. Because Kotler was well-known—even famous, in some circles. And he was well-liked, particularly by women. For the first time, however, Denzel was starting to realize that Kotler didn't keep close acquaintances. He knew everyone, but wasn't quite known by anyone. Except, of course, for Denzel. And that did put Kotler in a dangerous position—one where he could go missing for long stretches, and might not be noticed.

And something else bothered Denzel about this. It was dangerous for Kotler, for sure. But it also meant something about Kotler's life that Denzel hadn't put together until now.

Kotler was alone.

He didn't show any signs of that bothering him, of course. He had his trysts, and he attended all sorts of high society events. But some of his more meaningful romantic relationships hadn't worked out so well, in the time that he and Denzel had known each other and worked together. Evelyn Horelica had left Kotler long before she was kidnapped, during the whole scenario in Pueblo. And Gail McCarthy had turned out to be behind all the trouble surrounding the Atlantis discovery. Kotler didn't talk about it, but Denzel suspect that Gail's betrayal had hit harder than Kotler was willing to admit.

Kotler always came across as happy, and in a good humor. He was always making jokes or wry observations. He was always channeling his energy into doing something good. But all of that was hiding the fact that Kotler was as isolated as anyone could be, and still be out living in the world.

That was a discussion for a different day, though. And most of it wasn't any of Denzel's business. He would talk to Kotler about what they could do to make him a little less vulnerable to abduction. Kotler, being the epitome of a free spirit, would object to anything that might limit his movements.

Tough, Denzel thought. Something had to change, or Kotler would become a liability more than an asset. Or worse. Though Denzel wasn't entirely sure his motivation for pushing this on Kotler was really about liability.

Right now, he was just worried about his friend.

They cycled through more footage, and saw Kotler being shoved into the back of an SUV. "I'll run those plates," Holden said, "but I'd bet it's stolen."

"No ID on the driver," Denzel said. "He's not visible from any of these angles. We don't even know how many people are in that vehicle."

After several minutes of scrubbing footage, making notes, and putting in requests for information from various departments, there was simply nothing useful emerging. Nothing except a positive ID on Jack Harris.

Hours later, after Nick Peters had returned to AMSL and Jared Partano's lawyer had been given a heads up, Denzel was reviewing the report again, along with all the information his people at the Bureau could give him. There was a team on this now, and they were reporting to Denzel. Kotler might be just a consultant with the FBI, but he was still one of theirs. He was not going to be left behind.

Holden, to his credit, was also piling on resources. But his priority was the murder investigation. "I think we can bump Mr. Harris up to the top of the board," Holden said, taking Harris' photo from the large murder board near his desk, and putting it at the top of the suspect pool.

There were multiple investigations tacked to that board.

Unlike in the movies or on television, Detectives rarely had just one case to work on. Resources were too thin for that, and the case load was too heavy for one-at-a-time. Even as they sat reviewing Kotler's kidnapping, Holden. had taken several calls and answered a deluge of emails about other open cases. Mink's murder was high profile, and so it was getting high profile treatment, but his wasn't the only death crying for justice in the city.

Considering the near existential crisis Denzel had been having of late, he was seeing the bullpen of the precinct in a new light. He had never been a cop, but he'd now worked in law enforcement for the bigger part of his career. And he knew, even if he'd forgotten briefly, that there really are no small cases. Every case has its impact on the lives of others. And the work his department could do, solving crimes tied to misplaced history, could have a big impact on a lot of lives. It was important. He was doing good work. Worthy work. It eased something in his chest and stomach, coming to that conclusion.

Right now, though, he needed to focus on finding Kotler and the people behind all of this. In all the shuffle and all the chaos, there was a fact being lost, or at least put aside, though it might outweigh the lives of both Ashton Mink and Dan Kotler, in terms of importance.

The technology these people were after could do a lot of damage in the world.

Mind control. That was maybe the most dangerous weapon Denzel could think of. Turning someone from their own will, enslaving them, making them into a living weapon, subverting everything that made them human—Denzel shivered from the idea of it.

These are the people who have Kotler, he thought. He would do whatever it took to bring these people down.

CHAPTER 13

As kidnappings go, Kotler thought, *this one isn't so bad.*

The gunman from London was sitting in the seat next to him, in the back of a black SUV. Up front was a driver, wearing a hood and glasses that obscured his face. The three of them were the only ones in the vehicle.

"Phone," the gunman said, pointing his weapon at Kotler's stomach.

Kotler obliged, handing over his phone. He tried to tick off, in his head, the number of phones he'd had to replace over the past couple of years. Since starting his work with Agent Denzel, Kotler had put his phone insurance through its paces.

The gunman rolled down his window and tossed the phone out as they passed by a collection of trash cans.

If Kotler survived this, he would need to think of some way to supplement the phone as a tracking device. He knew that Roland would immediately ping the phone's location, but that didn't do Kotler much good if it was lying in a busted pile on a random sidewalk.

The SUV made several turns, seemingly at random. This was probably meant to complicate any search from video cameras, to break a pattern so it would be more difficult for the FBI or the police to keep track of where they went.

Kotler, on the other hand, knew exactly where they were in the city, and the gunman had made no effort to cover his eyes. A bad sign.

He didn't bother speaking during the ride. He already knew he'd be told to shut his mouth, probably with some colorful profanity in the mix. Instead of talking, then, he decided to spend the time running through everything he knew about the case, to see what new connections he could make.

With the murder of Ashton Mink, a whole series of events had tumbled into motion. At first, the murder seemed to be the starting point. But they had new information now. Patel's discovery of the Newton chamber. Dr. Lawny Bristol's death, and the locking of her records. The evidence that someone else had discovered and used the Newton chamber, long before Patel's arrival, but had apparently ceased operations sometime in the 70s. The as-yet-unnamed security guard who left AMSL just a week prior to Ashton's murder.

And, lest he forget the most intriguing and dangerous aspect of this case, there was the research and technology that could give someone the power to control the minds of others. Not a pleasant prospect.

Two new facts emerged for Kotler, however, as he ran through all of this.

First, it was clear that the London gunman was the former AMSL security team member. He was likely the one who killed Ashton Mink, and was equally likely to be the one who killed Lawny Bristol. His murder of Ashton, though, showed that he knew about the data card—something he'd only know about if he somehow had access to the AMSL servers.

The second emerging fact was that the gunman had someone else helping him. Someone on the inside. The security measures that Peters had in place were too next-level for someone like the gunman to hack into. He may have had some technical chops, but he didn't strike Kotler as being that level of hacker. He had to have help.

And Kotler's present situation proved that. Up to now, the gunman had operated alone, as far as Kotler could see. There was no evidence that anyone else had been in Ashton Mink's apartment, the night of his murder. And in London, the gunman had been alone with Patel, and alone when on the run.

But now he had a driver. Someone who knew how to remain anonymous. A professional, in other words. Far more professional than the gunman, though he showed at least some acumen for this business.

Kotler figured the gunman to be ex-military. That was an assumption based on his role with AMSL, which seemed to employ a lot of ex-military for security. He had training, then. He knew weapons, he had some hand-to-hand skills, and he could run within the parameters of an operation. But he showed no sign of being able to organize an op himself. He was too clumsy for that.

So, the driver was a hired pro, who probably had no idea who the gunman was, or even who Kotler was, for that matter. He was doing a job, he'd collect his pay, and he'd be gone, likely dumping the SUV in a river somewhere.

Or maybe not.

After a long stretch of random turns, the SUV finally pulled off the streets of Manhattan, into a parking garage with no attendant on duty. *Probably pre-arranged*, Kotler thought.

The garage was dark, and as the SUV pulled into an empty spot, the gunman shoved the nose of his weapon into Kotler's side. "Out."

Kotler got out, and was directed to climb into another vehicle—a generic looking tan sedan that had dark tinted windows and spinners on its wheel hubs. It smelled like pot and booze, and Kotler decided that it had been stolen as well, and meant to be as opposite to the SUV as possible.

The gunman joined him in the back, and the driver resumed his positon.

This time, almost to his relief, a bag was pulled over his head, obscuring his view. The engine started, and they were moving.

They drove for perhaps another 30 minutes, not taking many turns, until the sedan they were riding in stopped. Kotler was dragged out, into an elevator, and when he was finally forced into a chair and the bag taken off, he blinked at a series of bright lights. His hands were cuffed to the arms of the metal chair he was sitting in. A smart move, Kotler thought, since it made it doubly difficult for him to attempt an escape.

He couldn't quite make out where he was. The room was large, unfurnished, but very dark. The bright lights were spots, aimed directly into his eyes. Three lights—no … there were four lights. A detail Kotler wasn't sure mattered, but it seemed important at the time.

"Dr. Kotler," a voice said. It was distorted, playing through a speaker. Whoever was behind it didn't want to be recognized. Which told Kotler, immediately, that this was someone he knew. It could be a man or woman, thanks to the voice masking. He might be able to work out the person's gender by listening for certain affects, but that was tricky at the best of times.

"Hi," Kotler said, simply, forcing a relaxed affect.

There was a pause, which was what Kotler had hoped for. He needed to play for time, and to get as many details as he could, if he hoped to get out of this. He'd been grabbed after Denzel dropped him off, so it would be hours before anyone knew he was gone. If they knew at all.

"You have created some difficulty for us, Dr. Kotler," the voice said. "We needed Dr. Patel to complete the research."

"He's in London, but he should be back in a few days," Kotler said. "Maybe you can swing by and chat with Detective Holden. Scotland Yard will deliver Patel into his custody directly."

"I see you think this is a game," the voice said. "You may be overestimating your value to me."

"Right now, I figure you're planning to use me as leverage to get your hands on Patel," Kotler said, calmly. "But it won't work."

"And why is that?" the voice asked.

"Because Agent Denzel will find you first. And he won't let you use me as a bargaining chip. That isn't how he operates."

"Agent Denzel will be dead soon. I've already made arrangements."

Kotler felt his blood chill. "You really don't get how this leverage thing works, do you? If you kill Denzel, there's no way I'll ever cooperate with you."

"I don't need your cooperation, Dr. Kotler. Your value to me is as an item of trade."

"Trade?" Kotler asked.

"Someone has offered me an item I want, in exchange for you. It's a bargain, really. The only downside is they want you alive. But before you get it in your head that you're under some sort of protection, you should know that if you cause me any trouble I'll kill you anyway, and find some other way to get what I need."

"That doesn't sound all that efficient," Kotler said. "I mean, a bird in hand, and all that."

"I admit it will be easier if I can just trade you for what I want, but my timetable is flexible."

"What are you trying to do, anyway?" Kotler asked. "This technology you're after—you get that just trying to build it makes you kind of a super villain, right? Mind control is disturbing on every level."

"Do you know what it's like to be powerless, Dr. Kotler?" the voice asked.

This was interesting. Kotler had expected some sort of noncommittal retort, maybe something snide and derogatory, but had instead he seemed to have hit a nerve. "I'm a little powerless at the moment," Kotler said, pulling his tied hands up from the arms of his chair.

There was laughter, which sounded mechanical and eerie thanks to the voice modulation. "Now we both know that isn't true. You're exercising power even now. Oh, you're caught, and you're in trouble, for sure. You may not even make it out of this alive. But despite all of that, you're doing your best to control the situation, and even succeeding somewhat. I shouldn't even be engaging with you, but I just couldn't help it. Your recent activities in London have made things difficult."

"Well, in that case, I apologize," Kotler said. "I meant to make things *impossibly* difficult."

"I'm sure you did," the voice replied. "And that's exactly what I mean, Dr. Kotler. Even now you are reflexively trying to establish your dominance. Your power. Your privilege. You have it, even when you're at a disadvantage. What an injustice."

There was something about this conversation that was starting to buzz with Kotler. He wasn't certain why, but he was getting a vibe now, about the voice. There was something there, a fact that hadn't quite bubbled to the surface.

Your privilege, the voice had said.

"Well, this has been entertaining," the voice continued, "but I have work to do. There's a trade to arrange, after all. I hope you enjoy your accommodations for the evening."

With that, the bag was back over his head and the bonds were cut from his wrists, before he was dragged out of the room.

He didn't struggle. There were too many guns, even if he'd only seen one so far. And he had no idea where he was or how many people might be in on this. It was better to let things play out for now. He was safe, for the moment. The trade, whatever it would turn out to be, would be something of a guarantee for his safety, despite what the voice had implied. If he didn't cause trouble, he would be safe enough.

There was the sound of a key turning a large deadbolt, and Kotler was shoved through a doorway. He stumbled and fell, sprawling on the ground, just as the door slammed shut.

He pulled the hood from his head, but may as well have left it on. The room he was in was pitch black, without even a seam of light from the edges of the door.

Feeling around, he found a roll of blankets. No pillow, no cot, no anything else, that he could determine. The room was empty. He was lucky to have the blankets, perhaps.

He stood and felt along each wall, moving his hands up and down in sweeping arcs, trying to find anything that might be useful. The walls themselves were cinder blocks, with lines of grout forming a grid work everywhere Kotler touched.

In his sweep, he found no electrical sockets in the walls, no shelves, not so much as a leftover nail or screw, where a picture might have hung. And as he reached upward, he got no sense of where the ceiling might be. This space could have a ten-foot ceiling, or a fifty foot one. No way to know.

He wasn't sure what time it was, but it had to be late. He'd been nabbed from his apartment shortly before midnight, and that was starting to catch up to him. Jet lag was catching up as well.

He had exhausted every possibility he could think of, here in the dark, and so the last option was to take the gift of blankets, find a spot to rest, roll one up as a pillow, and go to sleep. He would need the rest. There was no way to know what tomorrow would bring.

CHAPTER 14

DENZEL HAD GROWN IMPATIENT WITH THE RESULTS they were getting, and was ready to try just about anything new.

They had scoured every security and traffic camera they could locate on the route taken by the SUV, but their search was going nowhere. The SUV had taken a series of random turns, looping around blocks at times, sometimes driving into areas of the city that had very sparse coverage. This wasn't London, after all. There weren't clusters of cameras at every city block. Denzel and Holden were relying on traffic cams, primarily.

Getting permission to access all those cameras was taking too long, of course. It had been twenty-four hours now, since Kotler had been abducted, and in that time, they'd only gotten court orders for maybe a third of the cameras along the SUV's route, most of which were associated with banks and ATMs. Denzel and Holden had resorted to calling individual branches and asking politely, hoping they could convince empathetic bank managers to cooperate and hand over footage voluntarily. Many did. Some didn't.

The video angle was coming along, but it wasn't producing much in way of results, and it was costing time. The crucial 48-hour window was closing. Denzel decided, after several hours of sitting in on review, that it was best to leave this part to the techs, and to go pursue new leads on his own.

The trouble was, there were no leads. Not in Kotler's disappearance.

"So, let's get back to Mink's murder," Holden said, gruffly. "That's the point, ain't it? Your boy was grabbed in connection to this murder, and this doohickey ... the, uh ..."

"Devil's Interval," Denzel said.

"Right. We solve this, we might have a better chance of finding your guy."

Denzel could only agree. He knew it deep down. Kotler's kidnapping was a complication in a bigger, ongoing investigation. Their best chance of finding him was to solve this case.

Only, parts of this case involved Kotler's expertise. How was Denzel supposed to fill in those gaps? He had nowhere near Kotler's insight into history and science. The closest he came to cultural anthropology and archeology and quantum physics was watching *Ancient Aliens* on the History channel.

He felt a gripping sensation in his chest and stomach, like what he felt in tight spaces. That's what this felt like, now. He was confined. He was in a tight space. He was in trouble.

Except ...

He took a few deep breaths. He had ducked into the men's room at the precinct, and he now splashed water on this face, rubbing his eyes and toweling off with paper towels. He slicked his hair at the temples, where it was starting to stick out a bit. He stood straight, tightened his tie, smoothed his shirt, and pulled on his suit coat. He was engaging the FBI agent within.

Because that's what he was.

Without Kotler, he had no immediate access to his partner's wealth of personal knowledge, expertise, and insight. But he was still an FBI agent. And he had a case to work. He would do his job the way he'd been trained to do it.

He left the men's room and found Holden, already pulling on his own soiled and wrinkled coat and brushing some crumbs from his shirt. Holden's tie was loose, as always, and the top button of his shirt was missing. He was, essentially, the opposite of Denzel's agent persona, but in his own way, he was doing just as Denzel had done. He was pulling on the uniform. He was preparing to go do the job.

"I was thinking," Holden said. "They grabbed Kotler right after your meeting with the AMSL people."

Denzel considered this. "They may have been watching Kotler's place. Waiting for us to arrive."

"But they knew who he was," Holden said. "They knew where to find him."

Denzel blinked. "That's right," he said. "I hadn't put that together."

"So that points pretty strongly to someone in the organization. Again."

"So, it's time to stop playing polite with these people," Denzel said. "They have a mole somewhere in their lineup, and we need to know exactly who it is. How's it coming with Jared Partano?"

"He's lawyered up, and isn't saying much. We didn't have anything on him, so I couldn't hold him. He's been released, but warned not to leave town. I have a unit watching him for the next 48 hours. And Nick Peters told me the kid's on leave until this is cleared up."

"What about the brother? Has he come out of it yet?"

"He's in a coma. You brained him pretty good," Holden said.

"He tried to shoot me," Denzel replied.

"I'm not saying he didn't deserve it. But the docs aren't giving him very good odds of pulling through."

Denzel felt a strange stab of regret at that. The man had tried to kill him, so Denzel had little sympathy for his current state. But he had information they needed, and it was Denzel who had taken him out of commission.

He shook it off. Things like this happened, during an investigation. Advantages and disadvantages were all part of the flow. Partano's coma, Kotler's abduction, a hidden mole within AMSL—these were all part of the puzzle. Solving this case would mean being able to think around the obstacles and limitations, and come up with a solution regardless.

"We need to go back to AMSL," Denzel said.

"And talk to who?" Holden asked. "We've already put everyone in that place in the spotlight. Whoever the mole is, they've covered their tracks pretty well."

Denzel thought for a moment, shaking his head. "What are we missing? There are pieces to this that we must be over-looking." He considered. "Did we ever get an answer on the question of who had access to Lawny Bristol's personal files, after she died?"

Holden took out his notebook. Hand-writing notes in a weathered reporter's notepad was a vice that he and Denzel shared. Kotler stored all his observations electronically, and usually well after the fact. The man had a near eidetic memory, which Denzel envied. But it was far too comforting to fall back to the handwritten notes, when he needed a refresher.

Handwritten notes.

"Wait," Denzel said. "What do we have on the notebook?

The one that Jack Harris grabbed in London? Have we seen any reference to that?"

Holden had glanced up at him, then riffled through his notebook again. "Nothing significant," he said.

Denzel was flipping through his own notebook now. "I have a brief statement on it from Patel," he said. "It wasn't something he knew about beforehand. It was older, though. He told me it contained notes in several different sets of handwriting."

"So, it had more than one owner," Holden said. "So what?"

"Where did it come from?" Denzel asked. "How does it factor into all of this? If we can pick up the trail on this thing, it might lead us to whoever is behind all of this."

Holden nodded. "So, we do need to talk to the AMSL folks again."

"Just one," Denzel said. "It's time that Nick Peters opened up everything he's got."

CHAPTER 15

"How many of these visits can we expect, Agent Denzel?" asked Ross Miller. He and Garrett Chandler were sitting with Nick Peters in the conference room once more, across from Denzel and Holden.

Miller raised a hand, waving off his own comment before Denzel could respond. "I apologize," he said. "I know that your partner was abducted, and that's adding to the weight of this. Of course, anything we can do to help, we will do. It's just ..." he trailed off.

"We have a company to run," Chandler said, with an edge to his voice. "And frankly, this investigation is starting to have an impact. We got something of a PR boost over Ashton's murder, but now the press is asking questions we're not even allowed to answer. If they get wind of your friend's abduction, and link it back to us, there's no telling how the public is going to react."

Denzel nodded. "I appreciate the predicament, gentlemen. But since we have a body and an abduction on our hands, I'm not particularly in the mood to give a shit about your PR."

There was a stunned silence in the room as everyone, even Detective Holden, reacted to Denzel's tone. He had delivered his words calmly and in the same professional way he might have asked about their whereabouts or alibis, and that somehow made his statement even more intimidating.

"Agent Denzel," Peters said, "We're cooperating. What can we do?"

"I need access to Dr. Lawny Bristol's archived files, and a list of everyone who had prior access to them."

"Already pulled that up for you," Peters said, sliding a smart tablet across the table.

Denzel took it and immediately started sliding through the data. "I also need to know if there was a handwritten journal in Dr. Bristol's possessions. Old. Leather bound."

Peters shook his head. "Not to my knowledge. We boxed her personal belongings and sent them to her family, in Chicago. Her sister. Name is Kate Bristol. She's all the family that Lawny had left, from what we could find. Her name was the only one listed in Dr. Bristol's employee file, anyway. She insisted that we ship everything to her home address. But the box we sent was small. Dr. Bristol didn't keep a lot of personal belongings here. Everything else was tied to her work, and so it's been archived."

"I'd like to see it," Denzel said.

Peters nodded, "Of course." He picked his phone out of his hip pocket and tapped out a message, presumably to someone on his security team.

Holden spoke up then. "I'd like the contact information for the sister. She probably took possession of Bristol's personal things, from her home."

Peters nodded, looked back at his phone, and after a few taps said, "I can email this information to both of you."

Holden nodded, though Denzel knew he'd prefer to hear it and write it down.

"Anything else?" Peters asked.

"Your man, Partano, is in a coma," Denzel said, glossing over the fact that it was he who put the man there. "We can assume he was in on all of this, so I'd like all of his records as well. Particularly his activities over the past few months. And those of his brother, too."

"That will take some time to pull together," Peters said. "Should we look for anything specific?"

"Anything to do with Dr. Bristol," Denzel said. "Particularly any time that Christopher had accessed her records."

Garrett Chandler spoke up. "You think Dr. Bristol is involved in this, too?"

"I can't rule it out," Denzel said. "Not based on what we have."

"Which isn't much," Holden grumbled.

"Right now, we're on the hunt for any hints about that journal," Denzel said. "And we want to track down the mole in your organization."

"Wouldn't that be Christopher Partano?" Chandler asked.

"I don't believe he acted alone. Based on the timing of Dan Kotler's abduction, and the presence of Partano in my home early the next morning, we believe someone else fed Partano and Jack Harris information on our movements. And, unless we discover that it was Partano who accessed Bristol's files and effects, there's still the matter of someone breaching your internal security."

"That system is beyond state of the art," Peters said, looking to the CEO and COO. "If someone did hack it, they had to have been inside."

"And who would be most likely to do that?" Miller asked.

"The list is short," Holden said. "And sitting in this room."

Miller and Chandler looked first at Peters, then at each

other, and finally back to Holden. "You're saying it was one of us?" Miller asked.

"That's my suspicion," Holden said. "It's also why I've brought this." He reached into the inner pocket of his coat and produced the search warrant, which Denzel had helped to expedite. "Warrant to search both of your personal access logs, your offices, and your homes. Officers are already doing all three."

Chandler stood first, his body tense with outrage. "What the hell? You couldn't have warned us?"

"Warned you for what?" Holden asked.

"I would have handed all of this over anyway," Miller said. "All you had to do was ask."

"I find it works better when the suspects don't know I'm coming," Holden said. "But don't worry, gentlemen. We're after some pretty specific things. Information, mostly. And your cooperation is both noted and appreciated. But for the time being, I'm going to ask that all three of you stay right here, in this room."

"Three?" Peters asked. "So, you're searching my offices, too?"

"Anything we need to know about?" Holden asked.

Peters smiled and chuckled. "Detective, everything is wide open. Go find whatever you can."

CHAPTER 16

KOTLER AWOKE TO THE DOOR SLAMMING OPEN, AND A flood of light pouring in from outside. The bright whiteness of it hurt his eyes, and he shielded them even as two men yanked him to his feet and pulled the hood back over his head.

He had to pee, but he doubted he'd be given the chance. He held it, hoping he could preserve his dignity long enough to at least be able to request a restroom.

He tried to keep pace with the two men, but found himself tripping and stumbling as his groggy brain struggled to send signals to all the right parts of his body. As a result, he was half dragged along the corridor, his arms and shoulders aching as two sets of very strong hands tightened their grip. In just a moment he was thrust into a chair again, his hands and feet tied for the second time in twenty-four hours. The hood was removed, the four bright lights shown, and Kotler realized he was back in the same interrogation room.

"Did you sleep well?" the voice asked.

"A bit rough," Kotler said, clearing his throat. "I could use a restroom."

"There isn't time, I'm afraid," the voice said. "I've come to an agreement with the other party. They should be arriving with my package any moment, and once it's verified I'll give you to them."

"That was quick," Kotler said. "I've had no time to request a rock hammer and a Rita Hayworth poster."

"You'll have to take it up with your new captor," the voice replied.

Kotler wasn't sure how to feel about this development, but he decided that the best course of action was to roll with it. He had a few moments with the disembodied voice on the other side of the lights, and this might be his only chance to glean more information.

"What is it I'm being traded for, exactly?" Kotler asked. "As far as I know, you have everything you need."

"Everything but Dr. Patel," the voice replied. "Thanks to you and your FBI partner. But I may be able to work without him. Your ... *benefactor* ... is offering a missing piece of research that Simon could never locate. He managed to recreate the missing information on his own. But with this, he might have completed his prototype years sooner."

"Something historic, I take it?" Kotler asked.

"Missing pages. From the journal."

Kotler nodded. "I've never seen the journal up close, but I assume that's what your man grabbed from the workbench in London? While we were in the Newton chamber?"

"It's been an invaluable artifact. It fills in all the gaps from Dr. Patel's previous research. All but the final component."

"The evil mind control component?"

"That would be the one. Now, you rest there, Dr. Kotler. My guest has arrived. Once I've verified the pages are authentic, you'll be handed over."

"Ok, but could we not do the hood …" His objections were cut off as the hood was once again pulled over his head.

He sat in the faux darkness, with only tiny dots of light bleeding through the pores of the hood. He concentrated on controlling his breathing, even meditating a bit. In confined situations like these, he could catch a glimmer of what Denzel must go through, in tight spaces. But Kotler had learned long ago, and practiced often, the meditative art of controlling his breathing and his anxiety. He kept his mind focused on each breath, until he was free to think and dwell upon other things.

He'd gotten quite a bit of information from his captor, during that chat. He wasn't sure how useful that information would turn out to be, but that was always the case. Information, data of any kind, was only useful in the proper context. And sometimes you needed to have the information first, and find the context second.

Right now, he had information that was clicking into place with data he already possessed. The story that was unfolding was different than he might first have imagined, but that served only to make new details stand out for him.

Of course, his exploration of all the new data was being hampered by the big question mark-shaped sword of Damocles hanging over his head. He seemed to be enjoying the 'good fortune' of having a benefactor—someone who wanted him for their own purposes. But those purposes were unknown, and could lead to him being in far more trouble than he currently found himself. Any comfort he might have taken in his relative safety from the night before was now dampened by fear of the unknown dangers that might be coming.

KOTLER HAD no way of knowing how long he'd sat there, hood over his head and bladder threatening to burst. His guru would have been proud of his composure, considering what a hard case Kotler had been during meditation studies. Kotler silently thanked God and sent blessings to his guru, who would surely be shocked to discover that any of his teachings had managed to remain in the skull of the impulsive and impatient archeologist.

Kotler heard two sets of footsteps, both of which had become familiar now, as they had entered and exited this room several times since depositing him roughly in this chair.

They cut his bonds this time, and Kotler immediately flexed and rubbed his wrists. They then pulled the hood from his head, and stood on either side of him.

He glanced up at each of them, then experimentally braced his palms on the arm of the chair and rose to his feet. He watched them, but they stood in stoic silence. They were two thick-necked and brutish men, each wearing long sleeved Henley shirts that were stretched tight across bulging muscles. They wore sunglasses, despite being both indoors and in a darkened room, though the bright interrogation lights might have been justification enough.

Kotler blinked into those lights now, shading his eyes, trying to see past them.

"You're free to go, Dr. Kotler. Your benefactor has a car just outside of that door."

Another set of lights came on, illuminating a set of double metal doors to Kotler's right.

"Who is it?" Kotler asked. "What do they want?"

"You'll find all of that out soon enough."

"And the pages? You got everything you need?"

"Everything," the voice said.

Kotler felt his guts twist. He glanced at the two guards—doubting they were mere mooks, and feeling safe in assuming they were well trained. He couldn't take them, he figured, without seriously hurting himself in the process. Maybe not even then.

He needed just a few more seconds. He needed to get as much information as possible, before he lost access to the person on the other side of the line. More importantly, he needed to see if he could do anything at all to stop what they were doing.

"Please," Kotler said, turning to face the lights and the disembodied voice beyond. "What you're building—it's more dangerous than you seem to realize. It's a weapon. It will hurt a lot of people. You have a chance to stop this. I'm asking you to take it."

"Dr. Kotler, you can either walk through those doors voluntarily, or my men will drag you through them and dump you on the other side. Your benefactor was not specific about what physical condition you should be in."

Kotler nodded. He turned to the doors and gingerly walked straight to them, his legs still a bit rubbery and his lower back aching. A night sleeping on a concrete floor, followed by hours of being tied to a hard-backed chair, hadn't done him any favors.

He wasn't sure, now, what frightened him more: The fate awaiting him on the other side of those doors, or the fate awaiting all of humanity if the Devil's Interval was completed. He decided his own safety and well-being were not as important as that of humanity, and with that he took a deep breath, calmed himself, and pushed through the doors like a Sheriff pushing his way into a saloon. Whatever was out there, he'd face it, and hope that he could escape, and somehow use what he knew to stop Devil's Interval from sending the world to hell.

The doors slammed closed behind him as he stepped away, out into the echoing chamber of a cavernous garage, or possibly some sort of hangar. The space was enormous, and there were large, cable-driven doors on either end, big enough for a plane or possibly construction equipment to fit through.

Before him, idling, was another black SUV, very like the one he'd been pulled into only last night.

On a hunch, he opened the back door to climb in, and suddenly found himself staring, shocked, his mouth agape.

"Well hello, Dan," a familiar female voice said. A voice he had not expected to ever hear again. "Get in."

"Gail," he said, dumbfounded.

Abigail McCarthy. The one that got away—from both Kotler and the FBI.

"It's been a few months," Gail said, smiling. "I thought it might be time for a reunion."

CHAPTER 17

THE SUV TOOK THEM STRAIGHT TO A SMALL AIRPORT
about half an hour outside of Manhattan. They pulled up to
the front of a large hanger, where a Gulfstream G650 was
waiting. The SUV drove into the hangar, just as the jet's
engines spun to life.

"If we're taking a trip, could I please use the restroom
first?" Kotler asked. "I'm really about five minutes away from
making a mess."

"That would be unpleasant," Gail said, shaking her head
in mock sympathy. "Get out."

Kotler got out, without challenge. He stood and
stretched a bit, his aching back finally getting some relief.

The two men who had been in the front seat of the SUV
climbed out and went to the back, opened the hatch, and
removed a suitcase and a small, metal attaché case. They placed
both on the floor of the hanger, between Gail and Kotler.

"I want you to know," Gail said, "I don't hold a grudge,
over Atlantis. As it turns out, things have gotten quite a bit
better for me, since then."

"You took over van Burren's smuggling network?" Kotler asked.

Gail smiled. "That, yes. There was so much more than I had expected, though. I think you'd be fascinated, Dan. But then, you're a bit too ... oh, I suppose 'moral' is the right word."

"Morals and ethics," Kotler said flatly. "Always getting in the way."

Gail laughed, lightly. "For some of us."

"Gail, I don't know what you're planning here, but it's not too late. The pages you traded for me—those people are building a weapon. A hideous and ugly weapon."

"Oh, I know. And I do feel terrible about that. But it was all I had to trade for your release."

Kotler was studying her, and wondering what she was planning. Her body language was always so tightly controlled —she was nearly impossible to read. Deceptive, even to her most minute movements.

"What do you want from me?" he asked.

She smiled, and walked around the suitcase, coming to stand in front of him. She looked up at him, her eyes sparkling, and then rose to kiss him on the lips. "I've changed some of my plans, and I think that one day you might consider joining me."

"Joining you?" Kotler said. "In what?"

"In life, Dan," she smiled, laughing again. "In the adventure."

"Gail, that isn't going to happen. You're ... well, you're a murderer, for starters. And a thief. A smuggler. I mean, honestly, you and I could not be more opposite."

"That's true," she said, smiling. "But right now, you owe me your life. Opposite or not."

"And what will I have to do to repay you?" Kotler asked.

"Where are we going?" He raised and hand, waving toward the plane.

Gail glanced back over her shoulder, then once again to Kotler. "Oh that? No, that's for me. You're staying here."

Kotler blinked. "I ... I am?"

She nodded to the attaché. "That's for you. Take it. You'll know what to do with it. And when you and that hunk of an FBI agent get all of this current nonsense figured out, saving the world and all that, I want you to focus your attention on this. Solve it, and you'll find me again. How's that for a promise?"

"What is it?" Kotler asked.

She laughed. "Dan, that's what I want you to figure out!"

She turned then, and one of the men grabbed her suit-case, carrying it to the plane. She followed him up the steps, with the second man behind.

At the top, she turned to Kotler and shouted. "The keys are in the ignition. Drive safely!"

With that, she and the two men disappeared into the plane, the doors closing behind them.

Kotler watched as it taxied away from the hangar. He took note of the numbers on the tail, though he knew it would do no good. Gail was too well connected, having taken over Richard van Burren's operation gave her incredible resources. They could trace that plane's flight path, but Gail was already out of their reach.

Kotler went to the attaché and picked it up, feeling its weight. The case itself was heavy—packed with fire retardant material, to protect the contents. It would be bullet proof as well, Kotler knew.

The hatch of the SUV was still open, and Kotler placed the case on the floorboard, opening it to see the contents.

Inside were three objects.

The first was a compass, made of brass and glass, and

roughly the size of the palm of his hand. It was old, judging by both the patina and the engravings around its edge.

The second object was a stone—somewhat opaque, and obviously, Iceland spar. Otherwise known as a Viking sunstone. They were used to navigate the seas even on cloudy days, according to legend. Recent facts had come to light which proved this to be accurate, and Kotler had studied one similar to this before, during his time at the Pueblo site. There had been a sun stone recovered among the Viking ruins, in connection to the Coelho medallion.

Kotler put the compass and sun stone back into the case, fitting them to their custom-molded places in the velvet-sheathed foam. He turned his attention to the third item.

It was a thin plate of brass, etched with symbols that Kotler thought might be Phoenician. In one end, there was a perfectly round hole, about the size of a dime, and encircled with text that was difficult to make out through what might be centuries of patina. Whatever this was, Kotler knew it was the riddle that Gail wanted him to solve. Something about this thin, brass plate held a mystery that Gail needed revealed. She was counting on Kotler's inborn curiosity to drive him, if nothing else. And she was right—he wanted to solve this, to determine what its secrets were. He also wanted to find Gail, to hold her accountable for all she'd done.

Kotler closed the case, and left it in the back of the SUV as he lowered the hatch. He wasn't sure what game Gail was playing, but if it meant he could get out of here safely, he was going to play along, for a while, at least.

He went to the driver's side of the SUV, and sure enough the keys were in the ignition. He took them, locked the SUV with the key fob, and then looked around, assessing.

He spotted what he was after in just a few seconds, and hurried that way.

Kotler was fluent in several languages, including many

that were long dead and out of use. But at that very moment, he was grateful that he understood one of the most universal symbolic languages on the planet: Even without translation, he could recognize the sign for "men's room."

CHAPTER 18

Denzel looked over Dr. Bristol's logs, related directly to Devil's Interval, searching for any sign that she may have ever had the journal in her possession. There had been nothing on the manifest of items removed from her office, which was to be expected: Even if she'd had it when she died, she might never have officially logged it.

If they were going to find the trail of this thing, they'd have to pick it up in the terabytes of notes and images and video that had been archived from Bristol's personal folder on the AMSL servers.

As Denzel sifted through all that data—admittedly not his strong suit but too important to leave to anyone else—Holden was busy trying to track down Bristol's sister in Chicago. So far, neither of them was having much luck.

"It's like she just vanished, after her sister's death," Holden groused. "The apartment she was renting has had a new occupant for months. No forwarding address. Her mobile phone gives me a deactivation message. Even her email bounces."

"Weird," Denzel said absently, running through some

video footage of Dr. Bristol—brunette, slender, a bit mousy at times—and was suddenly curious about a package that had been delivered to her through AMSL's internal mail system. She had signed for the package, which meant it would be listed in the building's logs. After that, she had looked around as if making sure no one was watching, and then went into her office and closed the door and the blinds.

Denzel scrubbed through the video, watching the office door, until it opened again awhile later, and Bristol walked out. She'd been inside for nearly an hour. From the vantage point of the camera, there was no sign of the package, and no way to know its contents.

He jotted some notes about the clip, including its time-code, and kept running footage.

"I'm going to see if I can get access to her credit card activity," Holden said. "Something's not right."

Denzel looked up then. "Credit card?"

"For the sister. Kate Bristol," Holden said, giving him a look like he'd known Denzel hadn't been listening. "She's missing."

"Any reports?" Denzel asked.

"Nothing. No one here ever asked who her employer was, since there was no reason to. So, I don't even have a place to start. But my gut is telling me there's something weird here."

"Do you think she may have been abducted? Over the journal?"

"Or worse," Holden said.

Denzel considered this, and looked back at the footage. Bristol's door still stood open, and he could see a bit of the interior. It was somewhat sparse, compared to other offices within view. There were a few items, mostly small objects on the desk itself. No sign of photos. And all the books and binders in the case behind the desk looked less than personal.

"Your gut's telling you something's weird," Denzel said. "I'm getting the same feeling."

He opened the manifest of personal belongings again, zipping through it with swipes over the surface of the smart tablet. It wasn't a very long list. A coffee mug and a travel mug, which seemed normal enough. A makeup bag containing lipstick, face powder, mascara, and chap stick. A grooming kit with nail files, trimming scissors, nail clippers, and a needle with a bit of thread. The list went on like this— mostly line items of minutia. The sort of bric-a-brac you'd expect from anyone's desk. No more, no less.

No photos. No handwritten notes-to-self. No books.

Where was the package?

The date on the video was only three weeks before Bristol's death. That was a blessing, Denzel knew, because it limited the amount of time he'd need to scrub through video. He ran the whole thing at double speed, stopping any time someone entered Bristol's office. He paid attention to every coming and going, looking at their hands, watching to see if they carried anything.

Eventually Nick Peters appeared on screen, shutting and locking the door to Bristol's office. This would be the day they learned of her death. Peters was locking everything down, including access to her files.

Denzel kept the video running at high speed until someone came to unlock the door. He ran this in real time, and watched everything very closely. Two of Peters' security team entered the room with a couple of file boxes. They loaded these methodically, going through every drawer, and turning to scan the shelves. Everything was removed from the desk, but nothing was taken from the book cases.

They left the room, locking it behind them, and Denzel followed them by switching camera views, trailing them digitally until they came to the secure storage area. They placed the boxes on shelves in that area and left.

Denzel ran the footage at high speed again, and watched as months sped by. No one touched the boxes until the day they were brought out for Denzel's inspection.

He had those very boxes sitting on the table next time now. Every item was accounted for in the manifest. No one had taken anything.

"So, where the hell is that package?" Denzel asked.

"What package?" Holden asked.

Denzel typed the timecode into the system and brought up the footage of Bristol getting the package, entering her office, and closing her door for most of the next hour. "From there, the thing just vanishes."

"Lot of that going around with this lady," Holden said.

Denzel blinked. "You're right. And that can't be a coincidence. You're running Kate Bristol's credit cards?"

"Yeah, I've already put in the request."

"Get her rental history, too. All known addresses. Everything you can dig up on her."

"That's going to take a court order," Holden said. "I'm pushing it with phone records and credit cards."

"Name her as a suspect," Denzel said.

"In what?"

"Ashton Mink's murder."

Holden barked a laugh. "You think the sister did it?"

"I won't rule it out. Not yet. It's like you said. Something isn't right. Bristol dies in an accident and then her sister goes missing? All around the time Bristol gets her hands on this package? And the package itself—what happened to it?"

"Could it still be in that office?" Holden asked.

Denzel stood and started for the door. Holden followed.

They were using a room in the security suites, and Denzel

stopped and rapped on Peters' door before opening it and barging in.

"Agent Denzel, you have free reign to look into anything you want in the building, but could you please respect me enough to let me answer before you barge in?"

"I need access to Bristol's old office," Denzel said.

"It's occupied now," Peters replied, looking at him strangely. "What are you looking for?"

"Is it the same desk? Same book cases?"

"The same," Peters answered.

"I want to inspect those."

Peters nodded, picked up the phone from his desk, and punched in an extension. He talked to the person on the other end, informed them that Denzel would be coming by, and to give the Agent complete access.

Denzel left then, with Holden close behind. Peters joined them before they reached the elevator.

The three of them rode to the research level where Bristol and Patel had worked, and Peters led Denzel and Holden to Bristol's old office. The current occupant stood aside and motioned for them to do whatever they needed to do.

Denzel started feeling along the edges of the book cases, tugging from time to time, removing books and binders to look behind them. He tapped the walls, looking for hidden compartments, but found nothing. He then started on the desk, opening drawers and feeling around within them, removing the effects of the current researcher to gain better access.

He felt the underside of the desk, and then the space beneath the file drawers. His hand brushed something sticky.

He dropped to his knees and peered under the desk, taking out his phone and using it as a flashlight.

There he saw remnants of tape, with a couple of pieces

hanging loose, as if whatever had been taken from there had been taken in a hurry.

"It was here," Denzel said. "The package. I'm betting it was the journal."

"It was taped under the desk," Holden said, nodding. "Ok. What good does that do for us? We still don't know who took it, or when."

"I've scrubbed all the footage. The only way anyone took it is if they closed the door and the blinds, which would block me from seeing. I've noted all those spots in the video files. I can get us down to a list of suspects. But I think I know who took it."

"Who?"

"Lawny Bristol," Denzel replied.

Holden shook his head. "Can you get around to some of this making sense?"

Denzel stood, brushing himself off. "I think she had the journal shipped here from London, keeping it secret from Patel and everyone else. She needed it here, for some reason. But when she got what she needed from it, she hid it until the time was right, and then took it with her."

"One problem," Peters said. "Everything gets searched, going in and out of this place."

"And who does the searches?" Denzel asked.

"Whoever pulls gate duty," Peters said. "Usually the ..."

He stopped, his eyes wide, looking at Denzel.

"Usually who?" Holden asked.

"The new guy," Peters said.

Denzel nodded. "Jared Partano."

"That little creep," Holden grumbled. He picked his phone out of his coat pocket and dialed his precinct, putting out a request to bring Partano in for questioning. "Good thing I had a unit on him," Holden said. "Otherwise, I'm pretty sure this kid would be in the wind. Although he's dropped in to see his brother a couple of times."

"That's what family does," Peters said, shrugging. "When your brother's hurt, you risk everything to see him. Nothing unusual about that."

Denzel frowned. "No," he said. "But there's something unusual about someone coming to collect her sister's things, and then disappearing. Unless she was abducted, where the heck did she go?"

"Working on that," Holden said.

Denzel was about to reply, to say he was mostly thinking out loud, when his phone rang. It was his home office. "Agent Denzel," he answered.

"Roland," a voice said. "It's me. Kotler."

"Kotler?" Denzel replied. "You're at my office?"

"It seemed to be the safest place," Kotler said. "I have some information, and it couldn't wait. I drove straight here."

"Drove? How'd you get away? Are you hurt?"

"No, I'm fine. I was … well, let's just say I was rescued by Gail McCarthy."

"Gail McCarthy?" Denzel started.

"It's a long story, and one I don't think I fully understand yet, but just wait, Roland. I think I've figured something out. My captor—the person running all this from behind the scenes—well, I think it was Dr. Lawny Bristol."

CHAPTER 19

KOTLER, DENZEL, AND HOLDEN WERE IN DENZEL'S office at the FBI. An agent had generously brought Kotler a change of clothes from his apartment, and he had cleaned up using the showers in the workout facility in the building. Kotler wasn't given to paranoia, or playing to fear, but Gail McCarthy had just shown she could get to him practically any time. She was sending him a message, about his vulnerability. It made him stop and think, at least.

They had debriefed each other, filing in missing gaps in information from both sides. Denzel and Holden told Kotler everything they'd learned during his 'absence.' Kotler, in turn brought them up to speed on everything connected to his abduction, including the appearance of Gail McCarthy.

"So, what's her game?" Denzel asked. "What were you able to learn from her?"

"Not much," Kotler said, sipping a cup of coffee he held in both hands. "I think it was some kind of show of power. She wanted me to know she could get to me."

"This is the same Gail McCarthy that is my primary suspect in Morgan Keller's murder?" asked Holden. He had his notebook open, and was jotting down details as Kotler could give them.

Kotler nodded. The Keller murder was an open investigation, and it was at the scene of that murder that Kotler and Denzel had first met Holden. At the time, none of them suspected Gail McCarthy as having anything to do with it, but as the affair with Atlantis progressed—something Holden wasn't aware of, just yet—it became clear that Gail was orchestrating things behind the scenes. She was responsible for at least two murders that Kotler knew about, as well as countless crimes of smuggling, gun running, and anything else she inherited from her mentor, Richard Van Burren. Who, as it turned out, was one of her victims.

None of this could be proven, exactly. Gail was far too careful. But she remained the lead suspect. Holden wanted her. Kotler knew the feeling.

"What about the attaché case?" Denzel asked. "I have a team going over every inch of it, looking for prints or any other trace forensic material."

"Tell them to be careful with the artifacts," Kotler said.

"What are they?" Denzel asked.

Kotler shook his head. "I'm not sure yet. I mean, I know what they are literally—all but that brass plate. But I don't know what they mean. Gail gave them to me hoping I would figure them out. She's promised that if I do, we'll find her."

"Seems like justification enough to dig in on them," Denzel said.

"Is any of this connected to the Mink murder?" Holden asked. "Is Gail McCarthy a suspect?"

"The security guard killed Mink," Kotler said.

"Jack Harris," Denzel said, nodding. "But what's his connection to Gail McCarthy?"

Kotler shook his head. "None, that I know of. At least,

none beyond the fact that she had Harris grab me in front of my own home, just so she could send me a message."

Denzel was studying Kotler, and Kotler picked up on his partner's micro expressions. "Don't worry," Kotler said, "I'm not losing it. I'm just playing a little closer to the shore now. If Gail wanted me killed, I'd be dead. She's up to something else, but I don't think it has anything at all to do with Ashton Mink's murder, or the Devil's Interval."

"You said you think Dr. Lawny Bristol is alive," Denzel said. "That she's the one behind this?"

Kotler nodded. "I have no proof, but based on the conversations I had with the disembodied voice, I strongly suspect it's her."

"What brings you to that conclusion?" Holden asked.

"I picked up on certain phrases that made me suspect it was a woman, masking her voice. She used the term 'privilege' to describe me, and in context she wasn't referring to my wealth. She asked if I had ever felt powerless, and then pointed out that I was exercising power just by trying to control the situation. Based on these statements, I determined that it might be a woman speaking, and that she was very intelligent. I didn't decide that it was Dr. Bristol until she showed some familiarity with Dr. Patel. She referred to him as 'Simon' at one point."

Holden scoffed. "None of that proves anything. You could have some bias in that."

Kotler nodded. "That's true. But I'm convinced."

"I am too," Denzel said.

"Why's that?" Holden asked.

"The package in her office," Denzel replied. "Her sister's disappearance. In fact, a whole lot of questionable things that have been creeping into this investigation, ever since we learned about her death. I think she faked her death as part of a long game. And I suspect you are going to find that Kate Bristol isn't even real."

"Not real?" Holden asked. He blinked, then scowled. "Shit, that makes sense."

"What makes sense?" Kotler asked.

"Everything I find about Kate Bristol goes back only about a year. The apartment lease, the credit cards, the phone, all of it. Before that, she's a ghost. I haven't done any deep background on her, but I bet I find nothing."

"Because she's just a cover for Lawny Bristol," Kotler said.

Denzel let out a long breath. "Maybe. I'm inclined to agree with you, but without proof, we can't really say for sure." He shook his head. "This case gets more complicated every minute. Ok, let me see if we can pull together the narrative here."

He stood up and went to a double-door cabinet on the wall, opening it to reveal a white board. He took a dry erase marker from the tray at the base of the board, and started jotting things down as he went.

"At the moment, we're working from the theory that Lawny Bristol is alive. She was brought into the Newton chamber by Simon Patel, who introduced her to the research he was using for the Devil's Interval project. She and Patel discovered a journal, leftover from the previous occupant, and Bristol stole it or snuck it away, then had it shipped back to her from London. Meanwhile, back in the US, she assists Patel in the research and development of the Devil's Interval technology."

Kotler interrupted. "I think we can assume she influenced the development of the technology," he said.

"What do you mean, 'influenced?'" Holden asked.

"I think that Patel's line of development was likely on track to do exactly what AMSL wanted it to do. It would aid the hearing impaired, allowing them to hear without surgically implanting cochlear devices. But Bristol ..." he glanced at Denzel, "or possibly someone else, found something in those journals, and saw an opportunity."

"That makes sense," Denzel said, jotting *DI Opportunity – Bristol?* on the board, and continued. "For the moment, let's assume it was Bristol. She uses AMSL to fund and develop the technology. Maybe she's lined up a buyer for it. There would be no shortage of interested parties. So, she keeps everything moving at AMSL, where there are resources she wouldn't have access to otherwise."

"And when the technology is close to completion, she makes arrangements to fake her own death?" Holden asked. "Why?"

"Cover?" Kotler offered. "If she's dead, no one will suspect her, if this technology emerges on the black market."

"Now we're up to Jack Harris and the Partano brothers," Denzel said. "How did they become involved?"

"That part's murky," Kotler said. "I don't think it's a coincidence that all three of them work in security. Harris is a natural, considering his past issues at the company, and his demotion. He has a technical background, so it's conceivable he came up with a way to access the system from the outside. He set things up so that Ashton Mink would do some of the dirty work, smuggling the memory card out of the building."

"The Partano brothers are more of a mystery," Holden said. "I dug into these guys. They're American heroes. Both have seen combat, and have exemplary records. Nothing about these guys suggests they'd be in on something like this."

Kotler sat up. "Were they special forces?" he asked.

"Both of them," Holden nodded.

Kotler looked at Denzel, who cursed. "Gail McCarthy," the agent said, nearly spitting the words.

"What am I missing?" Holden asked.

Kotler replied, "Gail inherited a network of smugglers comprised primarily of ex-Special Forces. Richard Van Burren and Edward McCarthy had been recruiting these guys for decades, and their network is probably still in place. These guys have turned mercenary. The money they get from smuggling far outpaces anything they'd get elsewhere, and it lets them use their special skills." Kotler shook his head. "The guys that Bristol has working for her—I should have put it together sooner. Other than Harris, these guys were power-houses. This explains how Gail became involved in all of this."

"Ok," Denzel said, returning to the white board. "So, Bristol starts reaching out, looking for a way to move the Devil's Interval tech, and somehow stumbles on to Gail McCarthy's network. Bristol hires some of McCarthy's mercenaries, and probably engages McCarthy to help find a buyer."

"Gail finds out that you and I are involved," Kotler said, "And decides to leverage the situation to get to me."

Denzel nodded. "But what about those pages? The ones she traded for you? Where'd she get those?"

Kotler thought about this, and shook his head. "There's no way to know that."

Denzel huffed. "Well, with her connections, she may have known all about the Newton chamber. Somebody had been using it for years, right up until the 80s. Maybe Van Burren discovered it, and was keeping it as part of his network. She would have learned about it then."

"Doesn't add up," Kotler said. "If she knew about the chamber, why did she only have pages from the journal? Why wouldn't she have had the whole thing? There are some valuable artifacts and scientific instruments in that chamber, but nothing on the level of the antiquities Gail typically deals with. I think those journal pages must have been part of a different lot. Whoever had been using that chamber must have torn them out, probably after realizing what kind of horror that information represented. But whoever it was must have had a respect for history and science, and couldn't bear to destroy them altogether."

"This is all conjecture," Holden said. "We can't prove any of it, and I don't know that any of it is really relevant to this case."

"Maybe not. But it's a useful narrative," Kotler explained. "It's a framework that helps us make sense of some of the confusing parts of this case, so we can move past them to the more relevant data."

Holden thought about this, and nodded. "Ok. Not exactly how I do things, but I can see the point of it. So now what?"

Denzel turned back to the board. "I think Ashton Mink's murder wasn't part of the plan," he said. "That's what set off the events that have led to us discovering all of this. I think Harris went a little rogue, and screwed everything up."

"That does seem to fit his M-O," Holden said. "Peters told us the guy is a hot head."

"So, Mink's murder was revenge," Kotler said. "Maybe Harris resented Mink's fame or wealth. Maybe he blamed Mink for his demotion. It really doesn't matter, in the end." He looked at the whiteboard, following the timeline from left to right. "The rest is actually unrelated. Not directly related, anyway. Bristol has the information she needs to rebuild the Devil's Interval technology. That's where we are now."

"If it really is Bristol," Denzel said. "And we're here with no leads, either way. We have no way to know where she is."

"Actually," Holden said, flipping through his notebook, "maybe we do have a way. Her 'sister' may have canceled her mobile phone, but I have records of all the calls she made from the time it was activated to the time it was shut down. And none of them were made from Chicago."

"You think she screwed up?" Denzel asked. "Left a trail to where she's hiding in New York?"

"We shouldn't waste any time," Kotler said. "I have a feeling she's prepared to run, now that she has everything she needs. She may be using Gail's network to skip out of the US."

"Then let me make some calls. We have photos of her, from her employee records. I'll put out a BOLO for every airport in the state."

"Gail would have her flying out of a private airport," Kotler said.

"Not so many of those around," Holden said. "I think I have enough people to cover all of them."

Denzel nodded. "Ok," he said. "Let's go bring in a dead woman."

CHAPTER 20

THE HUNT WAS ON, BUT KOTLER KNEW THEY WERE merely treading water. They had only sketchy evidence at best, leading them to the possibility that Lawny Bristol was not only alive, but somehow the mastermind behind a coup against AMSL, and a plan to create and sell technology that could negatively change the world overnight.

Kotler was as certain about his conclusions as he had been about anything in his life, but it would be a relief to find some actual proof.

He was riding in the passenger seat of Roland's car, watching the streets for familiar signs. "We're in the right neighborhood," he said.

"They didn't bag you when they took you out?" Roland asked.

"They didn't have to," Kotler said. "I was so focused on Gail, I didn't even notice where we were. It wasn't until we were already out of the city that I started to pay attention."

Kotler rubbed his eyes, pinching the bridge of his nose.

"You haven't dropped the ball, Kotler," Denzel said.

Kotler shook his head. "I'm not sure I agree with you. I

can't help feeling that I'm somehow responsible for Gail getting away. Again. She keeps doing that."

"She's smart," Denzel said. "Maybe as smart as you. Don't worry about it. Right now, we have to concentrate on getting some real leads in this case. Holden is taking heat from his higher ups, and my status reports are sounding a little flimsy, too."

Kotler smiled. "Well, at least I don't have to file reports," he said.

Denzel glanced at him. "You haven't been filing reports?"

Kotler blinked, then raised a hand, pointing to a building. "I think that's it!"

"Kotler, you …"

"We'd better get in there," Kotler said.

Denzel sighed and pulled the car to the curb. Kotler wasted no time getting out.

Denzel was close behind. "Ok, stay here. I'll go check the scene."

"Without backup?" Kotler asked. "I'm going with you."

"You're unarmed," Denzel pointed out.

"Yeah, about that. When is the FBI going to clear me to carry? I'm more than qualified—"

"I think you're right, this *is* the place," Denzel said, pushing past Kotler and carefully opening the street-level door, entering after doing a quick check.

Kotler sighed, and followed.

Inside, the building turned out to be a warehouse, once used for steel and other building materials. It was completely abandoned.

It took only a few minutes to find the room where Kotler had spent the night. Kotler saw it in the light for the first time—a small storage space that still had his blankets on the floor. The door was steel, and had a substantial lock. There was overhead lighting, but the lights were controlled by a timer dial outside the door. He'd had no shot at escaping that room.

They moved on, and moments later came to the interrogation space, which turned out to be a vacant shop floor. The lights and audio equipment were gone, but the chair Kotler had been tied to was still in place, the leavings of a few sets of cut zip ties scattered around it.

"This is the place, alright," Kotler mumbled.

"It's clean," Denzel said. "I'll have forensics run through here, but I doubt they'll find much. I doubt that Bristol was ever even here, judging from what you told me."

"I don't think she was," Kotler said. "I was just hoping. It was the only lead we had."

"Holden is still watching the airports," Denzel said. "We could get lucky."

Kotler looked at him for a moment, then shook his head. "This is bad. Gail gave Bristol—or whoever this is—the last pages from that journal. I have no idea what was on them, but it seems an awful lot like Bristol has everything she needs to complete Devil's Interval."

"What do you think she'll do with it from there?"

Kotler thought about this. "The first step will be to test it. And if she's planning to sell it, she'll test it somewhere very public. She'll need potential buyers to know that it's real, that it works."

Denzel considered this, then looked at Kotler. "She isn't leaving."

Kotler shook his head. "No, I don't think so. She doesn't have to, does she? She's dead, on paper at least. She's connected to Gail and her smuggling network, so she likely has access to some pretty impressive fake credentials. She may have a whole new identity we know nothing about. She could be living a block from here, and we'd never find her. Plus, she doesn't have to leave the country to sell the technology. Gail's network will take care of that. It's like eBay for super villains."

"So, we really do have nothing," Denzel said. "We're stuck waiting for Bristol to make her next move."

"Should we call Holden? Tell him to pull his people from the airports?"

"I'll let him know what we're thinking," Denzel said. "But we might want to keep the airports under watch for a while anyway. In the meantime, let's secure the rest of this building and get a forensics team in here."

Denzel busied himself with making calls back to his home office, and Kotler looked around the rest of the warehouse. He wasn't sure he'd find anything—in fact, he was sure he'd find nothing. But he felt somewhat helpless. He needed to do something, but every option for him felt like a dead end.

The warehouse wasn't all that large, and most its space had once been dedicated to inventory. The workshop would have been used primarily for repairing equipment. The offices, which were on the second level, and had windows overlooking the warehouse floors, were all empty but for a few abandoned desks and bits of paper, left behind by the former occupants. There was no sign of activity in any of them.

Kotler had turned and was going to descend the stairs, to find his way back to Denzel, when he spotted a small, brass plaque on the wall. Using his phone's flashlight, he read the inscription.

Donovan Metalworks
Est. 1972

KOTLER HAD NEVER HEARD of the company, but he felt a stab of grief anyway. It was sad to see a business close after so long. But progress was progress. It was hard to venture into a whole new world without leaving the old one behind. And, Kotler knew from studying ancient cultures, there was always some trace of the past. Artifacts—hieroglyphics and pyramids and stelae, in the case of ancient civilizations, or brass plagues in the case of old industrial warehouses—were always lingering, telling some faint version of the story of a place, a culture, a civilization. Even individuals would leave …

Kotler was half down the stairs when he stopped, then sped up, hurrying to find Denzel.

As Kotler rounded from the stairwell, he nearly ran into his partner. "There you are," Denzel said. "The van just arrived. Let's get out of here and let them do their thing."

"Traces!" Kotler blurted out.

"What traces?" Denzel asked.

"Bristol may have faked her own death, but she's left traces. Footprints. Her fake sister, the apartment in Chicago, the phone—Holden was on to something, when he brought up her phone records. That's partly how we found this place. But we're overlooking something."

"And what is that?" Denzel asked.

"We focused on where she was calling from. But who was she calling?"

Denzel's eyes widened, and he immediately took out his phone, calling Holden. They chatted for a moment, and Kotler felt his own phone buzz.

Holden had forwarded the phone records to both him and Denzel.

"Ok, Kotler," Denzel said. "Time to do some archeology."

CHAPTER 21

THEY WERE RACING THROUGH THE CITY STREETS, following the best lead they'd had in weeks. Kotler had a laptop resting on his knees, and was scanning through "Kate Bristol's" phone records while comparing them to research he was pulling up from Google.

"You're sure about this first address?" Denzel asked.

"Kate Bristol made hundreds of calls, but the most frequent was to this place."

"Kotler … it's a porn store."

"Adult entertainment complex, according to the website. And I didn't pick it for its virtue, Roland. I'm just telling you what the records are telling me."

They arrived at Big Johnson's Adult Entertainment Complex a few minutes later, and Denzel made sure to park the car in as discreet a spot as he could find. Kotler smirked at his partner's red face. "You really are a prude."

"No, I'm judicious," Denzel said. "And shut up."

They opted to enter through the front door, Denzel's coat buttoned to hide his holstered weapon. He had also pulled on a pair of dark sunglasses.

"You look like a Secret Service agent," Kotler said.

"Bite your tongue."

They had to be buzzed in through the front door, which was glass but had metal bars running from top to bottom. Inside, there was a veritable cacophony of sex sounds—porn running from dozens of different televisions all over the space. There were racks of DVDs in one area of the store's ample floor space, and the rest of the merchandise was comprised of all manner of paraphernalia. Kotler noted a great deal of dominance gear, as well as the usual stock of sex toys. Some items baffled him as to their purpose, however. He would have liked to ask questions, out of a cultural anthropology curiosity, but he didn't think Denzel would appreciate the data.

They approached the front counter, where a very bored looking clerk was all but napping, leaning back in a bar-height chair as he played a game on his phone. He made no move to talk to either of them, probably out of routine. People who came here probably didn't chat him up much.

"Is the manager here?" Denzel asked, producing his badge.

"I'm the manager," the man said. "I'm Guy."

"Guy, we'd like to ask you a few questions. Is there some place we can talk?"

"Can't leave the store unattended. People walk off with stuff."

Kotler looked around, and saw that there were a few customers lingering in some of the aisles, well away from the front counter. He also saw that there were multiple doors along the back wall, all with keypads next to them. Viewing rooms, paid for by swiping a credit card. No need for human interaction at all, beyond one human sitting to watch another perform lewd acts on the other side of a one-way mirror.

"This will do," Kotler said, exchanging glances with Denzel. "Believe me, this is probably the most private spot in the building."

Denzel glanced around, and nodded.

"Guy ... what's your last name?"

"Rivera," Guy said.

Denzel jotted this in his notebook. "Mr. Rivera, we're investigating someone who placed several calls to this ... establishment. Do you recognize the name Kate Bristol? Or Lawny Bristol?"

Guy thought about it, and shook his head. "Doesn't sound familiar."

Denzel nodded. "Ok. How about this number?" He flipped through the notepad, and showed the number for Kate Bristol's phone.

Guy looked at it, and thought. "I think that's Ingrid's number."

"Ingrid?" Denzel asked.

"I don't know her last name. She's tech support."

Denzel and Kotler exchanged glances.

"What do you mean? She fixes your computers?"

"Yeah," Guy said. "She also does the cameras. The video equipment. We do live shows, from the back. Ingrid set everything up, got us on the internet. We're making more money from that than we are from this shit dump."

"Ingrid comes here?" Kotler asked. "In person?"

Guy nodded.

Denzel took out his phone and made several swipes before holding up a photo of Lawny Bristol. "Is this Ingrid?" he asked.

Guy leaned forward and squinted. "Maybe. Looks kind of like her, I guess. Never seen her look like that, though. She's kind of goth, both the black leathers and the dog collar and stuff. Black lipstick. But that could be her."

"Could we see where Ingrid does her work?" Kotler asked.

"I can't leave the front," Guy said.

Denzel held up his badge again. "It's ok, Mr. Rivera. You just got all the permission you need."

"THIS IS INGRID'S WORKSHOP," Guy said, turning the key in the deadbolt and swinging the door open.

Denzel and Kotler both leaned into the frame of the door, cautiously, not sure what to expect.

The room was spacious, but filled with electronics equipment. There were dozens of server racks lining one entire wall of the space, along with terminals and access points. Kotler entered just as Guy flicked on the light switch, bringing a lot more detail into view.

Kotler stopped in front of a workbench that had everything one would need to build, modify, and repair circuitry, including soldering irons and an advanced oscilloscope. Scattered on it were bits of tech that were in various states of assembly. Kotler stooped to peer at a small casing, lying empty and open on the table's surface.

"What is it?" Denzel asked.

"Not sure," Kotler replied. The casing was just a bit bigger than the size of a key fob, like the one Kotler carried to access his building. It was made from plastic, and looking closer at it Kotler saw tiny ridges, like strata. He looked around, and spotted a 3D printer tucked into one corner of the room.

"I think this is the housing for …" he stopped, looking at Guy, who was standing in the doorway, staring with unabashed curiosity himself. "The tech," Kotler finished.

"*The* tech?" Denzel asked.

Kotler nodded.

Denzel turned to Guy. "I'm going to need you to return to the front," Denzel said. "And expect that a team of agents will be here soon."

"Hey, no problem," Guy said. "Is Ingrid in trouble? Is she making bombs? She's, like, a terrorist or something?"

"No bombs," Denzel said. "What was it she claimed to be doing back here?"

Guy shrugged. "Any time I asked, she said 'server maintenance.' The stuff she built for us was making us a ton of cash, though, so the owner let her do whatever she wanted, no questions asked."

"How often is she here?" Kotler asked.

"She comes in practically every week," Guy said.

"When was the last time you saw her?" Denzel asked.

"Yesterday. But I think she may have slept here. She came in the day before, locked the door, and I never saw her come out, even when I was closing up. She has her own key, so I didn't bug her."

"And she hasn't been back since yesterday?" Kotler asked.

"Not that I've noticed," Guy said.

Denzel took out his phone, and even as he dialed he said, "Go on back out front. When my team gets here, let them in. Also, you're closed for the day. You'll need to clear everyone out of here. Including the ... uh ... workers. The FBI apologizes for the inconvenience."

Guy gave Denzel an odd look, but said nothing as he went back to the front.

"I want first crack at this place," Kotler said.

"You'll contaminate the scene," Denzel said.

"I stand a better chance of knowing what we're looking for when I see it," Kotler said. "Roland, she's out there, and she's planning something. We're running out of time."

Denzel considered, then nodded. "Gloves," he said.

"I don't have any."

"I have some latex gloves in the car."

They left the workshop and went through the storefront. Guy had managed to wrangle all the customers and get them out the door, to grumbling protests. The girls working in the back were changing into street clothes, Guy assured them. They'd be gone in a few minutes.

Denzel and Kotler made their way to Denzel's car. The trunk popped open, and Denzel reached inside to take two sets of packaged, sterilized gloves out of the side pocket of a duffel bag. Kotler noted that there were still weapons, vests, and other paraphernalia in the trunk. A handy resource, as Kotler had discovered months ago at the Edison estate and museum. This cache had saved his and Denzel's lives.

"You keep forensic gear in here?" Kotler asked.

"Just some basics," Denzel said. "I added gloves and a few other things when you started tagging along."

Kotler chuckled and put the packaged gloves in his coat pocket. He'd pull them on inside the workshop.

He turned, surveying the street as Denzel put everything back in place before closing the trunk.

Across the street from them, only a few feet away, Kotler spotted Detective Holden.

It took him by surprise. They had updated Holden on where they were going, but they hadn't yet called to tell him what they'd found. As far as Kotler knew, Holden should have been investigating one of the other locations found in Kate Bristol's phone records.

"Detective?" Kotler called.

Denzel looked up, his hands on the lid of the trunk, just about to close it.

Holden raised his right hand, and Kotler spotted the pistol.

"Down!" Kotler shouted, turning to push Denzel back and away from the car.

Three rounds were fired, the sound of them echoing among the buildings on the street. Kotler and Denzel hit the sidewalk, falling with the car between them and Holden.

"What the hell is he doing?" Denzel shouted.

Kotler wasn't sure. But he suspected.

"We need to take him down without hurting him!" Kotler said.

Two more shots rang out and whined as they ricocheted from the sidewalk near their feet. They crawled quickly toward the front of the car.

Denzel took out his weapon.

"Listen!" Kotler said. "I think Holden is being controlled! Devil's Interval!"

"What?" Denzel said. "How?"

"I'm not sure, but we can't use lethal force. We have to find another way!"

Denzel cursed, and crouched at the front of the car. Peering over as Kotler joined him.

Holden had moved out into the street, angling to see around the corner of the car's back bumper. The trunk lid was wide open again, and it was blocking Holden's view somewhat.

"Why isn't he coming around?" Denzel asked.

Kotler shook his head, watching. Holden's body language was all off. He was clearly intent on finding and shooting the two of them, but he wasn't taking the sort of initiative he would have been trained to take. In fact, he was wide out in the open, with no cover, and behaving strangely. Kotler didn't know what the effects of Devil's Interval might be, but it was clear that the subject's free will was compromised to the point of making them less effective. Maybe Bristol hadn't perfected the technology yet.

Or maybe Holden was resisting.

"I think we may be able to rush him," Kotler said. "If we can come at him from an angle he isn't watching."

"How do we do that?" Denzel asked. "The second we leave cover he'll spot us."

"I think his reactions are slowed," Kotler said.

"You think?" Denzel replied.

"I'm open to other ideas," Kotler said.

Denzel cursed again, shook his head, and then took a few quick breaths. He then sprinted forward, running at full tilt across the street.

It did take a beat for Holden to react, but then he turned and started firing.

Denzel managed to make it to cover behind another vehicle, on the opposite side of the street. He looked back at Kotler with an expression that clearly articulated his opinion about Kotler being wrong.

Kotler, however, saw an opportunity.

Holden was now entirely focused on Denzel. The technology affecting him was overcoming the Detective's training and common sense, to a degree. He was leaving himself open from behind.

Kotler crawled back around the car and raised up to peer into the trunk. The bean-bag shotgun was there. An old friend, at this point. Kotler carefully reached in, took it, and loaded it. He heard two more shots from the street. There was no more time.

In a quick motion, Kotler stood, took aim, and fired a bean bag into Holden's shoulder.

Holden stumbled, and his weapon dropped to the ground. He turned, staring at Kotler, and stooped to pick up the gun.

Kotler fired again, this time hitting Holden square in the chest, knocking him back.

Denzel was on him then, pinning him to the ground and cuffing his hands. He had him up and leaning against the car where Denzel had taken cover.

Kotler, shotgun propped on his shoulder as if he were an old west lawman, smiled and ambled forward.

"Good work, Tex," Denzel said.

"All in a day's work," Kotler replied, tipping an imaginary cowboy hat.

CHAPTER 22

"OW! *SONOFABITCH!*" HOLDEN BELLOWED AS DENZEL helped him out of his shirt to observe the bruises. "Kotler, I'm going to get have you arrested and cavity searched for this!"

Kotler smiled. "You're welcome, Detective."

They were in the store again, and Guy had brought them a chair for Holden. Kotler, his hands now sheathed in latex gloves, was holding an evidence bag containing a smashed device, built into a casing identical to the one found in the workshop. It had been tucked into Holden's shirt pocket, and had taken the second hit from the beanbag gun.

Kotler examined the device, and then slipped into the workshop to do a bit of digging. He could hear Holden and Denzel talking about the incident, most of their conversation punctuated by Holden's cursing.

Kotler placed the evidence bag on the workbench, and started sifting through drawers and cabinets in the room. He found plenty of research material from AMSL, further proof that this might be Lawny Bristol. He also found a remote video feed connected to a voice masking microphone. This must have been where his mysterious disembodied voice had hidden out during their chats, when he'd been abducted.

Kotler kept searching, finding more and more evidence that this was where their suspect had pulled things together. There were notepads here and there, with scribble suggesting formulas and equations, alongside notes from phone calls. He found a phone number, which he noted for Denzel.

He was rifling through binders in one of the bookcases when he found the real prize.

He pulled an orange binder from the stack, and as he did so a heavy object fell and thudded to the floor. Kotler stooped to pick it up, and froze.

It was the leather-bound journal from London.

Kotler lifted it gingerly, and immediately spread it open on the workbench, turning a desk lamp to give him more light. He began flipping through pages, reading in quick sprints.

The journal was old. The first entry was dated June 16, 1923, and it was a set of notes about the Newton chamber, some mentions of research conducted by Newton himself, and something of a short mission statement, vowing to continue Newton's research and to discover "the curious effect of the Devil's Interval, and the latent influence of frequency and tone upon the emotions of man."

Kotler quickly flipped through, dipping into passages from time to time, before finally stopping at a section of loose, torn pages.

These must have been the pages Gail had traded for him, in her bid to show him she could get to him any time.

Kotler read these with a growing sense of dread.

He had seen some of Patel's research and development diaries for Devil's Interval. He knew some of the basics of it, though he was no expert in acoustics. He knew enough to realize that Bristol had all she needed to perfect Devil's Interval, and put it into play.

The key to Patel's technology had been the use of "gateway frequencies." These were frequencies that resonated with the cochlear and vestibular nerves, essentially transmitting vibration to them directly, while bypassing the cochlea. The effect was that sound could be transmitted directly to the brain, even if the mechanism for hearing the sound was damaged, underdeveloped, or missing entirely.

In that, Patel's work was a breakthrough of monumental proportions. It really was the cure for deafness, if used properly. The fact that Patel lifted his work from existing research, claiming it as his own, made the work itself no less extraordinary.

The side effect of mind control must have been an accident. Bristol may have thought she had everything she needed to replicate Patel's work, but she'd apparently lacked some crucial component. She couldn't replicate it. Not until she'd gotten hold of these missing pages.

Kotler read through them all, and was horrified to see that Patel's technology was not the first time this nightmare had raised its head in history. Whoever had kept these journals had discovered the same effect, and had cataloged exactly how to produce it.

Within these torn pages, Bristol had uncovered the missing component she needed to complete the technology, if not perfect it. And judging by Holden's attack on them, it was effective enough, as it was.

Kotler closed the journal, but didn't bother bagging it. He would need it. He would need to study it, along with any other notes on Devil's Interval, to find a countermeasure.

Again, this wasn't really his area of expertise.

But he knew there was someone who could help.

Kotler left the back room and found Denzel and Holden,

who was gingerly pulling his shirt back on. The forensics team arrived then, and Guy let them in without hesitation.

Kotler spotted Liz Ludlum, the Lead Forensic Specialist whom he'd met at Ashton Mink's apartment. She smiled as she passed, large forensics case in hand, and Kotler said, "It's good to see you again, Liz."

Her smile was positively beaming after that, and it didn't escape Kotler's notice, nor Denzel's as he gave Kotler a peculiar look that said, simultaneously, "this isn't the time" and "you incorrigible dog."

"I found the journal," Kotler said. "And it's as bad as we feared."

"Obviously," Denzel said, nodding to Holden.

"We need to figure out where Bristol is planning to publicly demonstrate Devil's Interval," Kotler said. "It's going to be big, and very noticeable."

"I have some leads on that," Holden said. "I had someone run down a list of big events in the city. Things that would be televised."

"Good," Kotler said. "We'll start checking into those. But first we need to get to your precinct."

"What?" Holden asked. "Why?"

"Simon Patel is arriving from London today, right?" Kotler asked.

"He should already be here," Holden said. He's being escorted to the precinct. You think he has something to add to this?"

"I do," Kotler asked. "I need him to see what I've seen, and I'm praying to God that he can think of a way to counter it."

PART 3

CHAPTER 23

PATEL LOOKED QUITE A BIT MORE HAGGARD THAN HE had back in London. His body language told Kotler that he had resolved himself to his fate. Whatever legal or career implications were coming, he had given himself over to facing them. His demeanor had 'shame' written all over it. Kotler had empathized with him as a researcher and scientist before, but now he could feel the pall of the man's life ending —at least, the life he'd always known.

"There's a chance to redeem yourself," Kotler said to him.

They were in one of the interrogation rooms. Kotler had requested that he have a chance to talk to Patel alone, and no one saw any harm in it. They were all watching, anyway.

Patel had been staring down at the table top, and looked up now, almost surprised. Even eager. "What do I have to do?" he asked.

Kotler slid the journal across to him. "Do you recognize this?" he asked.

Patel nodded. "Yes," he said. "It was in Newton's chamber, in London. I found it when I discovered the entrance, and I showed it to Lawny when I brought her in. It disappeared, though I had already gotten all I could from it. I was surprised, when that man, Jack Harris, showed it to me. He kept insisting I could use it, along with the data from AMSL, to recreate Devil's Interval. But there were pages missing. The information wasn't there. I didn't have enough to do anything."

"The pages have been restored," Kotler said. He reached across the table and opened the journal to the section where several loose pages had been replaced, their order restored even if their integrity was compromised.

That was what Kotler was offering Patel, in this moment. A chance to restore order, if not his integrity. He hoped the man would take it.

Patel reached forward. His hands were out of the cuffs, at Kotler's insistence. Patel represented no danger. In fact, he might not do much jail time. The British government was still weighing the charges, determining if any theft had occurred, and to what degree a punishment should be meted.

Denzel had already spoken to officials at Scotland Yard, and had arranged some leniency, if Patel cooperated in finding Bristol and the Devil's Interval technology. That was something Kotler was keeping in his back pocket, for now. He needed Patel to come to this on his own—to come to redemption under his own power, if at all.

If he was being honest, Kotler *wanted* Patel to come to it on his own. If Patel volunteered to help solve this, with no promise of reward, it would mean he wasn't too far gone. In Kotler's eyes, anyway. At that point, Kotler would push to have him redeemed legally as well.

For now, though, Kotler was holding out hope. He was trying to restore his own faith in the man.

Patel flipped through the journal, particularly examining the loose pages. He kept making fidgeting movements, as if attempting to reach for something that wasn't there.

"Do you need anything?" Kotler asked.

"Pen. Paper," Patel replied, distracted.

Kotler glanced to the mirror on one wall, and moments later Denzel entered with a legal pad and a pen. He also had the iPad that Peters had given them, containing all of Bristol's archived files. Kotler kept that close at hand, ready to hand it over if Patel showed a need.

Patel gratefully took the pad and pen, and began scribbling formulas and notes. "My God," he said once, and then made more notations.

Kotler watched, fascinated. He had a great appreciation for genius, and he knew he was watching it at work now. Patel may have stolen the ideas and the work of others, but it was clear he was just taking shortcuts. He was, by Kotler's estimate, every bit as brilliant as he had pretended to be. Which made his actions even more appalling and tragic.

Patel could well have built the Devil's Interval technology on his own, in time. His other patents might have evolved from his work as well. His self-worth was so intertwined with his success, however, and with the recognition of his genius from others, it limited his thinking.

By Kotler's estimate, Patel suffered from a fixed mindset. He had determined that his self-worth was based on his success, and on others perceiving his genius. If he came to an impasse, such as may have happened with his research into making cochlear implants obsolete, he would have faced that proverbial 'long, dark night of the soul.' He would have questioned his own intelligence, and with it his own self-worth. Faced with the prospect of losing himself through failure, he chose to lose himself through faulty integrity.

He gambled, in other words, that his brilliance was enough to justify stealing the work of others, since he would have eventually come to the same ideas anyway. The gamble had paid out for some time, but his luck had turned, as luck is prone to do. Kotler knew that luck made for a poor strategy, regardless of one's goals.

Patel worked through the remaining loose pages, and carried on into other parts of the journal. "This makes sense now," he said, looking up at Kotler. There was a slight sheen to his eyes, as if he had somehow rediscovered himself, finally, after losing himself in the dark.

"Can you counter the Devil's Interval technology?" Kotler asked.

"I believe I can," Patel nodded, smiling. "I also see, now, how this happened. The key is the set of window frequencies. We inadvertently used a frequency that not only directly stimulates the cochlear and vestibular nerves, it bypasses them to the temporal lobe."

"The part of the brain responsible for processing auditory stimuli," Kotler nodded.

"And memory, as well," Patel said. "I believe I know how this technology is effecting the free will of the subject. It stimulates the temporal lobe to essentially implant false memories, while simultaneously processing the sound of commands. The brain of the subject interprets the input, sifts it through existing memories to determine context and meaning, and discovers the simultaneously implanted memory. It misinterprets all of this as a command, bypassing the subject's will!"

Kotler shook his head. "This is fascinating, Doctor, and I would like nothing better than to sit with you and discuss this at length. But right now …" he paused. This next part was going to be a shock, and he didn't want to derail things further. But he felt that Patel needed to know this information. He needed to know what was at stake, and who might be behind all of it. He needed to know, in case knowing gave him an edge.

"Dr. Patel, there's something I need to tell you, and it's

going to be a shock." Patel was watching him, uncertain. But Kotler could tell by his body language that he'd been through enough shocks recently to give him a thicker skin. "There's a very good chance that Lawny Bristol is alive."

Patel blinked. "What do you mean? No ... She died months ago."

"We think she faked her death. Dr. Patel ... Simon ... we think she's the one behind all of this. She arranged for the murder of Ashton Mink. She recruited Jack Harris. She stole the data, and had you abducted and taken to London. And she's used the information from these journals to build her own version of Devil's Interval. And she's planning to use it, very publicly, and very soon."

Patel was staring at him, his mouth slightly open. He glanced back at the notebook, and then at his notes. He picked up the pen, tore a page from the back of the legal pad, and began scribbling. After a moment, he held out the paper for Kotler to take.

It contained a series of formulas, along with a crudely drown frequency curve. Below this he had written three frequencies.

"These will counter the Devil's Interval gateway frequencies," he said. "They will create a cancellation waveform. Similar to noise cancellation."

"How can we use them?" Kotler asked. "She's built devices. Small. Portable." Again, he motioned to the mirror, and Denzel again entered the room, this time with the evidence bag containing the smashed device that had been recovered from Holden.

Kotler took it and showed it to Patel. "She's built more of these. We saw first-hand what they can do, and this one was just casually planted on a police detective. How do we counter that?"

"The frequencies are very narrow," Patel said, "And they

rely on bone conduction, so the device would need proximity to the subject's cochlear and vestibular nerves. More than a foot or two away from the subject's cochlear nerve, and the effect would be too weak. The counter frequency can be a blanket broadcast, however. It doesn't require the same precision." He glanced back at his notes. "I could build something that can broadcast the frequencies as ultrasonic waves. It would need to be highly directional, for the effect to be strong enough, but if we can identify who is under her control, we can counter it from a distance."

"What kind of distance?" Denzel asked.

Patel shook his head. "Hard to say. Several feet. Maybe as much as thirty feet away."

"What do you need?" Kotler asked.

"My lab," Patel said. "Everything I need is already there."

Kotler looked up at Denzel. "We need to get him back into that lab," he said.

"We will," Denzel told him. "I'll take him there myself."

Holden opened the door to the interrogation room in a rush. "You'd better hurry," he said, huffing. "We just figured out what Bristol's plan is, and it's going down now!"

"What is it?" Kotler asked, his stomach clenching from dread.

"Ross Miller and Garrett Chandler are standing on the edge of the roof of the AMSL building, with a countdown timer being laser projected to the building across from them. It looks like they're going to jump!"

CHAPTER 24

PETERS MET THEM IN THE LOBBY, HAVING BEEN contacted by Denzel as they rushed to the scene. They had to navigate through police lines and throngs of people standing around, watching. The barricades started a block away, and members of the Press were already pushing against them, looking for a comment.

Holden had driven ahead of Denzel, his cherry light pulsing and his loud horn and siren doing a lot of the work of clearing people from their path. A squad car brought up the rear, having joined them *en route*.

As Denzel, Kotler, and Patel exited Denzel's car, it was like stepping into a lightning storm. Cameras flashed from thousands of photographers behind barricades at either end of the block. The front sidewalk of the building had been cleared of everyone but emergency crews.

"What's the sitrep?" Denzel asked the Fire Chief, who was directing his men.

"No way we could break their fall enough to save them, from that height," the Chief said, "but we're rolling out the mats anyway."

Kotler saw that two large, inflatable mats had been brought from one of the trucks, and rolled open as air hoses were attached. They would be inflated in a moment, but it was clear they weren't adequate to the task. At best, they'd prevent things from getting messy. From their current height, both men would reach terminal velocity quickly, and the momentum would make hitting those mats as good as hitting concrete.

This was more about showing the public that they were doing everything they could—more PR move than rescue effort, but necessary all the same.

Kotler looked up, and could barely make out the two men, standing precariously on the edge of the building. He glanced across the street, and saw the enormous laser projection of a countdown timer. They had less than half an hour before it hit zero.

"Will you have time?" Kotler asked.

Patel was also staring upward, and he was pale. "I don't know," he whispered.

"Get him upstairs, now!" Denzel shouted to Peters, who rushed forward with two of his men, escorting Patel directly inside.

"I'm going with him," Kotler said.

Denzel nodded.

Kotler rushed in and joined them just as the elevator doors were closing. The ride to the research level seemed much longer this time. All five men stood in complete silence.

"How did she get in here?" Kotler asked Peters. "How did she manage to plant the devices on them?"

Peters shook his head. "I have no idea. My team is reviewing all entry logs now, but so far, we show nothing from the time Miller and Chandler entered the building up to the two of them going to the roof together. They were basically in their offices the whole time."

Kotler thought about this. "She got to them before, then," he said. "She must have planted the devices on them before they entered the building. What about that timer?"

"It's being projected by one of our own pieces of equipment. Miller and Chandler hauled it to the roof with them. They also barricaded the roof exit itself. There's no way up there without a helicopter. We have one standing by, flying a couple of blocks away."

"No attempt to land yet?" Kotler asked.

"Our instructions were pretty clear. Make a move to rescue them and they jump early."

"Instructions?" Kotler asked

Peters pulled his phone from his pocket and showed Kotler an email. The sending address was masked, but it was using the AMSL domain.

"It was sent internally," Peters said. "I don't know how she's getting into our system. We can't find any back doors."

The elevator chimed and the doors opened. All five men filed out and rushed alongside Patel as he made his way to his lab. He stopped, suddenly, in front of the door, self-consciously patting his shirt and waist, looking for his security access card. Which, of course, he did not have.

Peters stepped forward, swiped his own card, and the door opened. They were inside, and Patel rushed to a workbench, preparing.

Kotler watched him as Patel moved quickly, turning on the oscilloscope, warming the soldering iron, and fishing through various cabinets for the components he would need. He was working fast, and had the scrap of paper, with the counter frequencies, spread on the table beside him.

Kotler wasn't sure he could offer much assistance in building the counter device, but he couldn't just stand around, waiting. He began thinking of the problem Peters had mentioned. "Do you have any theories, then? About how she's infiltrating your system?" Kotler asked.

Peters shook his head. "None. We have firewalls on our firewalls. Even the NSA has to get my permission to hack in here," Peters said gruffly, exaggerating of course. "According to her file, Bristol doesn't have the technical expertise to be able to hack in. Neither does Jack Harris, for that matter. But we've tracked every packet coming into our going out of this place, and we can't find her. It's as if she's hiding in the building somewhere."

"Could she be?" Kotler asked.

"I …" Peters started, then shook his head. "We've seen no sign of her. If she's here, how could she have gotten in without us noticing?"

Kotler thought about this, factoring in all that they had learned and all that had happened lately. "When Ashton Mink took the data from the AMSL servers, how did that go undetected?"

"He used his priority access," Peters said. "He just logged in and downloaded it. Nothing in our system would have prevented that, though we did track it. There was just no alert, because there was no protocol to demand on. He had complete and unrestricted access."

"But he would have had to empty his pockets if he went through the front door, right? Or the metal detectors would have gone off. The scanners would find that SD card. Ashton didn't want that. So, he left by helicopter, from the roof."

"Right," Peters said.

"And now we have your two top executives on that roof," Kotler said. "Your biggest security hole is up top."

"You think Bristol infiltrated us by flying in?" Peters asked. Then shook his head. "There haven't been any incoming helicopters since Ashton's death."

"I don't think Bristol infiltrated through the roof," Kotler said. "I'm starting to think something else entirely. You gave us access to the AMSL employee records, right?"

Peters nodded. "You should be able to get to them from your phone, I already granted you and Agent Denzel full access."

Kotler started sifting through emails until he found the one granting him access to the employee files. It took only a few seconds to find the information he was looking for. He turned to Patel. "The sooner you can get that countermeasure built, the better," he said. Then he turned to Peters. "Things just got weirdly complicated," he said.

"More weirdly complicated, you mean?" Peters asked. "What have you found?"

"For starters," Kotler said, "I think we've been very wrong about a lot of things, right from the start. We we're wrong about Lawny Bristol. She's not alive after all."

"What?" Peters asked. "How do you know?"

"Because she could never have gained the access she'd need. And she wouldn't have had the resources to track down Gail McCarthy. Plus, all the moles and leaks have been right here onsite—Jack Harris and the Partano brothers. And even after Jack and the Partarnos and Bristol herself no longer had access to the AMSL servers, someone was still able to gain access, without triggering any of your security measures. I was wrong before. She didn't get to Miller and Chandler before they entered the building, she couldn't have."

"Because we would have found the devices on them, as they entered," Peters said. He thought for a moment. "There's another inside man?"

"Actually," Kotler said, "Right now I think he's an *outside* man."

CHAPTER 25

"What are you saying?" Denzel asked.

Kotler held his phone in front of him, scrolling through the personnel file as he talked to Denzel on speakerphone. He and Peters were moving through the wings of the Executive Suite, the floor that housed both Miller and Chandler's offices, along with the other executives. The place had been evacuated except for Peter's security force.

"I'm saying we were fooled. Bristol isn't behind this. I don't even think she's alive. I think she really did die, months ago. Whether it was an accident, I can't say for sure. Not yet."

"Then who is behind this? Who has Miller and Chandler ready to jump?"

Kotler took a deep breath. "I think it's Garrett Chandler," he said.

There was a beat from the other side of the line. "C'mon," Denzel said.

"Seriously," Kotler replied. "I'm looking at his personnel file now. There are things we didn't quite catch. Or we didn't put together. That *I* didn't put together."

"Like what?"

"He's very active in the LGBT community, for starters. He has a portion of his salary allocated to the Equal Colors Fund. I had to look it up. They're an LGBT advocacy group —organizing protests, helping with legal fees for discrimination lawsuits, that sort of thing."

There was another pause. "Uh, Kotler ..." Denzel started. "I don't think we've ever talked about this, but you do know that it's not a crime to be homosexual, right?"

"Yes, Roland, thank you. But what I'm saying is, I read the voice from my abduction all wrong. I thought the voice on the other side of that tech was a woman, because everything I knew at the time suggested that was the most likely answer."

"But it *was* a woman," Denzel said. "We identified her with the manager from that porn store. I showed Bristol's photo, from her personnel file."

"I believe that Guy identified her because Bristol looked similar to Ingrid. They resembled each other, and that may have been intentional."

"So if it wasn't Lawny Bristol, who was it? We've determined that Kate Bristol didn't exist."

"She didn't," Kotler said. "I think Ingrid was Garrett Chandler."

Another beat. "What, in drag?"

"I believe he's transgender," Kotler said. "And hiding it from everyone. He has the background to build the tech, according to his file. He might not fully understand all the science of it, but he was an engineer, previously. Using the data he got from the SD card, and the frequencies from the missing pages of the journal, I think he was skilled enough to build a prototype, and then replicate it."

"But Bristol took the journal," Denzel said.

"To her home," Kotler replied. "Where all of her posses-sions were claimed by a sister she doesn't have."

"Chandler was pretending the be the sister," Denzel said, quietly.

"He would have had access to the manifest of Bristol's belongings. He'd know that the journal wasn't in her posses-sion. He also had access to her personal files, when they were archived after her death."

"You realize how this sounds?" Denzel asked.

"I do," Kotler replied. "But believe me, Roland. I think Chandler is using this scenario on the roof to run an end game. He's showing that the technology works, and then he's going to make his escape."

"How?" Denzel asked.

They arrived at Chandler's office, and Peters used his key card to gain access. Kotler scanned the room, looking for anything that might support his theory. Or anything that might tell him Chandler's next move.

He spotted a photo on Chandler's wall that made him stop.

"He's going to fly out by helicopter," Kotler said.

"What? How? There's no bird on that roof."

Just then, the sound of blades cutting the air filled the office space, dulled slightly by the thickness of the office windows. Kotler rushed to the glass, craning to look up.

Denzel spoke up from the line. "I see it," he said. "That's the bird they put in the air for support. It flew in from across town."

"I'd be willing to bet the pilot has one of the Devil's Interval devices on him," Kotler said. "And Chandler is a pilot. There's a photo of him behind the stick of a Bell 206. He can fly that chopper."

"Alright, I'm on it," Denzel said, hanging up. Kotler knew he would put in calls to bring more helicopters this way, filled with agents and police. He'd also lock down the airways. But Kotler knew it would all be too late. Chandler wasn't stupid. He had a plan.

And the countdown on the side of the building was just a distraction. A sleight of hand meant to fool everyone into being off guard. Chandler's demonstration of Devil's Interval was going to be more than simply the suicide of the CEO. He was going to show that he could outwit even the FBI.

"We have to get onto that roof," Kotler said to Peters.

Peters shook his head. "I told you, it's barricaded. It would take an explosion to open that door, and you might as well push Miller off the roof at that point.

He was right. Anything that might clue in Chandler that they were on to him would make him accelerate his plan. By this point, he'd already proven what the technology could do. Any potential buyer would be willing to risk the investment. So, the only thing saving Ross Miller, right this minute, was Chandler's showmanship. He was making as big a spectacle as possible, to erase all doubt in Devil's Interval, and he could end the show with just a single spoken command.

There had to be a way to get up there, though. There had to be a way to end this without Miller dying. Kotler refused to believe …

"How close are they standing to each other?" he asked.

"What?" Peters asked. "Who?"

"Miller and Chandler," Kotler said.

Peters shook his head. "I don't know exactly. A couple of feet."

"Less than two?" Kotler asked.

Peters nodded.

Kotler smiled, and raced away from Chandler's office, with Peters close behind. Kotler first thought he might skip the elevator and run down the stairs to the research level, but it was nearly thirty flights, and he was more likely to vomit than to make good time. Instead, he impatiently stood next to Peters as the elevator opened. They stepped in and glided down to the research floor. As the doors opened, Kotler sprinted for the lab.

The guards let him in without question.

"Simon!" Kotler shouted, as he was let through the secured door. "How difficult would it be for you to replicate the Devil's Interval tech?"

Patel looked up from his work, blinking. "I … I suppose I could do it in a couple of hours. But isn't it more important to create the counter measure?"

"We don't have a couple of hours," Kotler said. "At best, we have a few minutes." He patted his coat, and pulled out the evidence bag containing the busted Devil's Interval device. "Could you repair this one in that time?" He tossed it to Patel.

"Yes," Patel said, nodding. "But why?"

"Could you use it to transmit a signal to the device that Ross Miller is wearing?"

Patel paused to think, and again nodded, then smiled. "Yes, I can do that. And I have already built the transmission circuit we need," he said, nodding to his current work in progress. "It would not be very targeted, but I believe that is an asset at this point, yes?"

"Yes," Kotler said, grinning.

Patel got to work, removing the broken Devil's Interval device, and taking components of it carefully out of the shattered housing. He transferred these into the makeshift housing of his own device, and began soldering and connecting components. He replaced the damaged components from the bins of parts within the workshop, and after just a few minutes he waved Kotler over.

Kotler stood, bent and looking over Patel's shoulder as he pointed out the trigger for the device. "The range is not good," he said. "But if you can get within 20 feet, it should be fine."

"What about barriers?" Kotler asked. Will it work through a metal door?"

Patel shook his head. "The range will be dramatically reduced," he said.

Kotler cursed. "We're back to the same problem," he said. "No access to the roof."

"I think I have as solution for that one," Peters said. "Take that thing to the street, and I'll meet you there."

CHAPTER 26

Kotler, Denzel, Patel, and finally Peters, along with a handful of SWAT officers and FBI agents, exited the two elevators of a building directly facing AMSL's towering frame. This building was shorter by a third, but it would be enough. They rushed up a set of stairs and burst onto the roof.

SWAT members took positions, and leveled rifles on Garrett Chandler, across the way. The sound of the helicopter was louder here, as it had set down on the roof behind the two men and echoed through the city canyon. This was the end game, alright. They had only moments before Chandler gave the command for Miller to jump. Presumably he would rush to the helicopter then, taking it over from the entranced pilot. He would fly out, staying low within the canyons of the city to avoid being tracked by radar, and would make his way to whatever extraction point he had pre-arranged, likely letting the mind-controlled pilot take the chopper back into the air as a distraction.

It could be only seconds now.

"You got it set?" Denzel shouted over the din of helicopter noise echoing among the buildings.

"Set!" Peters said.

"I have looped the message we're transmitting," Patel shouted. "Once it is within range, it will be picked up and rebroadcast."

"Good!" Kotler shouted. "Let's get this in the air, we're out of time!"

Peters nodded, and as everyone cleared away he moved the levers on the control he was holding. The drone buzzed to life, rising quickly into the air.

"Come at him from above," Denzel shouted. "He's busy watching the street."

Peters nodded, and the drone continued to gain altitude, then tilted toward the AMSL roof.

In moments, it was across the canyon, and began to hover downward toward the two men on the roof's edge, its sound masked by the thrum of the helicopter.

They watched things evolve from the drone's point of view, as it got closer. Kotler realized that he had been holding his breath, and let it out.

"Ok," Kotler said. "We're within range. Trigger it."

Peters was controlling the drone, holding it in a steady position, as Patel used a handheld control to activate the device by remote.

There was no sound, no flash of light, nothing to indicate whether or not the signal had reached the device. Their only evidence came from across the way, and slightly above them. They saw Ross Miller's demeanor change, as did that of Garrett Chandler.

Both men suddenly took a big step back.

Kotler let out the breath he'd been holding. "Ok," he said, "I think we can safely breach the roof."

Peters nodded, lifted a radio from his belt, and issued the orders.

From their vantage point, they couldn't see beyond the roofline, but they had a clear view from the camera in the drone. The door to the roof was blown, and armed security and police rushed forward.

Chandler stumbled, moving away from Ross, and shaking his head. Kotler realized, suddenly, that their step back had moved them just out of range of the 20-foot field of influence from the modified Devil's Interval device. If its signal was still reaching the device planted on Miller, it wasn't strong enough to prevent Chandler from shaking off its effects.

Chandler turned, and sprinted away from Miller, headed straight for the helicopter.

They couldn't hear or see anything from across the way, but Peters was getting reports via radio. "Chandler has made it to the chopper! My team and the police are holding fire, to avoid hitting the pilot."

The helicopter rose swiftly into the air, then dipped low, following the corridor of buildings, turning out of sight a few blocks away.

"Dammit!" Kotler shouted. He turned to Denzel. "Is there any way to track him?" he asked.

Denzel was already on his phone, calling in the incident, requesting cameras, news helicopters, ground-level observers, and anything else he could think of.

Kotler was breathing heavily, as if he'd just sprinted up a set of stairs to get here. He felt his heart pounding, and the anger raging within him. He was as angry with himself as he was with Garrett Chandler. How had he missed the clues? How had he been so wrong?

A call came over Peters' radio. "We have Ross Miller," one of his men said. "He's safe."

"Good work," Peters replied. He issued more orders, informed his men to stand down and let the police and FBI do their work.

Kotler wandered away from everyone, still feeling rage over the missed capture. He spotted Patel, who was standing away from everyone, near the roof's edge, looking down.

"You helped us save Ross Miller," Kotler said.

Patel looked at him, his eyes wild. "I caused all of this," he said.

Kotler regarded him for a moment, then nodded. "Yes, that's true. But you also helped to stop it."

Comforting words. He wanted Patel to feel them, to know that he'd done some good. But Kotler himself wasn't feeling quite as hopeful about things. Patel may have redeemed himself, somewhat. His career might have a chance again. But the technology he created was now out there, representing a dazzling new threat in the world. Chandler Ross was out there, prepared to use it or to sell it.

What was his agenda? What was his motive for all of this? Kotler intended to find out. And then he intended to find Garrett Chandler, and put an end to Devil's Interval.

CHAPTER 27

ROSS MILLER WAS BEING EXAMINED BY PARAMEDICS IN his own office, having refused to go to ground level, much less the hospital. Letting the paramedics look him over was the only compromise he was willing to make, and he was more than a bit annoyed for having to endure.

He was also agitated and a bit skeptical over the news of his friend and fellow executive.

"I'm just having a hard time wrapping my head around all of it," Miller said. "I've known Garrett for years. It was on my recommendation that Ashton made him part of the company. I just can't understand why he'd do this."

"Money is the most likely motive," Denzel said.

Miller looked at him, shaking his head. "Garrett had money. His annual salary is seven figures."

"Not this kind of money," Denzel said. "He could buy his own country with this kind of money."

"Maybe it was more than the money," Kotler said. "I've been reviewing his personnel file, plus anything I could find online. He was very passionate about equal rights, and I think he felt some sort of shame or stigma about being a transgender, hiding in plain sight."

"I knew about it," Miller said, quietly. "We've talked about it. I ... I may be the reason he kept it low profile." He looked around at each of them. "I thought it might be bad for the company, to have its COO come out as a transgender. I told him it might be best to keep his private life private. But I encouraged him to support anything he felt passionate about."

"Judging by what I'm learning," Kotler said, "he may have resented you for that. There's this interview with him in Time." Kotler indicated his phone. "He goes on quite a bit about 'changing the minds of business leaders,' and 'imposing a new way of thinking on the world.' I may be just reading it as ominous, after the fact. But I think the idea of using mind control to further the cause of LGBT rights might have been tempting."

Miller shook his head, still shocked. The EMTs pronounced him fit, and left the building. He got up from his office chair and wandered out into the hall, with Kotler, Denzel, and Peters following close behind. He went straight to Chandler's office, which was currently taped off, as a forensics team swept it for anything they could find.

"He was my friend," Miller said quietly. "He tried to kill me."

"He sees himself as a warrior in a cause," Kotler said. "You were a sacrifice for the greater good. It was also strategic. With Ashton and you both dead, AMSL would likely fall into a tailspin. He was planning to survive the ordeal, and would have moved to take over as CEO. From there, he'd be able to reallocate AMSL's resources, to further this own agenda."

"But you figured it out," Miller said. "Just in time."

Kotler started to respond, but shook his head slightly. "Excuse me," he said, turning and walking away.

Miller was safe. Patel might receive a pardon for his help in this. And they now knew who was behind it all. But it was a pyrrhic victory. They'd won, but Chandler had escaped, along with his knowledge of the Devil's Interval technology.

"At least we have the countermeasure," Denzel said, catching up to Kotler at the bank of elevators.

Kotler raised his eyebrows, smiling wryly. "They teach mind reading at Quantico?"

Denzel smiled slightly, shaking his head. "You may be better at reading body language than anyone I know, Kotler, but you don't own the table on it. Besides, I know you well enough to know this was too close. You're kicking yourself."

"I had him, Roland. Just … too late. I was fooled. I let myself fall victim to cognitive bias. I was *convinced* I was talking to a woman, on the other side of that voice changer. Plus … well, I almost hate to admit it."

"Go ahead," Denzel said. "The elevator is taking its time."

Kotler took a deep breath, and exhaled. "It's Gail. She got in my head. Even before I knew it was her behind my abduction, I was already carrying around some baggage. It influenced me. It made me think the voice on the other end of that line had to be a woman, because lately women … well, I let my feelings for Gail cloud my judgement once before. I let my personal hang-ups color my perception this time, and it nearly cost Ross Miller his life. And it may have unleashed the most horrible weapon ever created on an unsuspecting world."

"First, I can think of plenty worse weapons. Losing your free will isn't something new, Kotler. People have been brainwashed and forced to do things against their will since the dawn of time. This technology just makes it easier for the bad guys, that's all. Second, it isn't your job to catch these bad guys, it's mine. Your job is to do exactly what you did. You put things together in a way I wouldn't have. You solved it, before it was too late. It doesn't matter how close to the wire you were."

"But Chandler escaped. We could have had him, but I didn't solve this fast enough."

"He's escaped *for now*. We haven't stopped looking. I have people looking into where that helicopter ended up. We will find this guy, Kotler."

The elevator dinged, and the doors opened. Kotler and Denzel stepped inside, and Denzel punched the button for the lobby.

They rode down in silence, and Kotler mulled over everything Denzel had said, wondering if he believed any of it.

THE STREETS WERE STILL BARRICADED as Kotler and Denzel made their way to Denzel's car. Members of the Press were clamoring for any soundbite they could get, and Kotler cringed to think of the headlines. "Viking Researcher Foils CEO Suicide," or some nonsense. It wouldn't go unnoticed that he was departing in the company of the FBI, and that was sure to create some sort of buzz. He might even be named as a suspect—there wasn't a lot of fact checking going on in the media these days

They had slowly pushed through the crowd and were a few blocks away when Denzel's phone rang. "This is Agent Denzel," he answered.

Kotler was staring out of the passenger side window, looking at the faces of everyone on the street. He wondered about all them—their lives, their families, their careers. Any one of them could be turned into a murderer in an instant, and all it would take was to plant a Devil's Interval device on them.

Denzel was right, of course. There were weapons that were far more horrible, in terms of their destructive power or the devastation they could generate. But to Kotler, who viewed free will as a divine gift, the idea of technology that could bypass it was abhorrent. He'd rather burn, rather watch his own flesh melt from his bones, than know he had been turned into a weapon.

"We have a lead," Denzel said. "The pilot of that chopper has been located. He put down just outside the city. He has no memory of when he took over, but there's a GPS in the aircraft. We can track where it's been."

Kotler nodded. Then shook himself a bit. This was good news. This was hope. "Let's get him," he said, smirking.

They drove to the location of the helicopter, which took some time. Police and even military were already on the scene. "What's the military doing here?" Kotler asked.

"Maneuvers nearby, so they offered an assist. We've been sort of all over the place, so it was a welcome bit of help."

The pilot was sitting in the back of a squad car, his hands in cuffs. Kotler glanced at Denzel, who stepped forward and showed his badge to the officer closest to him. "Why is he in cuffs?" Denzel asked.

"He has some story about mind control," the cop said, scoffing. "But he was flying the chopper that you guys were after. We're taking him in for questioning."

"I need to speak to him," Denzel said.

The officer looked hesitant at first, but shrugged and opened the squad car's door.

Denzel knelt, and chatted with the pilot for a while, asking for any details he could give.

Kotler stepped away, wandering among the police and military. He had his ID out, and clipped to the front pocket of his shirt. It seemed to do the trick, and no one stopped him.

He moved to the helicopter, where two technicians had plugged a tablet into the chopper's systems, and were pulling up GPS data.

"Find anything?" Kotler asked.

The technicians glanced at him, then at the FBI Consultant ID. "You're with the FBI?" they asked.

"Consultant. Working with Agent Denzel," he nodded to Denzel, who was standing now, dusting off and turning to look for Kotler.

"The helicopter took a pretty winding route through the city," one technician said. "But it did stop and hover in this location for a bit." He showed Kotler the map on screen. "There's a helipad on that roof. It's a hospital."

Kotler looked at the screen and nodded. But something didn't feel right.

"How long did they hover there?" he asked.

The technician checked some of the data. "Maybe three minutes. Long enough for your guy to disembark."

That was true. If the pilot took the stick, and hovered just above the helipad, Chandler could have exited in seconds. The pilot then continued his route to here.

"Why here?" Kotler asked, looking around.

"I'm sorry?" one of the technicians asked.

Denzel had walked up now, and had heard some of the discussion.

"Why here?" Kotler asked him.

"Why not here?" Denzel asked.

"The pilot was ... well, on autopilot. If Chandler exited at that hospital, why would he have the pilot fly all the way out here?"

"Throw us off the trail?" Denzel asked. "Get him as far away from that hospital helipad as possible?"

Kotler looked around. They were in an urban area. There was a large park nearby, and he could hear kids laughing and screaming as they chased each other. There were houses here —a neighborhood. And there were a few industrial buildings, small and squat, and lining the road running behind the park.

"He's here," Kotler said.

"What?" Denzel asked. "What makes you say that?"

"He's too smart. He wouldn't have left the GPS running. He'd know about it. He's flown this type of helicopter before. He didn't get out of the helicopter at that hospital. He paused there long enough to throw us off the trail. His goal was to get here."

"Why?" Denzel asked.

Kotler pulled out his phone and brought up a map of the area. "About ten miles from here, there's a private airport," Kotler said.

Denzel nodded, then yelled for the police and military, showing his badge and issuing orders. There was very little hesitation, as the officers and soldiers had been gearing up to leave, the mission and the excitement over. This would be action. They were onboard.

They were on the road and on their way to the airport, with sirens blaring. Denzel was calling ahead, making sure no planes left the ground.

Kotler, again, couldn't shake a feeling.

He wandered toward the playground, and the sound of the kids.

It was a pleasant day. The weather was a bit cool, but warm enough that many of the children were playing without jackets. Parents and nannies were seated and chatting with each other on the benches lining the edge of one of the playgrounds. Kotler smiled a bit. He thought of his nephew, Alex. He was a smart kid. Even had his own 'boy detective' agency, solving neighborhood crimes for a buck. Kotler talked to him often, and occasionally sent him something cool—a microscope or a replica of an ancient artifact, or anything that Alex might find interesting. Kotler's brother, Jeffrey, wasn't always keen on how well Kotler and his nephew got along, but at least he never tried to stop them from talking.

Kotler wondered what it would be like, to be a parent. His relationship with Alex was as close as he'd come, but he doubted it even compared in the slightest to the real thing. For starters, though Kotler was always concerned that Alex was safe, he figured that was nowhere near the near-panic worry he'd feel, if he was raising a child in this world: A world where monsters were real, and they were using technology to control the minds of others, to turn housewives into murderers. Or worse. Kotler figured he'd watch his child like a hawk, at all times, probably being too overbearing and too overprotective.

He paused.

His gut was telling him that something wasn't right, but his brain hadn't completely caught up to it. What was it? What was he seeing, that wasn't quite clicking?

The parents.

Most were casually talking to each other, keeping an eye on the kids without being too focused. This was just another casual day at the park for them.

But some of the parents were sitting rigid. They stared at the playground, unmoving, not talking.

One woman, off to herself with no one else sharing her bench, wasn't watching the playground at all, but instead had her head down, her hair obscuring her face.

Kotler moved closer, swinging around behind, and walked to the bench where the woman sat. She was staring at her hands, from what Kotler could tell.

"Chandler," he said.

Chandler looked up, startled. He was wearing makeup and a wig, and if Kotler hadn't known his face he would never have guessed this woman was AMSL's COO.

Chandler sprang from the bench and started running, and Kotler chased him, leapt, and tackled him to the ground.

They struggled, and Chandler got at least one good punch in before Kotler managed to take hold of his wrists. He had a knee on Chandler's stomach, pushing against his sternum. "Stop!" Kotler said. "It's over!"

"It's not over," Chandler hissed. He was smiling, and his mouth was bleeding, most likely from the fall. His teeth, straight and perfect, were stained pink with blood, making him look ghoulish. He laughed, and nodded toward the playground.

The parents that Kotler had watched earlier—three couples who had sat stiff and unmoving—were now on their feet. Each was holding a weapon, and each had it aimed at the children on the playground.

One of the other parents screamed, and a man ran forward, trying to tackle the nearest armed parent, but he was forced to take cover as the woman turned and fired at him.

It was clear. They had been programmed to take aim if Chandler were captured, and to fire at anyone who approached.

The children, within the meshed fence of the playground, had all hidden in the playground equipment at the first shot. Kotler could hear crying and whimpering.

"Let me go, or they die. All of them," Chandler said.

Denzel raced up then, his weapon drawn.

Kotler relaxed his grip, and stood, stepping away from Chandler.

"What are you doing, Kotler?" Denzel asked.

"He's controlling the parents," Kotler said. "They'll shoot the kids."

Chandler rose to his feet. His dress was torn and dirty, and the wig he wore was skewed. Blood pooled on his lip and ran down his chin. The whole scene was ghoulish and disturbing, and Kotler felt like throwing up at the sight of it.

Chandler started to back away, watching them as he went. "Let me go, or they die," he repeated.

Denzel kept his weapon trained on Chandler. "I can't let you leave, Chandler. Keep your hands where I can see them."

Chandler laughed. "I don't need my hands. The weapon's already been fired. I'm leaving, Agent Denzel. Do not follow me, or those parents start shooting."

He turned and walked away from the playground, straight to one of the squat industrial buildings, opened a door and ducked inside.

"Not again," Kotler said, gritting his teeth.

"We have a counter measure for the devices," Roland said. "I can get it here quick. We just have to keep those people from firing."

"You heard the rules," Kotler said. "Let Chandler go, and do not approach them." He looked at Denzel. "I can stop him," he said.

Denzel shook his head. "It's too dangerous."

"I'm going," he said. "You have to stay. You have to keep them from killing those kids. You're the only one with the authority to make those people listen to you." He nodded to the frantic parents, hovering close by. Any one of them might decide to do the wrong thing, to rush the people who had guns aimed at their children.

Denzel looked from the armed parents to the unaffected parents who were becoming more frantic.

He engaged the safety on his weapon, and handed it to Kotler.

"I'm probably going to be reprimanded for this. Or worse," he said.

"Tell them I took it when you weren't looking," Kotler said, smiling.

"That won't go over any better," Denzel replied. "Go. Stop him. I'll take care of this."

CHAPTER 28

KOTLER BURST THROUGH THE DOOR OF AN INDUSTRIAL building, where Chandler had disappeared from sight. He had Denzel's weapon leveled and ready to fire. There was no sign of Chandler inside, and Kotler rushed in, and kept low. He checked every side door as he went, but he was sure he knew Chandler's plan.

He must have had a car ready. And if Kotler wasted too much time, he'd lose him again.

He made a few quick decisions. If Chandler had a car ready, it would likely be outside, and probably on the other side of this building. The best chance was for Kotler to run full tilt, find the first exit he could, and hopefully catch up to Chandler before he got moving.

The building was abandoned, and looked vacant. The corridor Kotler ran down eventually ended at a T, and Kotler glanced from side to side, trying to find a clue to where Chandler would have run.

He caught a glimpse of light at the end of the corridor on his left, decided that was as clear a sign as any he could hope for, and raced in that direction.

At the end of the hall was a double set of doors, and Kotler pushed through these and to the outside in a rush. He blinked in the sunlight, weapon once again sweeping in front of him, and heard the car starting. He sprinted around the corner just in time to see Chandler squeal away.

Kotler dropped to one knee and took aim, then fired, and fired again. His second shot hit the car's rear tire, and the blowout was enough to cause Chandler to lose control and ram into a dumpster at the corner of the building.

Kotler raced forward, pulled the driver side door open, and was about to say something when a shot rang out.

Kotler rolled away, fell to the ground, and scrambled back to take cover at the rear of the car. Chandler, taking advantage of the opportunity, raced away and into the street.

Kotler ran after him.

"Chandler, you have to stop! It's over!"

Chandler answered by ducking behind a car parked on the street, and firing at Kotler again. It was clear Chandler was no marksman. He was aiming wildly, and though Kotler didn't feel particularly endangered, he worried for the homes nearby. A stray bullet could hit someone.

He had to end this.

He took aim, steadying himself, and fired.

The round grazed Chandler's shoulder, knocking him to the ground with a scream. He scrambled to his feet and fired three wild shots at Kotler, his aim even worse now that he was injured. But it was enough to make Kotler take cover, which gave Chandler time once again to run.

This time, Kotler hadn't seen which direction he'd gone. He could be anywhere, which made this situation even more dangerous.

Kotler had to move cautiously now, unsure of where an attack might come from.

When he reached the spot where Chandler had taken

cover, he saw blood on the trunk of the car, and spatters on the ground. He could track these, following the trail to the side entrance of one of the buildings. Kotler cautiously pulled a metal door open and ducked inside.

This was a furniture warehouse, filled with stacks of wood and woodworking machinery. Thank God it was closed for the weekend.

As Kotler moved deeper in, he passed through an area with large bolts of cloth, spooled in towering racks that made the room maze like. He moved cautiously and quietly, watching for signs of blood or any other trace of Chandler, and keeping himself hidden as much as possible.

"You know," Chandler's voice called out from somewhere in the room. It was hard for Kotler to pinpoint it. "I have to say, I'm very impressed with how you figured everything out."

Kotler said nothing. He didn't want to give away his position, but he also had nothing to say to this man.

"I meant it when I said I was a fan of your work," Chandler said. "I had followed your story, the Viking thing. But I knew of you before that. I read about you, years ago. About your family. About what happened to you."

This was a game now. Chandler was trying to rattle him, to get him upset or off guard. He was trying to level the playing field, since he was now injured. He figured he could get to Kotler through his past. But it was a mistake.

Kotler had come to grips with his past. He had learned to accept it as part of who he was. Just like the ancient cultures he studied—their tragedies were as much a part of the culture as their victories and successes. So were his.

He heard something to his right, and peered past a rack of fabric. He could see Chandler now, across the room, hold up in a space where he had decent cover on just about every side. He had torn some material and was using it as a compress, to staunch the flow of blood from his shoulder.

Kotler couldn't approach Chandler from here without being spotted. He wouldn't be able to take him down that way. If he alerted Chandler to his presence, even if he had his sights on him, this would turn into a protracted gun battle, with an uncertain outcome. Too dangerous.

Kotler wanted Chandler alive.

He wanted him to pay for Ashton Mink's murder. And he suspected that Chandler murdered Lawny Bristol as well. He should pay for these crimes.

Looking from Chandler to his surroundings, Kotler spotted a rolling staircase nearby. Possibly used to reach cloth from higher on the racks. It was currently sitting opposite of the rack of material that Chandler was using for cover.

Chandler had forgone the wig, and was pressing the compress against his shoulder. The material he was using had been bright yellow, but now was soaked red.

Despite the compress, however, Chandler still had the gun in his hand, and Kotler had no doubts that he'd use it.

Kotler moved away, and began to circle back around, trying to get to that ladder without being seen or heard.

He kept low, and struggled to keep Chandler in view, snatching quick glances of him from between gaps. It became increasingly difficult, however, as overlapping bolts of fabric formed an impenetrable barrier.

At last, Kotler reached the stairs. They were metal, and Kotler was certain they would make noise as he walked up. He looked around, and pulled at one of the bolts of fabric, but stopped when he saw a bin filled with scraps. He rushed to it, grabbed several of them, and ran back to the steps.

He laid cloth on all the steps he could reach, and carefully made is way up. It worked. The material dampened each step, and when he got to the second half of the staircase he laid down the rest of the fabric, and walked up to the top. Now he could crawl on top of the rack of cloth, and peer down at Chandler. He moved carefully, balanced himself, and managed to get to the top of the rack, with great effort. He carefully glanced over and …

Nothing. Chandler was gone.

He heard someone clear their throat from below, and looked down to see Chandler, grinning and aiming his weapon at Kotler, who was now in plain sight.

"It's been a pleasure, Dr. Kotler," Chandler said.

Kotler, reacting quickly, turned his weapon and fired, blind, as he fell backward. On his way down he grabbed at the bolts of material, yanking his arm and spinning himself jarringly. There was excruciating pain in his shoulder, and his weapon dropped from his other hand. His feet were aimed down, at least, and he was able to slowly lower himself to the floor. He recovered his weapon, and did a quick glance around the edge of the rack, to see if he could spot Chandler.

He swept with his weapon as he stepped around the corner, but lowered it immediately.

There was no need to worry now. His blind shot had been too true. He had caught Chandler in the chest, hurling him back against one of the racks and onto the floor.

Kotler engaged the safety on his own weapon, and tucked it into his belt. He limped a bit, toward Chandler. He rubbed at his own shoulder, which felt sore from being yanked hard during his fall. The pain was fading, but it ached.

He knelt and checked Chandler's pulse, to be sure.

He felt something.

It was a thread, a light flutter. Weak, but still there.

Kotler reached down and took Chandler's weapon, and then picked his phone out of the front pocket of his pants. He called 911 first, gave them the report of a man with severe gunshot wounds, and requested an ambulance. He also advised them that there was an FBI agent on the scene. No need to mention it wasn't Kotler himself.

Kotler had only basic medical training, but he put Chandler on his back, and started tearing bits of material from the racks to work as a compress and bandages. He wasn't sure if Chandler would survive, and the man had already lost consciousness. But for the first time since discovering that it was Chandler behind all of this, and possibly since the moment he'd seen Gail McCarthy back at that metalworks, Kotler felt some hope. He felt like justice might be served.

His next call, then, was to Denzel.

CHAPTER 29

Denzel was holding his badge up, hoping it would provide at least some assurance to the frantic parents. "Please, stand back!" he shouted. "If you approach them, they will fire!"

"Do something!" one man shouted.

"I have help on the way, sir, but for now we have to stay calm and stay away from them."

"That's my husband!" one woman cried, pointing at one of the parents who was aiming a handgun at the children. "Rob, what are you doing? Put the gun down!"

"He doesn't know what he's doing," Denzel said. "He's being controlled. It's a very long story, but these people are not responsible for their actions. As long as we do not approach them, they will not harm your children. Understand?"

Everyone was silent but nodding.

Denzel wasn't entirely sure what the play should be here. Nothing about this scenario was acceptable. He was unarmed, but even if he'd had his weapon, could he justify firing on these people? They were as innocent as the parents watching in horror.

He couldn't just let them keep their weapons trained on those kids, though.

One of the parents, the man who had shouted for him to *do something*, began to creep forward, toward the fencing around the playground. Denzel looked and saw a child—a little girl—crying and walking toward the fence.

"Daddy," she said, sobbing.

One of the armed and controlled parents shifted and started to aim her weapon in that direction, though Denzel couldn't decide if she was aiming at the man or the child. Either way, it didn't matter.

"Stop! If you go any closer, she'll fire!"

The man looked up, saw the woman, and looked with fright toward Denzel. "I can't let her shoot my daughter!" he said.

There was sobbing all around now, from both parents and children, and Denzel felt that drive again, to *do something*.

"Hey!" he said, waving his badge and stepping forward. "Hey! Over here!"

All the parents turned then, slowly, as if they were animatronic robots simply running on a pre-programmed circuit. Denzel was relieved to see that even the first woman had turned from the father and child, and was now aiming at him instead.

How far could he push this? How close would be too close? Would they fire eventually anyway?

It didn't matter. If he could hold their attention, their weapons weren't pointed at those kids. "Go around!" he shouted to the man. "See if you can find a gap on the other side of the playground. Stay hidden behind the equipment!"

The man nodded, and then he and some of the other

parents started moving. One woman ran to a minivan parked nearby, opened the hatch, and produced a tire tool with a pry bar end.

Denzel needed to keep the armed parents distracted, hopefully without getting shot.

He started shuffling to the side, angling away from the playground, but staying close enough, he hoped, that he would still seem like a pending threat.

The parents followed him, keeping their weapons trained on him. That was perfect.

The day was cool, and there was a nice, light breeze, but Denzel still felt sweat running down his sides. A drip of sweat rolled from his forehead, down to the tip of his nose. He dared not move to brush it away, in case the armed parents saw it as an aggressive move.

Right now, he was having a staring contest with a swarm of angry bees. No sudden movements.

He had called for backup, and had asked for the counter-measure to be brought along. It would take some time for anyone to get here, even if they came by helicopter. This was going to be a long battle. Denzel's hope was that the parents could somehow get the children out of the playground and safely away before something went wrong.

The children started moving, on the other side of the fence, and one of the armed parents noticed. They turned then, taking aim once more at the playground itself.

"No!" Denzel said, waving the badge and stepping forward once more.

There were six armed parents, and five were aiming at him. As he stepped forward, all five fired, and the sixth turned to aim at him again.

He gasped, closing his eyes, ready to feel the bullets tear into him. But nothing happened. He opened his eyes and saw that all five parents had shot at the ground at his feet.

Warning shots.

He was sure he wouldn't get another set. The next time those weapons fired in his direction, he'd be dead.

To his relief, however, he saw that all the children were out of sight, on the other side of a large structure that was festooned with slides and ladders and netting. The unarmed parents were also out of sight, and Denzel hoped that meant they were making progress.

If Denzel stood here, making no sudden movements, the kids should be safe. And so should he. Theoretically.

His phone rang.

There was no way he could answer it, and he silently prayed that it wasn't more trouble. Kotler had taken off after Chandler, with Denzel's weapon, and there was just no way to know how that scenario would play out. Kotler was trained, though. Denzel decided to trust that he could handle everything.

Sirens sounded in the distance. They couldn't be for him. His people wouldn't come in with sirens blaring, and they would still be several minutes out, by his estimate. Maybe someone in the neighborhood called the police.

This was going to get tricky.

From the corner of his eye he noticed movement on the other side of the playground. He turned his head, and saw that the parents had managed to get their kids out of the playground, and were running them to the opposite side of the park.

Denzel sighed with relief, and then took two steps back.

The armed parents turned again to the playground, aiming at the empty structures as if there were still children there. Apparently, Chandler's instructions hadn't been too thorough. Denzel wondered what he'd told them to do, simply aim at the playground and fire if anyone approached? That could still be dangerous for bystanders. But for now, he was willing to let them keep playground equipment hostage for as long as they needed.

The sirens grew louder, and an ambulance rounded the corner, headed down the block. Two police cars came from the opposite direction, and all stopped in front of a building just down the way.

Denzel checked his phone, saw that he had missed a call from Kotler, and called back with an uncomfortable feeling in his stomach.

"What took you?" Kotler said.

"I was babysitting," Denzel said. "You alright?"

"I'm good, but the police are coming in now. I shot Chandler"

Denzel sighed. "There's going to be paperwork. And yelling."

"I also told them there was an agent on scene," Kotler said.

"More yelling," Denzel said, sternly. "Mostly from me."

"I would just prefer not to be arrested or shot," Kotler said. "How'd things turn out on your end?"

"Kids are safe. The armed parents have a playground covered. It's not going anywhere, but no humans seem to be in danger. The countermeasure should be here soon, I hope."

As if on cue, Denzel heard a helicopter approaching.

"Kotler, show them your ID, and tell them that I left to come out here and deal with a secondary threat. Hide my weapon. They'll want a statement from you, but tell them you have to debrief with me first."

"Got it," Kotler said.

Denzel hung up, and went to greet an agent carrying a metal case. They placed it on the ground and opened it, revealing the makeshift device that Patel had built. "You know how it works?" he asked the agent.

She nodded.

Denzel pointed at the armed parents. "Those are your targets. Don't get too close, they're programmed to shoot at any threats."

The agent nodded again, took the device out of the case, and positioned herself in range. She activated the device, aiming it like a rifle at each of the armed parents. The highly directional beam had more range than the Devil's Interval device, which was fortunate. It took only an instant for each of the parents to come to their senses, and when they did they each tossed their weapons away as if they'd just discovered they were holding a snake.

Denzel let the agent on the scene handle them, and rushed to see if he could keep Kotler out of trouble. There would be a lot of explaining to do, but the circumstances and their victory would help.

He hoped.

EPILOGUE

KOTLER HAD SUNK INTO THE CUSHIONS OF A ROUNDED booth, and was enjoying both the scotch and atmosphere. *Hemingway's* was something of a theme bar, with an adventurer's motif. It had been here, on this spot, for more than fifty years. Updated from time to time, it had avoided being 'modernized,' beyond a few updates to the wiring and plumbing. The walls of the place were adorned with maps, photographs, and the occasional fly fishing rod. A set of books, leather-bound and all alleged to be signed by Hemingway himself, were on shelves at the end of the bar, encased in Plexiglas, and accompanied by a small, brass plague explaining their origin.

Kotler wandered in here from time to time—often enough that the bartenders knew him and considered him a regular. This, even though he would often disappear for months. Kotler had always liked that. He could go away for three months, and come back to find this place exactly as he'd left it, and with everyone recognizing him and greeting him with smiles and the occasional drink on the house.

But now he wondered if that was as good a thing as he

always thought it to be. These people knew of him, but they didn't *know* him. He could vanish this very evening, and they'd continue on with their lives as usual, maybe someday wondering "whatever happened to that archeologist guy?"

Denzel had slid into the seat across the table from him, looking uncomfortable. "How'd it go?" Kotler asked.

Denzel had a scotch of his own, but until that moment he hadn't touched it. He took a sip, took a breath, took another sip. "It went well enough, for an ass chewing. I was quoted regulations, more than once. More than ten times, actually. The Director let the Internal Affairs guys have at me for a solid hour before he stepped in."

"IA?" Kotler asked. "They didn't bring IA into my debriefing."

"They will," Denzel said. "You're up again tomorrow."

"Again? I've already told them everything that happened. Multiple times," Kotler said, his expression sour.

"Welcome to life in the Bureau," Denzel said, taking a more serious turn with his drink.

Kotler watched, then chuckled, and smiled. "That's the cost, then," he said. "At least we stopped Chandler."

"You stopped Chandler," Denzel nodded, and offered his glass up for a toast.

Kotler returned the gesture, they clinked glasses, and each downed the rest of their scotch in a gulp. Kotler motioned for the waitress, pointing at the two empty glasses, and she nodded and went to retrieve more.

Denzel relaxed a bit. "You did good, Kotler," he said. "I know we're taking a ration of shit now, but the Director is vouching for both of us. We managed to save Ross Miller, to keep a bunch of kids from being gunned down in a payground, and to take out Garrett Chandler without killing him. He's in critical condition, but expected to pull through."

"Good news," Kotler said, nodding.

"So why do I get the impression that you're not seeing this as a complete victory?"

Kotler regarded him for a moment, shook his head and smiled. "We won. I know that. I guess I'm having sort of an existential crisis. I'm wondering what I'm doing in the middle of an investigation like this in the first place. I'm an archeologist, not an FBI agent. All my career, I've dealt with artifacts and ancient texts and *research*."

"You've had your fair share of action," Denzel pointed out. "I've seen your file. You've been in some heavy activity."

"Not generally by choice," Kotler grinned. "But true."

"Are you having second thoughts, then?" Denzel asked. The waitress had returned with two new glasses of scotch. Denzel took his, staring into it for a second, then looking up at Kotler. "Are you thinking you'd rather not do this?"

Kotler shook his head, sipping from his glass. "Not at all. I'm thinking that I need to change a few things, if doing this is important to me."

"Like what?" Denzel asked.

"Like how I move around in the world. I don't really 'check in.' It sort of rankles me to even think about it, though. I like being free roaming, unattached. But ... well, maybe that's been part of my problem, in the past."

"You're not just talking about being abducted," Denzel said.

Kotler laughed. "No, I guess not. Evelyn. I was thinking about her and how things ended. They ended well before she was taken. And it was my fault. And I was thinking about Gail. She showed me she could get to me, but it was mostly possible because of how I live. She took advantage of my freedom, and used it to shackle me." He sipped his scotch, then shook his head. "I don't think I can change entirely, Roland. I like my life. I like how I live. But I see that I need to compromise a bit, if I'm going to keep finding myself in situations where a sociopath might have a gun on me."

Denzel nodded. "I was going to ask if you'd agree to a sub-dermal tracker."

Kotler choked then laughed, a loud bark that brought some eyes their way. "I was thinking I should probably just check in more. You want to tag me like a seal?"

"It would only be used if you went missing and I needed to find you," Denzel said. "I'm getting one, too."

Kotler shivered. "I don't know. That doesn't sound appealing at all. Makes me feel … leashed."

"I could make it a condition of your contract," Denzel said.

Kotler gave him a hard stare. "You could," he replied.

The rest went unspoken, but was still clearly understood. If it became a condition of Kotler's eligibility to consult with the FBI, it would be the end of that consultation. Kotler was willing to put on a leash, but it was going to be a very long leash, or none at all.

Denzel nodded. "Voluntary is better," he said.

Kotler felt the muscles in his neck and jaw loosen, and the smile returned to his face. "Voluntary is always better."

"Will you do it?" Denzel asked.

"Give me some time to think about it," Kotler said. "For now, I'll promise to check in regularly."

It wasn't enough, Kotler knew. This new role would require Kotler to be in the line of fire more, and it meant he would have to make some compromises.

What if he just went back to his old work? It was true, the gatekeepers of academia and science had more or less blackballed him, in terms of publication. But Kotler could go it on his own. He could publish his own work, in much the way men like Graham Hancock or Erich von Däniken continued their work despite garnering jeers from their peers.

These were brilliant men, pushing the boundaries of what was known about human history, offering new perspectives and new theories about who we were as a race. And they were brave enough to take the heat for it. Maybe Kotler could follow their example.

Or maybe he could do both. Working with Denzel had opened new opportunities for him, and provided him with a new cause. But it didn't have to be his only work. He had stipulated, from the start, that he would consult but would also continue his own work. It was how he had been able to spend weeks at the Atlantis site. Maybe he would make that more of a regular thing, with his FBI consulting becoming less prominent in his life.

Maybe.

He was feeling better now. Nothing was entirely resolved, but he could feel that resolution coming. He would work this out.

"So, what about the Devil's Interval technology?" Kotler asked. "Were we able to determine whether Chandler sold it to anyone?"

"So far, things seem clear. We're still looking for Gail McCarthy, to see how much she knows. That's just one more note in her file, though. She has a lot to answer for."

Kotler nodded. "I'll start looking into those objects she gave us. She's baiting us, but there's something to that."

"Careful," Denzel said. "Don't do anything without looping me in."

"Of course," Kotler said, smiling.

Denzel studied him, a look of doubt on his face, but went on. "Holden called me this afternoon to say that he's arrested Jack Harris."

Kotler's eyebrows arched. "He tracked him down?"

"It wasn't hard, once we knew that Garrett Chandler was behind everything. Holden ran all of his records and found several rental properties, inside and outside the city. Harris was holed up in one right here in Manhattan. He had a burner phone with Chandler's number programmed in. He'd been waiting for instructions, he said."

"Did he confess to Ashton's murder?" Kotler asked.

Denzel nodded, sipping his scotch. "He did. And to Lawny Bristol's murder."

Kotler whistled. "Two murders, with confessions." He shook his head, then thought. He looked at Denzel, who was staring back at him. "You're kidding … he cut a deal?"

"He had contact with Gail McCarthy's network. It's how Chandler found out about it. He has information we need."

Kotler felt his face flush. He wasn't given to being angry, but lately the injustices were piling up. "So he walks? Two murders, two confessions, and he gets off?"

"He'll do time," Denzel said. "It'll just be a nicer prison. And if he screws up, even once, it's off to harder times."

Kotler shook his head, unbelieving. He had studied humanity all his life, but sometimes it could still surprise him. He sighed, sipped his scotch, and brooded for a moment.

Denzel, apparently sensing Kotler's frustration and wanting to shift the conversation, changed gears.

"As soon as Chandler wakes up, we'll have a lot more questions for him. But it looks like his motives were primarily aimed at aiding his cause. I think he was planning to use any money from the sale of the tech to fund a new operation, to keep exploring how to use this technology to effect larger numbers of people."

"That would fit," Kotler said. "He somehow became radicalized. And it's not too hard to see why. History is filled with instances of oppressed classes rising up, and it's almost always a bloody revolution."

"I don't know that he's part of an oppressed class," Denzel said.

Kotler shook his head. "He isn't. Not really. He has rights, and he has more wealth than most. But he thinks he's oppressed, and that's the reality that matters to him. There are possibly millions of others who feel the same way. Look at the state of things, in the US. The media can't seem to report anything without connecting it to something homophobic or repressive to women, transgender, blacks, or someone else. These good people are being told, every day, that they're victims, and that turns them sour. It's no wonder there's so much tension and hatred growing. It isn't good. I've studied human cultures my whole life, and I can tell you that this isn't a new phenomenon. We're watching an 'us versus them' mentality gain a strong foothold in the world, and eventually it will boil over into conflict. Chandler's move to use Devil's Interval may be one of the first volleys, but it won't be the last."

Denzel considered this, and nodded. "It's sad," he said. "I fought for this country, and for the values of it. I want people to have the kind of freedom that lets them choose who they want to be, and to be that, without hesitation. If it doesn't harm someone else, or infringe on someone else's rights, then it should be that way, I believe. Somehow, that's been twisted, and even militarized."

The two sat, somber, sipping their drinks, until Kotler smacked the table with the palm of his hand. "Enough," he said. "We won. We celebrate that. No more crisis, no more lamenting."

"Agreed," Denzel said.

They finished their drinks, and Kotler paid the tab. They left Hemingway's exactly as they found it, moving out into the Manhattan night.

Kotler decided, on the ride back to his apartment, that

the world needed someone to occasionally point out the repeating patterns of history, and to sometimes act to protect humanity from its own fears and prejudices. History was a pretty remarkable guide for that, in Kotler's estimate. And if assisting Denzel in solving cases and unlocking mysteries and sometimes saving the world with a gun in his hand was the path he was on, then for the moment, at least, he could live with it.

He would continue his research and keep publishing. He would keep traveling the world, exploring cultures first hand, and connecting disparate ideas of history and science to understand it all. He would be himself, and the best version of himself that he could think to be. And he would try, as hard as he could, to avoid being kidnapped or shot, in the process.

STUFF AT THE END OF THE BOOK

When I first started writing Dan Kotler's adventures, I figured they would end up like all my other books. I love what I do, and I love the stories I've crafted. They're a part of me, and it pleases the hell out of me when they become part of the readers as well. But all my previous books have become more like family you only see on holidays. You still love them. You're still excited to see them, when they come around. You still cherish them and want them to do well. But they aren't part of your daily life anymore.

In some ways, that's a bit sad. It's the way life works, though.

I once had an employer—a cantankerous attorney with a big heart and a bigger mouth—tell me, "I don't buy people, I rent them." This was said in answer to some comment I must have made, maybe casually stating the fact that it was clear I wouldn't work for him forever. I liked him, quite a bit. I respected him. But I knew from day one that he and I weren't going to be lifelong partners in anything. And this was his way of saying he knew it, too.

And I think that's the way a lot of our relationships work.

We're in it for seasons, not lifetimes. There are souls who come into our lives for a season, and we enjoy each other's company, drinking and laughing and spending time together, and then we move on. That season may come around again, some day, but for now, the world keeps rotating and revolving, and we're hovering just above it, letting it pass beneath our feet, on to new people, new relationships, new adventures.

This applies to the work, too.

These days, I'm a thriller writer. Previously, I was a science fiction writer, and a fantasy writer. I can still pen a sci-fi or fantasy story any time I want, but that's more like buying your Christmas gifts in April, and wrapping them in July. It's sweet. It has meaning. But it isn't the season.

There's something about thrillers that has really caught on with me, and I think it comes to me from multiple directions.

First, the nature of the thrillers I enjoy writing is that they are tied to some bit of history. And not just any history, but "out of place history." I love the idea of a character who is as versed in history as anyone in academia, but is obsessed with finding the oddballs and the out-of-places. I love, as well, that this character might have other interests that are weighted equally with his love of history—interests such as quantum physics, and the study of how the universe itself is stitched together. In a way, both disciplines are identical, in that they both entail looking below the surface, studying and making observations, and connecting disparate ideas to form a cohesive whole. They're both about pursuing meaning by studying the world around us.

I'm neither an archeologist nor quantum physicist myself, but I've long enjoyed reading about both fields. I've studied whatever I could find, absorbed what I could, maybe come to my own conclusions, for good or ill. I'm as intrigued by the lost civilization of the Maya as I am by the potential existence of multiple states of reality. What I lack in the academic foundations of each discipline, I supplement through research and study and, frankly, imagination. I'm a fiction writer, after all.

In a lot of ways, Dan Kotler represents me, in his universe. We share a dry wit, and a propensity for both getting ourselves in over our head and figuring out a way out of it. We both share a love for the unusual among the unknown. We both get bored with pure research, and want to shove our hands in the muck just to find out what's under there. Dangerous, sometimes. But fun. And fuel for more stories than I can write, I think.

I owe a tremendous debt to Nick Thacker for goading me into this direction for my career. I've seen more success come from publishing these Dan Kotler stories than I saw from the entire rest of my catalog of books, which his nice. But more important to me, and the one thing that can motivate me back to the keyboard every single day, is the fact that I love telling these stories, more than I loved even my first generation of books—those once-close friends and relatives whom I occasionally see on holidays, or follow on Facebook.

I have ideas for non-thriller stories all the time, and it's likely I will write those books, or novellas, or short stories, here and there. But I have fallen in love with this genre, due mostly to its range. It's just the right fit for me.

I can tell virtually any type of story in this genre. Science fiction? Fantasy? Romance? All that can fold in nice and neat within a thriller. If I have a daring and capable hero who can solve a mystery and save the day, I can fold in all the additional elements I want, as long as I put a gun in someone's hand, and aim it at the protagonist at just the worst possible moment. It's possibly the most freeing genre of them all.

Which isn't to say it doesn't have its challenges.

Get a gun wrong, and you will hear about it. Get the history of a culture out of whack, and you will receive letters. Make your science too soft, or too detailed, or too esoteric, and you lose readers right away. Thriller readers, in my experience, tend to be brilliant and attentive, and utterly unforgiving *if you get it wrong*.

God bless 'em.

I love that about them, though, because I've come to think like that myself. I can be very forgiving of an author's work—I can overlook typos and grammar gaffs, if the story is good. I can even overlook farfetched ideas with no basis in reality, because it is fiction after all. Tougher to swallow, though, are errors regarding real-world concepts. Get the guns right. Get the cultures right. Get the science right. And if it's wrong, give me a good reason to accept it, to overlook it, and to go on. Write a fantastic story, and I'll forgive you.

I have plenty of critics. Some have very good points. I listen and weigh every bit of criticism that comes my way, and though I probably ignore 90%, I implement about 10%. Call me a softy.

But I say that to point out that the important component of a thriller, to me, is whether I've grabbed a reader to the end. Thrillers have more movement than just about any other genre. They're a river. And if that river doesn't have a strong enough current to carry you all the way to the end, the book has failed. If it carries you, but there are slow bits where you could get out if you choose, and you stick around anyway, that's a win. I've had plenty of readers write and complain about "scene X" or "scenario Y" or "grammar gaff B." But what I weigh their comments against is whether they finished the book. I can fix errors in the next release of the book, but if the story didn't keep them, there's little I can do but start over with the next tale.

Dan Kotler has been compared to Indiana Jones, Robert

Langdon, and numerous other thriller protagonists. My writing has been compared to Clive Cussler, Dan Brown, David Morrell, and others. I love all those comparisons, but more importantly they're telling me that these books hold up. They fit. The gut instinct I have about Kotler and Denzel and these stories is right on. I've found the niche that I fit best. For a season, at least.

I have more of these on the board, ready to be written. In 'Devil's Interval,' I laid the groundwork for the next book, for which I've already done a great deal of research. That research, itself, is a powerful motivator for me, because it means immersing myself into books and films and television programs about a topic I'm already interested in, and exploring it from every angle. Most of what I learn won't be used in the book, but it sure helps to feed the background of the story. It feels good, actually, to write a scene and reveal certain details, knowing (as Kotler knows) a whole lot more about the topic than time permits me to say.

All of this to say, I truly enjoy writing these books, and I enjoy even more hearing that you like them, too. I feel I'm still learning and growing as a thriller author, but it's an education I'm very happy to embark upon. And I'm so grateful to you for being a part of this, and helping me to grow into the role. Thank you. I owe you a lot for it.

Kevin Tumlinson
    Pearland, Texas
    June 21, 2017

ABOUT THE AUTHOR

Kevin Tumlinson was born in Wild Peach, Texas, in 1972. He spent most of his childhood running barefoot in places no sane human would tread even with boots on. With only three fuzzy channels on television and the invention of game consoles still slightly out of reach, Kevin learned at an early age to keep himself and his family and friends entertained with stories and anecdotes. He did not always tell his family and friends that these were stories or anecdotes.

Kevin has been writing professionally since he was twelve years old, and has an ever-growing library of novels, novellas, and non-fiction books to his credit. He is an award-winning copywriter, and once endured a shockingly long career in marketing, media, and documentary television. He's also a renowned expert on pants jokes, with over a thousand in his repertoire--far greater than the actual number of pants he owns.

Learn more about Kevin and his work on his website, and get three of his best books for free when you register at kevintumlinson.com/starterlibrary

Connect with Kevin:

kevintumlinson.com
kevin@tumlinson.net

HOW TO MAKE AN AUTHOR
STUPID GRATEFUL

If you loved this book, and you'd like to see more like it, I can totally help with that. And there are some things you can do that will help *me* help *you*:

(1) REVIEW THIS BOOK

Go to Amazon, Goodreads, Apple's iBooks Store and anywhere else you can think of and leave a review for this book. Seriously—**I can't tell you enough how much this helps!**

The more reviews a book has, the more discoverable it becomes. Help me build and grow an audience for the books so I can keep writing and publishing them!

(2) BECOME A SLINGER

Slingers are what I call the people who are on my mailing list. They get the latest updates on new book releases, blog posts, podcast episodes, and (coolest of all) FREE GIVEAWAYS.

Best of all, if you sign up, you can get the Kevin Tumlinson Starter Library for FREE.

Go to http://kevintumlinson.com/starterlibrary download your free books now!

(3) TELL YOUR FRIENDS

Without readers, an author is just some guy with a really crappy hobby. Long hours at the keyboard. Tons of money spent on editing, layout, cover design. Even more long hours waiting for reviews and sales and bits of praise on Twitter. Honestly, a fella could take up fishing.

So please, spread the word. If you liked this book, tell a friend. Send them to that link above and let them download some free books. Help me grow this author business, and I promise I'll do everything I can to keep you entertained as much as possible!

Thanks for your help. And thanks for reading.

Nomad

YA & MIDDLE GRADE

Secret of the Diamond Sword — An Alex Kotler Mystery

Watch for more at kevintumlinson.com

DANVILLE PUBLIC LIBRARY

DANVILLE PUBLIC LIBRARY
Danville, Indiana

WITHDRAWN

52050298R00166

Made in the USA
San Bernardino, CA
10 August 2017